GREED

THE DAMNING BOOK 1

KATIE MAY

EXPRESSO PUBLISHING, LLC

Cover Design by Melody Simmons

Edited by Meghan Leigh Daigle of Bookish Dreams Editing

Dedicated to my daddy. Thank you for refusing to read my books so I could remain your angel.

CONTENTS

ONE

Z

I crouched on the roof, a protruding air vent obscuring me from the bustling street. The air was uncharacteristically cold, and the trees seemed to be cooperating, their branches skeletal. I fiddled with the zipper on my jacket, turning my attention towards the people below me.

The city itself—if you could even call it a city—was small. Buildings and houses, once vibrant in color but now washed-out by the scorching sun, filled up every available space. The majority of them were doorless and windowless, a product of both vandalism and inconsistent weather. Intermingled with each building were stalls, which sold everything from trinkets to bread to clothes. Humans manned most of these stalls, but a few nightmares were present as well. I spotted a mermaid splashing happily in a tiny, inflatable swimming pool. Her face, however, was dirt stained, despite the water, and her eyes flickered rapidly from one face to the next.

Crazed. Feral. My heart ached as I stared at her. Even nightmares were not immune from the societal standards of normality. If you were different, or human, you were forced to live in poverty, barely making enough money to support yourself, let alone a family.

It was a fucked-up system. Unfortunately, it was one that was gaining traction by the day.

The man I was looking for was standing in front of a stall that sold silk scarves. His long black hair was pulled into a braid, and his hands moved animatedly as he spoke. The vendor, a woman I knew to be Mali Estba, had her arms crossed over her chest as she listened to whatever the man was saying.

The man, Luca Leon—an oh so original name for an oh so original mage—took a step closer to Mali and brushed at her hair.

My hands clenched into fists as I stared at the figure, silhouetted in the waning sunlight. I hated him with an intensity that surprised me.

A thief. A rapist. A murderer.

He didn't deserve to live.

B had said as much when he'd delivered the file. His eyes had gone cold, colder than usual for B that was, and his lips had pursed into a thin line. I could practically feel the anger emitting from his body. I had accepted the case greedily, like the vindictive bitch I was.

"I knew I could count on you, Z," he'd said, a bright smile wrinkling the skin around his eyes. I had smiled back instinctively, though I imagined mine had appeared more bloodthirsty and feral than anything else.

Now, I flipped through the pictures of Luca's victims in my mind.

Juliet Beat. Human. Seven years old.

Missy Devlon. Human. Ten years old.

Ali Bennet. Human. Twelve years old.

I hated cases that involved kids, but someone had to fight for them. That someone was me.

It was the family of the last girl, Ali Bennet, that had come to see us, nearly hysterical with grief and demanding that we take their case. While most families would have mourned the death of their daughter, these parents were different. Vengeance was a dangerous emotion to have, but it was one I was all too familiar with.

With a heavy breath, I turned back towards the monster in question. Mages, vampires, genies, shifters, mermaids, incubi, and shadows. They were all monsters to me. Nightmares.

And it was my job to eliminate them.

I reached for my bow, the only weapon besides a dull knife us humans were permitted to have. Of course, the council didn't believe that we would be stupid enough to use it on one of their own. It was a tool, they had told us, not a weapon. Misuse of their "generosity" would lead to a nationwide ban.

They saw us as weak and pathetic—creatures born to serve in the natural hierarchy they created. I knew that not all nightmares were bad, just like not all humans were good. There were facets of light and darkness in every aspect of nature.

But this man...this Luca...

He was bad.

And he deserved to die.

I grabbed an arrow out of my opened pack, hand steady despite the horrendous act I was about to perform. I reminded myself that he was a nightmare, a scum, a fungus, and he didn't deserve my time or affection. With my job, you couldn't afford to show pity. It made you weak, and a show of weakness got you killed. That was a lesson B had drilled into my mind since I first started training to become an assassin.

I froze when I saw a group of people gliding towards Luca and Mali. They all wore matching black cloaks with different colored hoods.

Green for the mages.

Red for the vampires.

Purple for the genies.

Gold for the shifters.

Blue for the mermaids.

White for the shadows—and yes, I saw the irony in that.

Pink for the incubi.

The council.

Shit.

Burrowing myself further into my hiding place, I eyed the approaching figures cautiously. What were they doing here? Council members rarely, if ever, involved themselves in the mundane aspects of life, especially in a primarily human settlement. It was beneath them. If you weren't royalty, you weren't deserving of their time and attention.

Bracing one hand against the gilded edge of the roof, I hissed. This was proving to be an extra difficult mission. I just hoped that the vampire and shifter representatives had their enhanced senses turned off. It was a little secret they didn't think us humans knew. Apparently, it was like a switch inside of their minds that determined whether or not their senses were activated. It was a conscious decision, the equivalent to a human choosing to lift their hand. I imagined it would get tiresome to hear and smell the entire world day after day with no relief, thus this switch was created through evolution.

Fumbling in my pack, I grabbed my hearing chip. Powered with magic from a mage ally, the chip would allow me to hear conversations from any distance, as long as I focused. Unfortunately, it only had a lifespan of ten minutes before it had to be recharged.

Just one caveat of working with magic.

After the bud was comfortably in my ear, I focused on the figures below me.

"...opportunity, yes?" Mali was saying almost tentatively. I rolled my eyes.

Mali was anything but tentative. A vampire and an ally of the Alphabet Resistance—a stupid name given to us by the nightmares—she had quickly become the annoying sister I never had. I loved her to death, but her acting skills were subpar at best.

"It should be considered an honor," an icy voice said. Even with my enhanced hearing courtesy of magic, I strained to understand his words. Shadow. Only one species was conceited enough to speak in whispers.

Not all of us have super hearing, asshole.

"How long?" Luca asked.

"Two months, though you may be eliminated earlier," another voice said. This one was husky, the telltale sign of a shifter.

I knew immediately what they were discussing.

The Damning. It had another name, a fancier name, but us humans only referred to it as the Damning. I was pretty sure the name stuck, though, and now, even the kings called it that.

Every five years, the baddest, meanest, and deadliest nightmares were chosen to participate in this contest. The winner would become the royal families' personal assassin. The losers? Well, it wasn't pretty. There was a reason we called it the Damning. In a span of weeks, it went from one hundred competitors to one winner. Ninety-nine deaths.

And apparently, good old psychopath Luca had been picked to participate.

How fucking great.

Pinching the bridge of my nose to control my erratic breathing, I narrowed my eyes at the slimy figure. I watched as he took the invitation presented to him by the mage representative.

A few more words were spoken, but I tuned them out.

B would be pissed if I both did and didn't complete this task. On one hand, the families of those little girls deserved justice. On the other, it was an immense risk to take out someone chosen for the Damning. Like, *head on a pike while your body is burned alive* type of risk.

Ugh. Fuck me.

I listened to the swish of their robes as the council retreated, each movement agile and graceful. All of the nightmares were.

Contemplating quickly what my next course of action would be, I once again envisioned three faces staring back at me. Three little girls, all with their lives snuffed out because of this maniac. My resolve settling, I muttered under my breath, "Do it."

Mali nodded slightly, the only indication that she'd heard me with her advanced vampiric hearing.

"That's so exciting," she gushed, turning her attention to the scumbag beside her. I didn't even have to see his face to know he was wearing a cocky ass smile. The idiot was *excited*. Didn't he realize that he was going to die? Or was he dumb enough to think he had a chance of winning?

"Hard competition this year," he said easily. Mali laughed, a high-pitched sound that made me squirm. I would most definitely tease her about it later.

"Come on. I want to show you something."

I knew she would be putting a hint of persuasion into that final sentence. All but shadows were helpless to a vampire's allure and compulsion. He went to her willingly, a fly caught in a spider's web. I licked my lips as I watched them walk down a dark pathway, closer to where I was crouched.

"What do you have to show me?" he asked suggestively. I gagged. Literally gagged.

Before he could say anything else vomit inducing, I allowed my arrow to fly. It spliced through the air with a blistering speed, accurately finding its target's heart. I heard him gurgle as blood filled his mouth. His body fell, hitting the ground with a barely audible thump.

Smiling with grim satisfaction, I jumped onto the nearest awning before landing beside Mali and the now dead mage in the alleyway. The shadows from the nearby buildings provided a flimsy shield between us and the outside world. It obscured us from the throng of people walking the streets and their way too curious eyes. Even with that small protection, we would have to make quick work of disposing the body and portaling away.

My best friend was glaring at me, eyes narrowed into thin slits.

"What?" I asked innocently, removing the arrow from his chest. Up close, he was even more disgusting. White, ashen face and dark eyes. He might've been considered handsome, if I didn't know the horrors he'd committed.

"Did you really think that was the best idea?" she snapped.

Frowning, I felt along his coat until my searching fingers came across his gold-trimmed invitation.

I snorted.

Please accept this one-way ticket to death. We make it extra pretty so you know that you're special before you're murdered.

Damn nightmares.

"He was chosen for the Damning," Mali hissed. Her foot tapped with increasing speed the longer I ignored her. I didn't know what she expected me to say.

Sorry for killing him?

"He deserved to die," I settled on at last. I placed my arrow, still bloody, into my backpack. I would have to clean it when we got back to headquarters. The longer we stayed there, the higher our chances were of getting caught.

"He would've died during the competition," Mali said in exasperation. "Now you just drew more attention to us. How do you think the royals and council members are going to feel when their beloved sociopath doesn't make an appearance?"

"They'll think he's a wimp that ran with his tail between his legs," I said, reaching into my pocket and pulling out a cerulean blue tablet. It was made by a mage, Diego, for this exact purpose. "Besides, this was much more satisfying than a competition death would've been."

I dropped the tablet onto Luca and watched as his disgusting body diminished before my eyes. Nobody would ever find him again.

Perks of magic.

I had asked Diego once what happened to the bodies, but he'd merely smiled wickedly. I decided I didn't want to know.

Huffing, Mali turned her back to me and dropped her own green pill. These created portals, designed to take you to the place you considered home. Pretty fucking cheesy if you asked me, but useful for my day job.

The portal glimmered a combination of silver and red, encompassing nearly the entire alleyway.

"B's going to be pissed at you," she said a second before she stepped into the portal. I watched her retreating back and spoke softly.

"I did what I had to do."

———

THE COMPOUND WAS BUSTLING when we stepped through. The dank, drooping walls of the cave were leaking water, indicating it must've rained before we arrived. The buffet line curved around the walls of the cafeteria, where we landed, and a pungent smell assaulted my senses. Some type of meat. Kids and adults alike were enjoying their meals at the various wooden tables.

All eyes flickered towards us when we stepped through.

If I didn't know any better, I would've said they were afraid of me.

Ridiculous.

Absently, I pulled out my bloody arrow and began to wipe it off on a napkin from the nearest table.

I was just a lovable human being who just happened to like pointy things.

Satisfied with my now clean weapon, I gently placed it next to my other arrows.

"Where's B?" I asked the young man swaggering towards me. Behind him, looking like demented ducklings, were numerous children I had never seen before. They all had dirty faces and clothing that were two sizes too big. New recruits.

Their wide eyes fixed on me as if I were the nightmare.

It was rather rude, if you asked me.

"His office," T said. He stopped in front of me with a teasing smirk that made his dimples appear. Stepping to the side, he gestured towards the kids that trailed behind him.

"Kids, meet Z. Z, meet our newest recruits."

One kid dared to raise her hand in a wave. I decided I liked her.

Chuckling at their less than enthusiastic response, T asked me, "Is there any advice you want to give the newbies?"

"Don't sit down when you have a knife in your waist-band. It might accidentally go up your asscrack and then you'll receive a lot of embarrassing questions," I responded seriously. Mali, beside me, jabbed her elbow into my stomach.

"Well, that's adorable," T said with a wink. I think one of the little kids pissed his pants. Oh well. At least I wasn't on laundry duty. "Come on, chicks! Let me show you to your bedrooms!"

That caught the kids' attentions. Their eyes widened significantly, and tiny smiles formed on their faces at the thought of having a room to themselves. Joke was on them.

The "bedrooms" were nothing more than row after row of cots in a sweltering hot room. Each room fit approximately fifteen cots.

Yup. Living the good life.

"I'm going to talk to B," I told Mali.

"Do you want me to come with you?" she asked hesi-tantly. As head of this mission, it wasn't necessary for me to bring her along for the debrief. However, I could use the moral support when B got on my ass about protocol.

"I'll be fine," I said instead. I nodded towards the buffet line. "Go grab me a plate."

Smiling gratefully—Mali was as afraid of B as I was of nightmares—she skipped in the direction of the heavenly smelling food. She, of course, wouldn't eat any of it. She had her own supply of animals to drink from in the lower levels of the caves.

Taking a calming breath, I headed in the direction that housed B's office. The light in the cave got scarcer and more unreliable the farther I ventured, until they were flickering intermittently above me.

Fortunately, I knew my way through the tunnels by heart.

I arrived in front of B's office door, heart pounding, then raised my fist to knock. Before it could connect with the wood, the door was yanked open.

B stood in the doorway, arms crossed over his bulky chest and his receding gray hairline revealing his true age. This life had taken its toll on him—already, I could see an ancient despondency to his creased face that went centuries beyond his forty years. His eyes were sharp, though, as they traced my features.

"I heard that there was an incident on your assignment," he said at last.

"How did you...? Never mind."

I forgot that B knew everything.

"Normally, I would get on your ass about killing a Damning competitor, but I'm rather grateful that you did."

I blinked. I'd expected him to yell at me for risking both myself and the organization because of a stupid vendetta. This? Saying the word *grateful*? Unheard of.

"It provides us with an opportunity," he continued, moving to sit behind his stone desk. A single hanging bulb illuminated the bare walls, casting the room in shadows. Hesitantly, I walked farther into the sparsely lit area. I wasn't usually a timid individual. I was more of a *stab first and ask questions later* type. With B, I turned into an entirely different person. What could I say? The man scared the shit out of me.

"Opportunity?" I parroted. There was a single seat in front of his desk, but I knew better than to sit before he allowed me to. Instead, I rested my hands on the hardwood—not a sex joke, you pervs—and watched B's face turn thoughtful.

"You know about the crowned princes? Correct?"

I nodded mutely. Who didn't know them? A prince from each nightmare royal family, all the same age. There were numerous rumors concerning these men—that they were monsters, murderers, worse than their parents, who created and enforced human slavery.

And there was also the prophecy.

I didn't know the exact wording, no human did, but the message was clear—these princes had more power than any nightmare that had ever existed. This excessive power could be used to either bring equality to all the races...or completely destroy the world. There was no in-between.

What I wouldn't give to get my hands on those men, those monsters...

"You have the invitation, I presume?" B queried. I nodded and produced it from my pocket. B's smile was positively radiant, making him look years younger than his actual age at that moment. "Did you know that the invitation is designed specifically for each person? The council gives it to a killer, and the killer is obligated to join the Damning. It was created by a group of very powerful mages."

"Okay?" I wondered where B was going with this. He had a tendency to speak in riddles, especially when he got overly excited.

"People will kill others in order to receive an invitation," he continued. Again, all I could do was blink at him like an imbecile.

Look at me—a badass assassin confused by an old man's ramblings.

"This will be the perfect opportunity to take them out from within," he finished gleefully.

Again...the hell?

Seeing my confusion, B let out a grunt of annoyance.

"Read the invitation."

Frowning, I stared down at the piece of paper I was holding. The blood drained from my face as I read the words once. Twice. Three times. The words were intricately written, as if someone had spent time creating each individual letter.

Surely there was a mistake.

Surely I had read it wrong.

Surely...

But the letters didn't change, no matter how much I willed them to.

Z, you have been chosen as the competitor of the Damning. Please report to the capital in five days' time.

"When you killed Luca, the magic transferred itself from him to you. Congratulations, Z. You're now an official competitor of the Damning."

Oh fuck me.

TWO

Z

I leveled another punch at the black bag. It swung like a pendulum, the movement almost rhythmical and hypnotizing. I couldn't help but wish that the punching bag would fight back. I wanted to feel the pain, the adrenaline, the excitement of a fight. I wanted blood to cascade down my face, to feel something other than this numbness tightening my lungs.

I was afraid.

It was an emotion I hadn't experienced since I was five and was forced to watch my parents die at the hands of nightmares. I remembered the copper taste of blood in my mouth as my little hand grasped my mother's desperately. I remembered hiding behind her clothes in the closet, waiting for the bad men to finally leave.

I hadn't only lost my mother and father that day. I lost a little piece of myself as well. My innocence. My humanity.

The nightmares had destroyed it all.

I thought of S then as well, his shirt soaked with blood and his hand reaching for me. His eyes had been anguished when they met mine, but they still held more love than I deserved. Especially since I was the one who'd gotten him killed.

Just the thought made my blood boil. I rapidly punched at the bag until my knuckles were scraped and bleeding. The pain...I needed more of it.

How did B possibly expect me to compete in the Damning, let alone assassinate the royal darlings? Even *I*, certifiably insane, knew it was a suicide mission. Either I would die in the competition just because I was a female human, a prime target for fucked-up nightmares, or I would die by execution after I killed the royal family. My only option seemed to be death.

Yup. Not a big fan.

It wasn't as if I was afraid of death, per se, but more so of the implications behind it. Where would a person like me go? Certainly not heaven, and I wasn't ready for a hell worse than the one I was currently living.

I stared at the rivulets of blood cascading down my fisted hand. I barely processed the pain as I thought about what I had to do.

There were rumors about the royal families, though most of them were only that. It was the type of gossip you would hear in bars and clubs. I reckoned no one actually knew the families that were supposedly devil-sent to lead us.

Each group of supernaturals were descended from one of the Seven Deadly Sins. There was a lesson that us human children were taught religiously. *Don't mess with the nightmares. They're descended from the devil himself.*

Shifters were the most volatile and dangerous of the species, given that they were descended from Wrath. If a shifter became angry enough, frightened enough, passionate enough, they would shift. Fortunately, it wasn't something they could do at will. When they transformed, it was immensely difficult to separate the man from the beast. The two became one and the same.

The royal family of shifters consisted of a king, a prince, and a princess. The queen, the king's soulmate, had died years ago at the hands of hunters, aka people like me. Apparently, the loss of his mate made him completely unhinged. He had always been cruel, but her death made him evil. He was one of the biggest proponents of human work camps. His son, twenty-three and with the dumbass name of Lupe, was one of the elite seven. The seven princes, all born within minutes of each other. All destined to either save the world...or destroy it.

Our profile on Lupe consisted only of photographs, all of which showed the big man in the capital's library. So far, he hadn't found his mate. I hated him more than the others, despite knowing next to nothing about the beast of a man. It was a shifter who had killed S, and it was a shifter I would enact my revenge upon. If that shifter happened to take the form of a prince... Well, I never said I wasn't a greedy, vindictive bitch.

The mages were descended from the sin Sloth—read as, they were lazy sons of bitches. Their magic actually developed through evolution, as it was difficult to get them to do anything that involved moving. They required a simpler way to enjoy the pleasures of life, thus the creation of magic. Their prince was named Sebastian, or Bash to his friends, and was the stereotypical party boy. I was willing to bet what little money I didn't have that he'd never worked a day in his life.

Most people had to work for what they wanted, but not him. Not any mage. They snapped their stupid fingers and the world fell at their feet. There was only one mage I had ever met that actually worked for what he wanted. He was my other half, my best friend. An asshole, yes, but still ten times better than any other person in this fucked-up world, nightmare and human combined. Diego may have had his flaws, but he was one of my best friends.

The vampires were the offspring of Gluttony. According to Mali, it felt as if you were constantly thirsty. As if you were wandering a desert for days on end, unable to reach that lake of water in front of you. No matter how much you drank, how much you consumed, you always wanted more. She described it as a painful burn in the back of her throat that only diminished when she fed. The relief would last for an hour before the pain began once again in earnest.

Out of all the nightmares, vampires were my favorite. That could've been because I was partially biased towards that species. After all, I really couldn't hate the species of my best friend. What type of racist bigot would that make me?

Their prince, next in line for the throne, was Jax. From what little intel we'd gathered, he was engaged to marry the shifter princess, Atta. She wasn't his mate, but that didn't seem to matter in the supernatural political world. After all, the chances of him actually finding his mate were slim to none. It was quite literally like looking for a needle in a haystack.

Genies were the race most likely to interact with humans. They needed us to live, needed our greed. As descendants of Greed, genies thrived on human fantasies and dreams. They picked apart every desire, every wistful thought you ever had, and kept it as their own.

I had once met a genie—Lin the Asshole—and even asked him to help me avenge my parents' death. Stupid ass genie. I'd also made the idiotic mistake of falling in love with said genie.

Not one of my finest moments.

Seriously, if I had a time machine, I would use it to slap the stupid out of younger, hormonal me.

The genie prince was Devlin. Not much was known about this prince, since he constantly traveled the world to grant wishes. Like all genies, he was considered selfish and smug. He created contracts with so many loopholes, it was impossible to catch them all until it was too late. I'd heard more than one horror story of people getting cheated by Dev the genie.

Incubi were the love children of Lust, as you could have probably guessed. They fed off the sexual energy of others. They needed sex to survive, like vampires needed blood and genies needed greed.

Their prince was some tool named Killian. As you would expect with any incubus, he had a different lover every night. Apparently, a string of hookups was required for an incubus to survive until they found their mate.

I sometimes wondered if I was half incubus. Mad respect for them. Using their species as justification for lots of sex? Yes, please.

The mermaids were another interesting creature that I yearned to study. They were the descendants of Envy and were forced to spend twelve hours in the water and twelve hours on land, never fully a part of either world. They were jealous of the creatures in the water, the natural way they were able to adapt, and envious of those on land, the relationships, the technology, the life they would never be allowed to have. I might've pitied them if their royal family members weren't raging dicks.

Their envy towards humans caused them to back the shifters' proposal for human work camps. If they couldn't be happy, no one could.

Dair was their prince. Again, not much was known of him. When he was human, he hid away from the world. Rumor had it that he appeared more fish than human, that his life was tied more to the water than to the land. Others believed he was so beautiful, with the siren allure common in most mermaids, that he had to hide his face away to keep women from falling head over heels for him.

Pretty damn vain if you asked me.

Finally, we had the shadows, the most mysterious group of nightmares. They were direct relatives of Pride.

This pride kept them hidden away from the rest of the word. They didn't believe us peasants should have the pleasure of knowing their names or seeing their faces. I'd heard rumors that the shadow prince had a name that started with a R. Ryan? Ryland? Rachelle?

The world may never know.

They had never, not ever, talked to a human. We were so beneath them that we didn't even register on their stupid importance scale. We were the scum beneath their feet, the disgusting virus they vaccinated themselves against.

The seven royal families. The seven princes. And it was my job to kill them.

No pressure.

I found myself on the dusty ground, my back against an old treadmill as I stared at the makeshift gym. It was empty at this time of night, though I knew the morning would bring in dozens of people. Everybody wanted to train. To fight.

To kill.

I didn't know how long I sat, wallowing in my own self-pity, before T came looking for me. Without a word, he sat beside me, his knee touching mine. His auburn hair hung in his face, in desperate need of a cut. Almost absently, he brushed a strand behind his ear.

I always startled at the resemblance between T and his brother, S. If I were to squint my eyes, I could almost believe that S was sitting beside me once again, laughing at one of my poorly timed jokes or attempting to make me smile.

T's own smile turned sympathetic, as if he knew the direction my thoughts had headed. Knowing him, he probably did. I would've liked to say that I trusted T based on his merit alone, but that would've been a lie. If he hadn't looked like the man I once loved and lost, I wouldn't trust him as much as I did. He would never own my heart, but he would always hold a piece of it in a way that only close friends forged from a shared trauma could.

"Are you going to say anything?" I asked after the silence became unbearable.

"Are you?" he retorted.

"I don't know what to say." My finger traced patterns across the stone flooring. It was something I had always done, a way I had found to escape. Draw. If only it was possible for me to draw my pain away. "I don't know if I can do this, T. I don't know if I'm ready to die."

T was silent for a moment, his eyes intensely trained on my finger moving across the floor. It was the first time I'd admitted my own thoughts out loud.

"You don't have to do this if you don't want to," he finally said. He leaned forward to rest his long arms on his knees. His head tilted to the side, expression thoughtful. "That's what makes us different from *them*—free will."

I considered his words, the connotations of something so apparently simple. Free will. Did anyone really have it? Did I have it?

Sure, I could walk away at any time, but would that be the right decision? Would I be able to live with myself if I had the opportunity to change the world but chose not to? Morality, I realized, prohibited free will.

T nudged my shoulder with his, breaking me out of my thoughts.

"I actually came down here for a reason," he said at last. "B wants to talk to you."

I groaned.

B wouldn't be expecting an answer. He already knew

what my answer had to be. The world needed fighters, not cowards. I knew this. I honestly did.

But the fear of death settled in my stomach heavily.

Nodding in resignation, I followed T to B's office. Each step forward was weighed down, my feet dragging against the stone hallway. A leaden, miserable feeling settled over me as I spotted B talking with Diego.

The mage smiled when he saw me.

"Hey, hot stuff," he flirted. I glared.

"I will kill you with a butter knife."

Diego grabbed his chest in mock offense.

"One day, Z, you will fall in love with me. One day."

"I'll let HH know."

Diego blanched at the threat. HH was his mate, a cute human boy and the reason Diego had joined the resistance in the first place.

"Not that I'm not glad to see your sexy face," I teased back. "But what are you doing here?"

Diego turned towards B expectantly, and I did as well. T leaned against the back wall, arms crossed over his muscular chest.

B's face was grim as he dropped picture after picture onto his desk.

"What...?"

I trailed off, unable to tear my eyes away from the horrendous sight before me. A young girl, her lower body mauled off as if she had been attacked by a bear.

Or a Shifter.

Two teenagers with their skin removed.

A male with no eyes.

A baby with—

"Enough." I swiped the pictures off the desk, watching as they fluttered to the floor. I took a calming breath as if that one small gesture could erase the images already tattooed into my brain. "Why did you show me that?"

My stomach threatened to expel the contents of my dinner.

"Those were the victims of your fellow competitors. You will be competing against murderers. Monsters. You, and only you, have a chance to end it all." B slammed a fist onto his desk, and Diego startled beside me at the sound. "How can you not want to take a stand against such horrors?"

I bristled at his implication.

"You know I would do anything to rid the world of such disgusting creatures." I glanced at Diego out of the corner of my eye. "No offense, Diego."

"None taken."

Turning back towards B, I straightened my shoulders imperiously. "I'm just not sure I'm ready to die yet."

He rolled his eyes. "Quit being so dramatic."

Dramatic?

I was going to castrate him. Where was he when vampires started a blood-trafficking trade? Where was he when the mages decided to experiment with new spells on runaways? Where was he whenever the nightmares attacked?

He was safe in his fucking office, that was where. Hiding. And he dared to call me dramatic? He dared to imply that I was a coward?

Before I could threaten bodily harm, he continued on.

"You fear that people will target you if they know you are human, correct?"

I nodded mutely, too angry to speak.

"Did you know that a couple of humans are chosen for the Damning each year it's put on?" he asked, moving around his desk gracefully. He leaned against the front, arms and ankles crossed. He was the epitome of calm... the epitome of everything I was not.

"I didn't know that," I muttered through gritted teeth.

"They're *expecting* humans to compete. It's a part of the natural order of things. A way to determine who is higher up on the food chain. Being human is not an issue, as there is always at least one human disgusting enough to be chosen. Now, there *is* an issue with you being a female." His voice was impassive, revealing nothing.

"So what do you plan for me to do about that?" I snapped. And no, I wasn't willing to do a sex change. I rather liked my vagina, thank you very much.

A small smirk pulled up B's lips. He nodded towards Diego, who eagerly procured a silver necklace.

"Jewelry?" I asked, quirking an eyebrow.

Diego gasped. "Not just jewelry, you filthy whore. A spell." He handed me the necklace enthusiastically, though I failed to reciprocate such an emotion. Holding the chain tentatively, I glanced at B, unsure of what he wanted me to do.

"Have you never put on a necklace before?" Diego quipped. Without waiting for a response, he used one hand to hold up my hair while the other snapped the necklace into place. It felt heavy between my breasts.

"Okay...?"

"Press down," Diego instructed.

"On?"

"The pendant, dumbass."

Rolling my eyes, I did as he said.

I didn't feel the change. I wouldn't have even realized something had happened if I hadn't caught sight of my reflection in the mirror.

A black cloak was now obscuring the curves of my body, the hood pulled up. My face was covered by a white, intricately detailed mask. It was outlined in silver, two pinprick black dots in place of my eyes. I looked badass, yet I felt no different. I couldn't feel the weight of the cloak, nor the sharp plastic of the mask digging into my face.

I sucked in a breath as I considered the ethereal figure before me. My identity would remain a secret. Nobody would know that I was a female.

And, if shit hit the fan, I could run.

I could run, and no one would know who to look for.

There was still fear, still stomach curling terror, but now I felt something else as well. Something akin to hope.

I could compete in the Damning. I could kill the monsters that plagued this Earth. By eliminating the royal families, we might actually have a chance of winning this war. I could sneak into the capital unde-tected. I could do this.

"Only you can compete in the Damning. You killed

Luca, and the magic transferred itself to you. This is your choice, Z, but I hope you make the right one."

B must've seen the decision in my posture, the sinking of my shoulders in resolution. A brilliant smile crossed his face.

"That's my girl. I knew you would make the right decision."

THREE

Z

I fiddled with the hem of my dress, wondering if I had somehow died and gone to hell. How did women wear these damn things? Didn't they need to breathe?

"Stop fidgeting," Mali hissed. "You look great."

"You look sexy," Diego corrected, flashing me a smile. "*Sex on a stick* type of sexy."

I flipped him off, turning to stare at the scenery through the car window. The grassy fields slowly transformed into mountainous ranges, and the car swiveled side to side as it attempted to maneuver through the horrendous landscape. My stomach churned and tightened as we made another sharp turn.

"Fucking shit," I muttered, squeezing my eyelids shut as if that could somehow quell the nausea.

Definitely hell.

"We're going to be there soon," Diego said, acknowledging my discomfort. He casually threw his arm around the back of my seat, squeezing my shoulder in the process.

"Why can't I push the button?" I moaned, absently caressing my beautiful, badass necklace that hung around my neck. Diego referred to it as the ninja transformation button. I couldn't help but agree with him.

"We've been over this," Mali said, yanking the steering wheel to the left. The movement propelled me into Diego's warm body, and I placed my hand over his mouth before he could make another dirty joke. "You should only wear your ninja badass costume when you're competing. We need to be careful that people don't draw targets on your back. Outside of the competition, you're Zara the maid. Not Z the assassin."

A tiny smirk pulled up my lips.

"Ninja badass costume?" I teased. Mali's cheeks flamed, and she reached behind the seat to swat at my knee.

"Shut up."

The plan had been drilled into my head by B until I could practically spew it in my sleep. Each competitor was allowed three personal employees, called the assistants. Mali and Diego were posing as my maid and driver, respectively. And me? The dress wearing, non badass me? I was some bimbo named Zara. I know. Awful.

Z was the assassin.

Zara was his caretaker.

"But why a dress?" I whined, fidgeting. Mali cast me a look of disgust. She'd never understood my aversion towards dresses and jewelry. She was the type of female who would wear elaborate gowns and high heels while relaxing around the house. Her closet held more clothes than both mine and Diego's combined.

"Because *Zara* wears dresses," she stressed, reminding me of my alter ego. I snorted.

"*Zara* wants to punch you in the face."

"*Zara* needs to learn that threatening people isn't always the best course of action," she retorted. Before I could respond, Diego clamped his hand over my mouth. When I narrowed my eyes at him, he grinned sheepishly.

"You talk too much, darling."

In answer, I merely bit down on his palm.

He cried out, instantly removing his hand from my face.

"So savage," he muttered, eyeing me darkly. I gave him a shit-eating grin.

"Holy crap, guys!" Mali squealed. Her attention diverted from the road to face the magnificent building resting in a steep decline. I cursed, whacking the back of her head with my hand.

"Eyes on the road!"

"But...shiny..." she cooed. I turned to face what had so thoroughly captured her attention.

A large, golden mansion sat in a valley created by the mountains. From this distance, I could see nothing but a dozen or so pillars holding up a grand arcade and a wrought iron fence. A soft glow emanated from the various windows running along the brick siding. A large body of water was adjacent to the building, no doubt hosting the visiting mermaids.

I'd heard rumors of this place. A place that no human

has ever lived to tell about. A place where nightmares lurked in broad daylight.

A place where the Damning was held every five years.

With my mouth agape, I allowed my eyes to roam over the nightmare's capital. Directly between all seven kingdoms, this was considered the most important building in the entire world. All of the important nightmares resided here, including councilmembers and royalty.

The assassin in me began to fangirl.

"You're swooning," Diego whispered, nudging my side. I reluctantly pulled my eyes off of the building to face him.

"I don't swoon."

"I'm pretty sure you just did." He lifted a finger to touch the edge of my lip. "See? Drool."

"I'm not..." I rubbed at my mouth.

Dammit. He was right.

We pulled in front of wrought iron gates, stopping the car in front of a small guard booth. A large man with broad shoulders and a shaved head ambled towards the driver's window. One look, and I knew he was a shifter. They were always freakishly large, regardless of what animal they transformed into. I'd heard a story about a three-hundred-pound killer who shifted into a mouse.

"Identification." His voice was gravelly, unsurprising given his impressive stature.

Mali turned towards him, flashing a singularly beautiful smile.

"I'm Mali Estba. That is Diego Kenny. And back there is Zara Winters."

I blinked.

Zara Winters.

Zara. Fucking. Winters.

Why did that name evoke images of baking cookies and dusting off shelves? It was most definitely not a name that an assassin like me should ever be associated with. I shuddered just hearing it.

"Matching or Damning?" the guard asked. His eyes were penetrating as he surveyed the occupants of the car. When they rested on me, I met his stare with an imperious set to my chin.

It suddenly occurred to me what he had said. I knew what the Damning was, everyone did, but I'd never heard about the Matching.

And what was up with these dumbass nicknames? Whoever was the event coordinator really needed to get fired. What was next? The Eating? The Talking? The Stabbing?

On second thought, the Stabbing did have a nice ring to it.

"The Damning," Mali answered without missing a beat. "We're the personal assistants of Z." She flashed him the invitation, and he quickly scanned it, confirming its authenticity.

"Personal assistants, huh?" he asked, wiggling his eyebrows. Nobody could miss the suggestiveness in his voice. I shouldn't have been surprised. B had warned me that people would assume we were the lovers of Z—that was what all the assistants were. Hired lovers.

So he was pretty much insinuating that I would be considered the lover of...myself. Not a horrible lover, as lovers could go, but there was only so much a finger could do before it got repetitive.

Diego, beside me, began to chuckle, no doubt coming to the same conclusion I had. Sick, perverted bastard.

"Where is Z?" the guard asked, searching the car once more. His eyes zeroed in on Diego and narrowed.

Of course he would assume it was the guy.

Fucking shifters.

"Z doesn't like to show his face," Mali lied smoothly. The shifter's nostrils flared, and I knew what he was doing. Sniffing for a lie. There were a lot of things shifters could sniff—heightened emotions, smells miles away, sweat glands when one began to lie. Would they be able to smell every fart that had ever existed?

My mind turned over this newfound information.

How did one separate the farts from all of the other smells? Was it just a constant background smell that they had to get used to? Could a shifter die because of a fart?

Could a—

"Zara," Diego snapped, elbowing my stomach. "Where did your mind go?"

I shrugged. "Farts."

Diego glanced at me oddly. "You really are a psycho bitch, aren't you?"

I chose not to respond to that rather fitting statement, turning back towards the window instead.

We had pulled away from the guard booth and up a paved driveway that circled around a marble statue. The opulence of both the building and the yard was almost nauseating.

There were no other cars when we arrived in front of large glass doors, though I wasn't surprised. B had wanted us to arrive early to scope the place out.

A wicked smile turned up my lips.

As long as I could kill some nightmares, this entire shit show would be worth it.

FOUR

KILLIAN

I listened to the sated moans, muffled through the closed door. Around me, women and men alike ambled through the brothel's halls, drunk, both from alcohol and pleasure.

I watched a particularly dazed woman leave one of the many bedrooms adorning the hall. She was completely naked, her breasts covered in bites and bruises. A man immediately followed behind her, face carved from marble and red hair neatly trimmed.

Vampire.

Upon seeing me, the woman made an immediate beeline in my direction. I blanched, attempting to disappear into the wall. What I wouldn't have given to be a shadow at that moment. The vampire glared at me, grabbing the woman's arm and pulling her back towards the bedroom. I heard the woman's sigh of pleasure.

Lust. Pleasure.

I breathed it all in. Immediately, my fatigued body

thrummed with unsuppressed energy. I felt as if I could run for miles.

The couple behind the door I was sitting in front of let out loud, earsplitting screams. The power from their shared orgasm breathed life into me. I knew color was returning to my cheeks, and my hair, which had been greasy and disheveled, began to shine as if it had a garnet sheen.

Feeling immensely satisfied, I picked myself up from the floor and headed towards the entrance of the brothel.

Madame Delong, an aging woman and the owner of this establishment, regarded me from where she was perched behind a wooden counter. She was a mage, with graying hair and a hard expression. I imagined life had chipped away at her smile. She lost her mate when she was only a teenager and had been alone ever since. Alone...if you didn't count her string of lovers.

"Killian dear, are you sure I can't interest you in any of our girls?" she asked slyly. It was the same question she had asked numerous times, and, as always, I declined profusely.

"Not tonight, Madame," I said smoothly, running a hand through my red locks. She gave me a knowing, all-seeing look. I had the distinct feeling she saw me more clearly than I saw myself.

"If you change your mind..."

"You'll be th-the-eee...first-t-t...to know," I assured her. Her lips turned up slightly at hearing my stutter, and I automatically winced.

An incubus with a stutter.

An incubus who was still a virgin.

Could I be any more of a disappointment?

My brothers assured me that it was normal, but I knew they were only trying to placate me. None of them understood my desire to save myself for my mate. Hell, I didn't even understand it. It was an innate need inside of me, something that I couldn't entirely explain.

All I knew for certain was that I didn't want to be like my father.

I glanced at my reflection in the window. My hair was glossy, radiant almost, with golden tendrils and darker red streaks that heightened the auburn color. My skin was muscled, almost obnoxiously so. It was just another perk of being an incubus. The main perk? Tattoos. They arrived the second I reached puberty, twining down my arms and across my defined eight-pack. Hurt like a bitch. While the intricate design may have seemed pretty to some, I hated them. They were a constant reminder of what I was and what I had to be.

With a sigh, I stepped out of the small building and into the bustling town. It was a unique blend of old and new, past and present, existing in an almost uncanny harmony. Broken shacks stood adjacent to large glass buildings. Some patches of the road were nothing more than dirt, while others were paved asphalt. It smelled of fresh baked bread from the local bakery and smoke from one of the many factories.

In the distance, I could see the mountains that surrounded the capital. It was that time of year again. The Matching.

And the Damning, though that didn't concern me.

Every year, our fathers would bring every eligible

maiden to the capital in the hopes that we would find our mate. It was a futile effort, I knew, and more of a power play than an assurance of our happiness. A mate had the capability of enhancing our powers. A lot was resting on this Matching, especially for Jax. This was his last year to find his mate before he would be married to the shifter princess. I pitied both of them.

I also pitied my brother Devlin, though he would probably stab me if he knew I felt such an emotion.

The door behind me pushed open, and a familiar figure stumbled out. I recognized his ash-blond hair, lightly curled, and verdant green eyes immediately. He had his arm around the waist of a petite redhead.

"Brother!" he slurred, coming to grab me in a hug.

"Bash," I replied. I stumbled under his weight.

Sebastian regarded me, eyes glazed, before turning towards the girl beside him.

"Killian, this is Rachel," he introduced.

"It's Allison," she hissed.

"That's what I meant. Alexis."

I smirked. It was no surprise that Bash was intoxicated. It was also no surprise that he was found at a brothel the day of the Matching.

He claimed it was because he didn't want to meet his mate, that he didn't want to be tied down. I secretly suspected it was because he was terrified he *wouldn't* meet his mate. The asshole was a hopeless romantic.

"We need to get back," I said, allowing him to put his weight on me. Bash was a heavy bastard, that was for sure.

"Bye, Ariana!" he cooed to the girl behind him, and

she hurled obscenities at him that would make even my mother blush.

"We need to check on Jax."

"Jax?" he muttered drowsily. I could already see that I was losing him. Dammit. I wasn't in the mood to lug his heavy ass back to the capital.

I considered, briefly, leaving him on the road. He would sober up rather quickly and be able to walk himself back. I decided against it. Someone had to look after my dumbass brothers, and unfortunately, that person was me.

"Come on," I said. "Let's get you to the car."

Believe it or not, Bash wouldn't even be the worst problem I had to face that day.

JAX WAS NAKED.

Again.

That was a sight I *never* wanted to see.

He stood in the middle of his room, his back to the doorway as he watched the cars slowly creep up the long driveway.

Devlin was leaning against the far wall, pinching the bridge of his nose.

"Jax, we talked about this. You need to get dressed." He sounded more annoyed than anything, as was common with Devlin.

Jax continued to stare out the window, ignoring Devlin completely.

"The hills go up and down. Up and down. Around and around and around and around..."

Devlin cast me a helpless look, and I rolled my eyes. I hated always having to be the one to deal with our eccentric brother.

"Jax," I said soothingly. I learned long ago that he only reacted to soft, honey tones—a drastic contrast to Devlin's strident voice.

"Around and around and around and around—"

"You need to get dressed. It's the Matching, remember?"

I stepped carefully in front of him, being extra cautious to avert my gaze from his dick. There was only so much I could deal with before I had to bleach my eyes.

For a second, his face flickered with a brief flash of coherence. It was there and gone too quickly for me to be certain.

"The lovers with the cord?" he asked.

"The mate cord? Yes."

He nodded his head seriously. Before I could say anything else, he turned towards the doorway.

"You need clothes on!" Devlin shouted after him, but Jax continued walking. I rubbed at my temples, my head already throbbing.

"He needs to feed," a cold voice said, and I jumped, though I shouldn't have been surprised. Ryland crouched on the windowsill, twenty feet above. I couldn't decipher any of his features, since they were obscured in thick shadows. Still, his voice rang out clear in the silent room.

"He won't," Devlin said. "Not that I blame him."

I stared at the open door where Jax had disappeared

through. His mind was in shatters, and there was nothing I could do to piece him back together again. This wasn't just a case of bandages and tape. The damage done to him was permanent and irreversible.

"Can somebody please get that crazy asshole dressed?" Devlin pleaded. "I have somewhere I need to be in like five fucking minutes." Both him and Ryland immediately turned towards me.

"Fuck you both," I mumbled, flipping them off. With a sigh of resignation, I left the room to track down my crazy brother. Hopefully, I could get clothes on him. I didn't want another repeat of the last Matching ceremony.

FIVE

DEVLIN

The last thing I wanted was to be heading into this meeting worried about Jax. I told myself repeatedly that Killian would handle it, that the situation would find a way to remedy itself. I had to be the leader. I had to act like I actually had my shit together so nobody would question my decisions.

Control.

I reminded myself that I didn't always need to have control.

The mantra played on repeat in my head as I straightened my tie. Violet, of course, which heightened the purple in my eyes. My dark hair was slicked back, showcasing my sculpted cheekbones and curved jawline. As always, I was impeccably dressed in a gray, formfitting suit.

My brows furrowed in the mirror as I considered myself. Dark circles under my eyes, a permanent scowl etched across my face, deep lines crinkling my forehead.

I was the spitting image of my father.

To some, that might've brought them immense joy. For me, however, I wanted nothing more than to completely eradicate any resemblance I had to that disgusting creature. If that meant shaving off my hair, then so be it.

Squeezing my eyelids shut, I changed the mantra in my head from *control* to *calm.*

Calm. I had to remain calm. My temper had a tendency to flare at these meetings, a fact that failed to escape the attention of my too observant father. One more outburst, and I would be punished.

She would be punished.

No, it was better for everyone if I got a handle on my eccentric emotions. They had an uncanny resemblance to a rollercoaster. I would rise higher and higher in what felt like elation, only to fall suddenly and be rendered immobile by a crippling depression. Sometimes, I would survive the fall, while other times, I lost tiny pieces of myself. The extremes in my emotions had been more prominent the last few years, a never-ending ride of twists and turns, ups and downs.

Control.

Calm.

Taking a deep breath, I headed to a section of the capital that housed the conference hall. It was a room I was intimately familiar with.

The door was opened as I entered, bright sunlight emanating from the opened windows. I allowed all thoughts of my brothers to drift from my mind as I took stock of the scene before me.

It was a familiar sight—a long table crafted of

obsidian stones, a dozen leather chairs positioned in a semicircle around the table, and a single podium in the direct center of the room.

Each chair was already occupied when I ventured inside. Genies, all with the violet eyes common for our species, chatted amongst themselves. Someone had brought a box of donuts, and coffee was being served by the waitstaff.

To anyone looking in, it appeared to be a normal day in the office. What they failed to realize, however, was that they were seeing things through a distorted, funhouse mirror. Nothing was as it appeared, and this seemingly innocent meeting of individuals was an example of that.

My father sat at the head of the table, eyes flashing purple. Up close, no one could deny the similarities between the two of us. Same olive-toned skin. Same cascade of disheveled brown curls. Same violet eyes, a few shades lighter than the average genie and the telltale sign of our royal lineage. As if he felt my eyes on him, my father turned towards me with a sly smile. His eyes remained chips of ice.

He was just another thing seen differently through the funhouse mirror. Hundreds of smiles couldn't hide the coldness in his eyes.

With my father, it was all about perception. There was the way he wanted the world to see him, the way the world actually saw him, and the way he acted behind closed doors. Not one of these personas was the same.

Only when he slid his eyes away from mine did I finally feel like I could breathe again. My breath left me in a swooping exhale, and I very noticeably slumped in my seat. Just as quickly, I straightened my spine and lifted my chin. No weakness.

Control.

Calm.

My resolve strengthening, I turned my head towards my father. As always, he had already garnered the attention of the entire room.

They perceived him as the supreme ruler, the just and fair king.

Perception.

It was always perception.

"Case number 23X73B," he said, his strident voice echoing in the grand room. "Please enter."

A backdoor slid open at his command, and two genies entered carrying a trembling human. They shoved him in front of the podium before resuming their positions against the far wall.

The poor man couldn't have been older than thirty. His hair was so blond, it was almost white, and his piercing green eyes flickered anxiously from face to face. If he was looking for a supporter, he wouldn't find it in this group of people.

My hand clenched into a fist at what I knew was about to transpire. As always, I was helpless to stop it. I couldn't risk her life.

Calm.

Control.

Calm.

"Jonathan Goodrich, you are accused of violating your contract with the genie Laurel Payne. How do you plead?" My father paced in front of the podium, looking oddly like a feline shifter in that moment. He could've been a lion out for the hunt, desperate to take a bite of the pathetic deer who dared to encroach on his territory.

The man, Jonathan, noticeably gulped.

"Contract?" he whispered. His eyes flickered towards a petite brunette, the girl I knew to be Laurel, sitting closest to the podium. She flashed him a flirty smile and a wink. She, like my father, was enjoying this. She enjoyed seeing the man squirm, sweat, cry.

Beg.

She would always make them beg.

Smirking once more at the poor human, she moved to her feet and procured a scroll from her jacket sleeve. I recognized it as a genie contract, created by our magic and bound by our blood. With an elaborate flourish, she unrolled the yellowing paper.

"On July 7th, you rubbed my lamp and demanded three wishes, is that correct?" she asked confidently. Jonathan began to tremble.

"Yes, but I—"

"Did you or did you not wish for three things? A new car, a new apartment, and a million dollars in cash." She ticked them off on her fingers as she spoke to emphasize her point.

"I did, but—"

"Did you or did you not sign a contract with me before said wishes were made?" When he remained silent, Laurel continued on dogmatically, "And did I or did I not provide you with what I promised?"

The man alternated between nodding and shaking

his head as if he was unsure of what the appropriate response was. Finally, he nodded jerkily.

"Then what seems to be the problem?" my father asked. The same sinister smile I was familiar with twisted his face into something almost unrecognizable. It was most certainly not something I would ever see in the mirror. Only our smiles distinguished us from each other at that moment. "Laurel upheld her part of the deal, and now it's your turn to uphold yours."

Before my father had even finished speaking, Jonathan was already shaking his head.

"No. I didn't agree to that. No. No. No."

"You signed the contract," Laurel said with feigned innocence. "It's not my fault you didn't read it beforehand."

"I didn't know you would ask for my soul!" he exploded. Tears welled in his eyes, and he turned his attention towards the other genies present in the room. His eyes begged us to stand up for him, to plead for him, to be the defender he so desperately needed.

My nails created crescent-shaped indents in my skin. Still, I pressed down tighter, willing blood to be drawn. Pain. I needed more pain.

Calm.

Control.

Calm.

Remain calm.

My breathing was harsh to my own ears. I didn't want to watch this again. I couldn't. There was only so much a person could take before they snapped. Still, I forced myself not to look away as my father strolled up to the trembling man.

"You made the deal, son, and I would hate to set the precedent that there will be no consequences for someone backing out of one. Do you understand? It's nothing personal." Turning away from him, my father addressed the bloodthirsty crowd. "As supreme ruler and King of the Genies, I find Jonathan to be guilty of breaking his contract. To remedy the wrongs he created, I require his soul to be handed over to Laurel, effective immediately."

The man began to scream then, and the sound would haunt me. If only I wasn't such a damn coward. If only I had the strength to stand up to my father and protect the people I loved.

Expression gleeful, Laurel grabbed her lamp and mumbled a familiar incantation. As I watched, transfixed, a sobbing Jonathan began to be pulled by an unseen force towards the lamp. His body turned into a cloud of purple smoke, and his features blurred until they were nearly indistinct. Still, I could clearly see his mouth opened in a cry of agony before he dematerialized into Laurel's lamp and the mist receded. His soul was now hers.

My stomach churned painfully, threatening to expel what little I had eaten for lunch.

I thought of my own lamp just then.

And the soul...

A violent shudder shook my body.

No, my lamp was lost. Stolen. I couldn't think about that and everything I had lost when it was taken from me without completely spiraling into a depressive episode. It was better to think of nothing at all.

I listened to conversation continue around me. A few people reached across the table to grab another donut, and someone in the distance poured another cup of coffee. The person beside me, Brad something, asked the table if we could smell the fire wafting off of him. Fire. As if that actually had a smell. When someone asked him what the fire was from, his lips curled up wickedly.

"Not even family is immune to the consequences of our deals. Had to burn my own mother for trying to renege."

Just another day in the life of a genie. Another day in the dissonant chaos that was my reality.

SIX

Z

"If I die...this right here would be the reason why it's worth it," I said, flopping onto the spacious bed. It looked as if it could easily fit ten people, which I supposed was the point, given the nature of most nightmares. Exclusivity only existed between mates, and even then, it was a rarity. I supposed nightmares were like people in that way. They craved companionship, if not necessarily love.

"Don't be dramatic, Z," Mali said, and I prepared myself for her to launch into a speech on how I'm not going to die. Instead, she said, "The fridge is ten times better than the bed. See? Fresh O-negative blood."

"Well thanks, She-Who-Has-So-Little-Faith-In-Me," I said dryly, and Mali flashed me a grin.

"Don't worry. Diego will whisk us out of here before you can die. Right, Diego? Diego? Diego!" Mali pinched his ear, and he turned from where he was wistfully surveying the walk-in shower, visible through the opened bathroom door.

"It massages your ass," he whispered dreamily. Mali rolled her eyes, a standard reaction for dealing with both Diego and me.

"You know who else will massage your ass? Z. If she lives."

"Yeah...no... That will be a hard pass by me."

Mali turned to give *me* a look, as if she were shocked and slightly offended by my refusal to give Diego an ass massage. After a moment of studying me, she shook her head.

"Anyway, this is considered Z's room, not Zara's. We have rooms in the servant quarters," she said, and Diego glanced longingly at the shower.

"But..."

"Come on! We need to settle in." As the two of them moved towards the door, I remained sprawled across the bed. Mali turned on her heel when she noticed I wasn't following her, one hand going onto her hip. "Are you coming?"

"I think I'm going to be Z tonight," I drawled lazily. "This bed is comfy."

Mali's eye began to twitch.

"No. You're supposed to be *Zara* when you're not competing."

"Well *Zara* wants to give Z a little loving."

Diego's brow furrowed, as if he were attempting to solve a difficult math equation. Mali just rolled her eyes. Again. I imagined they would become stuck like that if she kept it up.

"So Zara and Z..." Mali trailed off.

Diego said, "I am so confused right now."

I would rather not explain the basics of masturbation to him, but if someone had to take the fall...

With an exaggerated huff, Mali grabbed his arm and pulled him out of the room.

Alone at last, I allowed my mind to wander.

For obvious reasons, I had a feeling that I was going to die. A human had never won the Damning before. Hell, not even a woman had won before. I didn't want to think I was weaker than my competitors, but I knew the truth. They had supernatural skills. I had a mean right hook.

Could a human like me really last in a fight against a nightmare? I was no match for a shifter's strength, a vampire's speed, or even a mage's spell. Humans were the roadkill in this day and age. I could only hope that my death would be semi painless...and that I would be able to take out a few nightmares before my time came.

I stretched my taut muscles. The car ride had been grueling, and my body ached. I glanced longingly at the shower before turning towards my closed bedroom door.

Zara would indulge herself in a hot bubble bath.

But Z? She would assess the situation. How many rooms? How many exits? How many competitors? I was already at a disadvantage, and I couldn't afford to go into this competition blind. Z would act like she actually had her shit together, so people would stop worrying about her eventual, inevitable demise.

Rolling out of bed, I tentatively touched my neck-lace. I debated whether or not I should dress as the assassin but quickly decided against it. If people only thought of me as Zara, a poor, defenseless assistant, I would be less of a target. Granted, women, particularly human women, were always viewed as prey by night-mares, but I hoped being at the capital would quell such crude behavior. It was a chance I had to take to keep my identity a secret.

The lady who'd brought us here had explained that all of the competitors would be spread out throughout the numerous halls and buildings that made up the capital. I couldn't understand why they felt the need to separate us, though I figured it was to lessen the number of fights that broke out.

A hundred deadly creatures.

A hundred strong personalities.

We were considered the meanest, nastiest, scariest people from all seven kingdoms.

I snorted. And then there was me. Blonde-haired, blue-eyed, and a few inches over five foot. I looked more likely to cuddle you to death than to strangle you.

Looks could be deceiving.

I fucking loved it when they underestimated the little guy, when they underestimated me.

The hallway was empty when I stepped through the doorway. The light here was sparse, as if they hadn't invested in as many lightbulbs as they should've. I glanced in one direction where I knew the entrance to be, and then down the opposite hall.

I had already surveyed the area between my room and the front door when I was led here. It seemed to be rooms of various sizes, none of them occupied, if the noise level, or lack thereof, was any indication.

Smoothing down my black dress, I followed the flow-ered carpeting down a long hallway. That, too, consisted of nothing but empty rooms. I had knocked on a few of the doors to be certain, but no one had answered.

Strange.

It was only after I made two rights and a left that I began to hear excited chatter. My fellow competitors, perhaps?

But no. All of the voices sounded feminine. Happy. It wasn't the type of emotion you would expect people to feel before their inevitable death.

The slave—excuse me, *servant* quarters? Again, those were supposed to be on the opposite side of the capital, down two flights of stairs.

A woman ran out of a room, nearly barreling into me. She didn't pay me any mind as she grabbed at her skirts and ran down the hallway. Her hair was stylishly braided, and she wore a glorious gown that likely cost more than my entire life savings.

What the hell?

I stared after her in confusion but couldn't find it in me to care. If she wasn't a competitor, then she wasn't important.

"What are you doing?" a strident voice demanded. The voice belonged to a gray-haired, stern-faced woman. She hurried from the direction the girl had run down, lips pursed and eyes calculating. "All of the girls are already in place. Go!"

"I, um..."

Before I could protest, she grabbed my arm and propelled me into a large ballroom. It was a beautiful room with three-tiered chandeliers and an opulence nobody could even attempt to replicate in my poverty-stricken hometown. Standing against the far wall were dozens of beautiful women.

All different colors, ages, heights...

All beautiful.

And all nightmares.

Had I been wrong? Were these the competitors for the Damning? I surveyed each made-up face and carefully constructed hairstyle. I knew my brows were furrowed in confusion, but I obediently stood in line between two tall brunettes.

Both of their nostrils flared when I came close to them, identical expressions of distaste marring their faces.

"Human," one of them said snidely.

"Shifter," I greeted.

What in the actual hell was happening?

Surely I had missed a memo somewhere. This felt more like a beauty pageant than an assassin competition. My hand instinctively clenched around the handle of the knife I always kept up my sleeve. If this was a trick—or worse, a trap—I would be prepared. For now, I had to remain as Zara Winters and see where that would lead me.

"Ladies!" The woman who had led me here clapped her hands together. The usual whisper and fidgets immediately settled down like a flame being blown out. Each of the girls leaned forward expectantly. I, on the other hand, was searching for any escape route.

"My name, as most of you know, is Mrs. Grinshaw. My assistant, Laura, will be coming around with a potion I brewed. You will all be required to drink it."

Potion. She must've been a mage, though I hadn't

heard of one making a potion in hundreds of years. It was too much work for them.

None of the girls looked scared by this revelation, but I felt my muscles tense. The last thing I wanted to do was put an unknown substance into my body. Hell to the no.

Casting a quick look in both directions, I saw that the only exit was the door I had entered in. Across the ballroom.

Fan-fucking-tastic.

Perhaps if I explained the situation...

The assistant, Laura, stopped in front of me. In her hands was a golden chalice. Before I could even begin my improvised speech about how I was nothing more than a little maid, my hand snapped forward and grabbed the cup of its own accord. I felt as if I was a doll, incapable of moving myself without the help of a puppeteer. My eyes narrowed on my traitorous limb, even as my lips parted to drink from the cup. Out of the corner of my eye, I could see Mrs. Grinshaw moving her own arm in tandem with mine.

The liquid was bitter, but not entirely unpleasant. It felt warm where it tickled the back of my throat.

Glowering, I handed the chalice back to Laura and crossed my arms over my chest.

"Fucking mages," I said at last.

Every head whipped in my direction. Some held amused expressions, while others looked positively livid.

"What the hell? I didn't mean to say that out loud!"

Mrs. Grinshaw smiled. It wasn't a pleasant one, all sharp teeth and crooked edges.

"That's the point of the potion, my dear. It lowers inhibitions. Makes you speak your mind."

"Well, fuck," I cursed, and a few of the girls gasped.

Really? Had they never heard someone swear before? *Pansies.*

I must've spoken that out loud as well, as the two shifters on either side of me stuck their noses into the air. It was this type of mentality I hated the most with nightmares. They acted as if they were creatures to be revered and respected, so superior to little humans like me. They rode on fucking high horses in order to justify their bigotry. Let me get something straight—no horse was high enough to condone such behavior. You couldn't demand respect, you had to earn it.

"Don't worry. The spell should wear off soon," Mrs. Grinshaw said with a pointed look in my direction. In answer, I gave her the finger.

Shit. Shit. Shit.

"I want all of you ladies to remain very still. You will allow them to do what they want with you. Is that understood?"

All of the girls nodded eagerly, obviously understanding what she was referring to, but I felt my stomach twist unpleasantly.

I really did not like the sound of that.

And that was the second thing I hated about Nightmares—the assumption that we would want to do anything and everything to please them. It wasn't just humans that received the grunt of this, but nightmare females as well. There were these defined gender roles that had only been reinforced over time. There were also preconceptions of victims and perpetrators in this sexually charged world, where the female population was continually dwindling. Fucking disgusting, if you asked me. It was one of the many things I fought to fix in this male-dominated society.

Mrs. Grinshaw spoke some more—*this is the first stage, blah blah blah, this doesn't automatically mean you're not a match, blah blah blah*—but I zoned her out. I had obviously walked into something I wasn't supposed to. Add into that my lower inhibitions? It was an ass kicking just waiting to happen. As in, my ass being kicked. Painfully.

"...Lupe Shifter!" The name brought me out of my frantic thoughts. My eyes turned towards the doorway Mrs. Grinshaw had indicated, even as all of the other women broke into enthusiastic cheers.

The figure who entered was undeniably a shifter. He was tall, nearly two feet taller than me, and was built entirely of muscle. It appeared as though his hand was larger than my entire head.

And I had a pretty damn big head.

Dark hair, short on the sides but longer on the top, showcased an arresting face of chiseled cheekbones and light blue eyes. Dark stubble coated his jawline. Even I could admit that he was handsome, but there was something about him, something quiet and almost deadly in his apathetic gaze, that caused my heart to clench in fear. A shifter. *The* shifter. He wasn't the nightmare that had killed the man I loved, but he was still a monster. How many defenseless people had he slaughtered? How many lives had been cut short by his hand? The wrath of a shifter was undeniable. I'd read a story about a man who had slaughtered his entire family, including his two young kids, after his wife had forgotten to pick up milk from the grocery store.

This one, however, seemed almost bored as he walked towards the first girl at the end of the line.

"Lupe," she said dreamily, and I resisted the urge to gag. It was unsurprisingly difficult, given the whole lack of inhibition thing I had going on.

The man, Lupe apparently, paused in front of the woman who'd spoken. He leaned forward, eyes locked with hers, and sniffed her hair.

Sniffed. Her. Hair.

What the hell?

There was no way I was going to get sniffed by a damn shifter. No way in hell.

My nails dug into my palms as I attempted to calm my racing heart. Fear and anger warred for dominance.

Lupe, expression impassive, made his way down the line of girls. Each girl would smile at him seductively, but the second he would pass them, their faces would fall. It was actually kind of comical.

When one girl broke into tears, I laughed sharply, quickly trying to smother the sound with my fist. I obviously didn't do a good job at it, if the glares directed my way were any indication.

Lupe raised his head, eyes meeting mine, and I held his stare defiantly. I could've sworn that his lip twitched, but that would've been impossible.

He was the shifter prince. Evil.

He was evil.

I had to remember that, even if my body's reaction towards him was contradicting what I knew to be true.

Finally, he was standing in front of me.

"Look, I have to warn you that I didn't shower today," I said briskly. The more I tried to stop myself from talking, the more I talked.

Damn mages and their stupid potions.

"So you can just skip the whole sniffing thing with me. For both our sakes."

Lupe's face was only inches from mine. I could see a splatter of freckles across his nose and strands of obsidian in his brown hair. He leaned forward, and I braced myself.

"Do shifters get mad if someone smells? Is that a thing? Because I promise you, I would've showered if I knew I was going to be sniffed. Why are you even sniffing me? And why am I the only one freaking out over this?"

Before I could say anything else, he sniffed me.

And then he sniffed me again.

And again.

Something emitted from his chest, a sound that was barely audible.

A purr.

The giant man was purring?

My fight or flight response must've been broken, since it added on a new choice to the equation—fuck. And right then, my body really wanted to do just that. With a giant, purring, murderous shifter.

"What is actually happening right now?" I asked in exasperation. I was no longer scared. That emotion had diminished the second my heart rate decided to settle back into a normal rhythm. If anything, I was annoyed.

Lupe straightened suddenly, eyes narrowing on my face and full lips parting.

Before he could say anything, the door to the ballroom opened and closed. I heard the patter of footsteps, but I refused to break eye contact with Lupe. The air around us seemed to practically shimmer with electricity.

"Zara Winters!" Mrs. Grinshaw snapped. "You're not supposed to be here!"

"Well, no shit!" I quipped before I could stop myself. I finally broke free of Lupe's penetrating gaze, looking over his broad shoulder at the older woman. Mali was standing beside her, expression wary. "I tried to tell you—"

"Leave!" She pointed a finger towards the doorway, and I let out a breath of relief. Without giving her the chance to change her mind, I hurried towards where Mali was waiting for me.

"Thank god," I whispered to my friend, linking my arm with hers.

"How the hell did you end up in the Matching?" she asked, voice barely containing her laughter.

"Don't ask."

Despite the eyes I could feel on my back, I kept my gaze forward. I had a competition I needed to focus on.

And I had some princes I needed to kill.

SEVEN

Z

The sky was gray as I stepped into the grassy clearing the next morning, the large clouds threatening rain. My black cloak swooshed around my feet with each step I took, though I barely processed it. Diego had done his spell well. I couldn't even feel the mask obscuring my face, let alone my heavy clothing. If anything, it felt like an extension of my body. I still couldn't get over the fact that Diego had created this spell. *Diego.* He must've really loved me for taking the time to create such an intricate design when I knew he would rather sit on the couch and waste the day away.

My bow and arrow were slung over my shoulder, and I kept three daggers on my person—one on each leg and one on my hip. I'd wanted to bring my machete, but Mali had insisted that it was overkill.

After a long argument, I had eventually conceded. What she didn't know, however, was that Diego had masked my machete so it hung from the shoulder opposite of my bow, utterly invisible. I still felt the weight, but the weapon itself remained unseen.

Thank you, Diego.

I wasn't the first to arrive at the clearing, but I also wasn't the last. My timing was, as always, impeccable. It was ingrained within me that I had to be like my machete —invisible. It was crucial for my survival.

I got a few glances when I arrived, no doubt for my badass getup, but nobody commented on the fact that I was a female or a human. Once again, Diego had saved my ass.

I nonchalantly spun a dagger through my fingers, being extra cautious not to do anything too amazing. If I were to win, I had to be in the middle of the pack, at least at first. The top competitors would turn on one another near the beginning stages of the Damning, as well as eliminate those they deemed as easy or vulnerable. It was vital that I didn't fall into either one of those categories.

I looked at the various men spread out along the clearing. And that was what they all were—men.

A few had their feet dipped inside the nearby lake. Mermaids, no doubt, attempting to get every last drop of power the water was willing to give them.

Some of the men were large, the size of tree trunks, while others were small and wiry, almost sinewy, in appearance. Still, I knew not to be fooled by their less than impressive physiques.

One guy in particular caught my attention. He was tall and lightly muscled, nothing extraordinary compared to the immense beast of a man beside him. Despite his skinny frame, there were numerous scars adorning his face, as if he had fought more battles than I could comprehend. His eyes were cold, devoid of emotion. It wasn't like the indolent expression Lupe had worn earlier. It wasn't an impassive mask one would use to hide their true selves away from the world. This man just looked dead, a mannequin with painted on eyes and lips.

It was unnerving.

Another man stood a little bit away, watching the competitors with an amused tilt to his lips. He had blond hair nearly down to his ankles, and his violet eyes glowed. Only one species had violet eyes

Genies.

The devils themselves.

I hated him immediately.

That point was only reinforced when he spoke.

"Is this everybody competing? There's no pussy?"

The rest of the men jeered and laughed, and I mentally added each and every one of them to my shit list. Okay, maybe shit list was the wrong word. I preferred to call it my kill list, as in, I was going to kill every last one of them. Painfully. And with a variety of weapons.

I mentally flipped through the information I'd received from B on all of the competitors. The man with the dead eyes was named Zack. From what I knew about him, he made me ashamed to have a Z name. A serial killer, he was recently released from prison for the sole purpose of this competition. He didn't have empathy, nor did he have a moral compass, though I supposed you could argue they were one and the same. Either way, he would be a deadly foe.

The giant of a man beside him, with a shaved head

and numerous tattoos, was Griffin. A shifter and a renowned rapist. Like Zack, he was recently released from prison.

The blond genie was named Sammy. It was such an innocent name, completely in contrast to the horrendous crimes I knew Sammy committed. He had convinced a high-up political figure, Geneive, to eradicate every human in her territory, as if we were a disease. And that was how the humans died—with diseases wished for by Geneive and granted by Sammy.

My stomach churned, and my hands curled into claws. I wanted nothing more than to run at those monsters and stab them with one of my many daggers.

In time, I told myself. Karma was a bitch.

An imposing man with graying hair and broad shoulders stepped onto a small stage set up near the center of the field. He wore a black robe with a blood red hood, indicating him as a delegate, if not the head delegate, of the vampires.

"Good evening." His voice was as icy as his features. His lips were curled downwards, as if he was disgusted by the sight before him. For the first time, I couldn't blame him. "Welcome to the Damning."

Hoots and cheers erupted from the masses, and I resisted the urge to roll my eyes. Did they not realize that all of us but one were going to die? I sure as hell realized that. My death was imminent, as was theirs. I could only hope I went down fighting.

"Every five years, we have the Damning to select our new assassin and torturer."

Oh joy.

Though my thought was sarcastic, the enthusiastic cheer that emitted from the crowd was very much sincere. I was surrounded by a bunch of psychopaths, all intent on being the last man standing. Fun. Fun.

"There will be one competition, one trial, one chance to prove yourself as the most worthy. The pride and joy of the kingdoms."

Way to butter up the crowd.

"The competition is simple—a fight to the death. In a span of two months, all but one competitor must be dead. The remaining man will receive fortunes beyond his wildest dreams and a chance to serve his kingdom."

The crowd began to murmur amongst one another. I saw a set of twins exchange careful, calculated glances.

"Now I know what some of you are thinking. The easiest solution, and consequently the safest, would be to hide away like cowards. I would like to inform you that one of the requirements of being the winner is having five kills yourself. No outside help."

He allowed that to sink in, cold eyes roaming over each face in the crowd. He paused when his eyes rested on me, and even from this distance, I could see his brow quirk. Just as quickly, his expression smoothed over to be replaced with indifference.

"Five kills. Two months. Last one standing wins. All competitors are required to stay at the capital until the Damning ends. Are there any questions?"

This felt more like a damn lecture at school than a fight to the death announcement.

The silence in the field was suddenly pronounced. Charged, almost, as if an electrical current were running rampant through the air. I felt myself shift from one foot to the other, searching for any person that moved too quickly, moved too suddenly. I may have been fated to die, but I wasn't ready to die *yet*. Give it a few weeks.

"No questions? Then I would like to formally declare that the Damning has commenced!"

The cheers from the crowd were sudden and roaring. My hands were clammy by my sides. Two words echoed through my head over and over again like a song on repeat.

Fuck me.

Before I could even move, a dagger flew through the air, landing directly in Sammy's forehead. The genie's eyes glazed over, mouth parting as if he were preparing to scream, before he crumpled to the ground.

I froze, staring at the body only a few feet away from me. Blood coated the ground, as bright as the vampire's cloak. He was dead. The legendary Sammy was dead, brought down by a simple knife to the head.

In the distance, eyes cold as he surveyed the body, was Zack. Without a word, he grabbed the dagger from Sammy's body and wiped the blood on his pants.

"One down. Ninety-eight to go."

EIGHT

Z

I was attacked approximately two times on the way back to my bedroom.

The first one was in the form of a dagger, nicking my ear as it flew through the air and impaled itself into the wall. I immediately went on alert, surveying the halls for the source. The only indication that someone had been near was a flash of blue from the now opened window.

The coward had left. He hadn't even been willing to face me. *At least*, I thought, slightly sardonically, *he had poor aim.*

The second attack consisted of two shifters cornering me in the hallway. After I rendered one of the men unconscious, the other had changed his focus and had ripped the throat out of his fallen comrade.

Apparently, not even alliances were sacred in this game.

By the time I was back in my room, my hair was disheveled and shifter blood coated my clothes. Diego and Mali both glanced up from where they were chatting on my bed. Diego was only wearing a towel—that asshole had used *my* shower. Mine. If he'd used all of the hot water, I was going to castrate him.

"What the hell happened?" Mali screeched, running towards me. Her nostrils flared as she took in the splotches of blood, and relief was evident in her sagging body when she concluded that the blood wasn't mine. "What happened?"

"I take it that the Damning didn't go well?" Diego drawled lethargically. He sprawled out on my bed, still dressed in only a towel, and propped himself up on his elbows.

"Wow. You don't fucking say," I quipped.

I really needed a shower.

Pressing the button on my necklace, the disguise disappeared, leaving only "Zara" in a white, blood-stained dress with messy blonde ringlets. Unfortunately, Diego's spell didn't magically cleanse me of all the blood. Shame. That would've been handy. And hugely profitable.

Maybe I could convince Diego to invest in an assassin-slash-serial killer store. I could see the tagline now. *Blood be gone!*

Smiling wickedly, I stripped out of my dress until I was standing in the center of the room naked. Neither Mali nor Diego even blinked. That was a surprise. Usually, Diego would've taken this opportunity to make a remark about my sexy but emotionally unavailable body. He must've really been worried. I summarized the events of the day.

"The Damning is a fight to the death. Two months. Five kills required. Fun times."

"We need to leave," Mali said suddenly. She anxiously chewed on her bottom lip, teeth sharpening into keen points as they always did when she experienced a heightened emotion.

"We can't leave."

Walking into the bathroom, I absently scanned the toiletries provided. I needed bodywash, shampoo, and a nice razor. If I was going to die, I'd be damned if I died hairy.

"Then you can only be Zara. Not Z. Never Z," she proclaimed, following me into the bathroom. Her voice gained more conviction as she spoke. I eyed her, grabbing a fluffy white towel and a delicious smelling bottle of shampoo. It was a shampoo designed specifically for men, but I wasn't going to be picky. Anything was better than the sweet aroma of copper.

"These competitors are monsters, and they have to be stopped," I reasoned. Without looking back at her, I fiddled with one of the many dials in the shower. Warm water immediately rained down, and I smiled contently. Stepping fully into the small box, I allowed the water to cascade over my skin. It felt wonderful. Almost better than sex.

Almost.

And ten times better than shower sex. I'd never understood that appeal. For one, it was difficult to find a shower large enough to fit all the people participating in such an...activity. Secondly, there was this little thing called "height difference" that was often overlooked. Men failed to realize that they had to aim lower than they anticipated. And don't even get me started on the slippery floors.

"Are you even listening?" Mali's voice bordered on a scream, as if she couldn't decide if she wanted to be angry or amused.

"I know what you're going to say," I said. "And I know what the risks of staying are. I know that there's a good chance that I'm going to die. And you know what? I'm okay with that. If I die, I don't want it to be fucking passively. I want to... I don't... Okay, look. I want to make a difference, and not just *build a shitty home for the poor* type of difference. I want lives to be saved. I want the world to be better because, let's face it, the world currently sucks ass. I want... Look, this world is full of monsters. To some, I might even be considered one, and I'm okay with that. Humans are a dying breed, and I want us to survive and... I don't even know what I'm saying. Ignore me."

Some people were capable of giving eloquent speeches at the snap of a finger, but they were far and few between. Realistically? People were blubbering messes. I couldn't even tell you what I had just said, let alone if it made any sense.

The silence was almost stifling. It was Mali who broke it first, voice terse.

"Fine. I'm going to message B and let him know the plan. Will you two be good here alone?"

"Don't worry. I can protect Diego," I teased. I heard him make a rather unflattering remark.

"Rude," he hissed.

"True," Mali and I both pointed out. I heard rather than saw my bedroom door open and close once again.

"You know," Diego began conversationally once Mali had left. "She's only worried because she cares."

"I realize that." I tilted my head back, water pelting my face. "But she does understand my job description, right? People like me don't have long lifespans."

"Don't say that." His voice was as serious as I'd ever heard it.

"It's true. I knew what I was getting myself into when I signed on."

"You didn't sign your fucking death certificate, Z. Stop thinking like that," he snapped. Turning my head, I could see his silhouette through the foggy shower screen, pacing across my bedroom floor in irritation.

"I'm an assassin, Diego. It's a kill or be killed type of world."

He would never understand. Not only was he not human, not a species so low on the totem pole that we were considered scum, but he also wasn't an assassin. Extensive training had to be undertaken before you could be initiated. Even the leader of the resistance, the baddest, most dangerous assassin I'd ever met, had died before he turned thirty. A had been more than a friend, but a father to the poor orphan girl he'd plucked from the streets. Our newest assassin, RRR, had to train for five years before she was even allowed to tag along on a mission.

I was familiar with death. We were old acquaintances, death and I. I had been face-to-face with it more times than I could count. I'd lost people—people I loved.

They had been ripped brutally away from me by the seductive pulls of death.

Was I afraid?

Most definitely.

Would I allow that fear to consume me?

Maybe.

"Just...don't die, okay?" Diego pleaded. "I don't know what I would do with myself if something happened to you."

My throat closed up at his confession.

"Don't get all sappy on me," I said roughly. He snorted.

"You started it, bitch."

"You're the bitch."

"You're the—"

Diego was interrupted by the rapid knock of knuckles against my bedroom door. I stilled, immediately switching the water off. I told myself that it couldn't be a competitor. What type of assassin would knock before they killed you?

A polite one, I reasoned.

"Stay back," Diego warned. "A lot of the competitors saw me with the other assistants. They know I'm not Z."

Now it was my turn to snort. If he really thought I would stay on the sidelines, he didn't know me at all. This was my fight, not theirs, and I would never forgive myself if I pulled them into the crossfire.

As I wrapped a towel around me, I became aware of voices speaking near the main doorway—far enough away where the intruder wouldn't be able to see me in the shower, but close enough where I could hear two, distinct voices. Both male.

I recognized Diego's immediately as he introduced himself to whoever had stopped by. I heard the second voice ask for Z.

"I want to thank him for participating in the Damning," he stated.

His voice was familiar. Raspy, almost, as if it had been used frequently. There was a slight lilt to his words. I would've liked to say it was an accent of some sort, but I knew it came from an accident in his early years.

But it couldn't be. What would he be doing in the capital?

My traitorous heart pounded beneath my ribcage. My brain fought against my heart. It was completely illogical to assume he would be here. What would be the reason? Was he a competitor?

I prayed that I was wrong. I didn't know what I would do if I saw him again.

"The crown would like to thank him for his service," he continued, and Diego said something else in reply, but the words were lost to me.

Assured that I was mistaken, I steeled myself and stepped out of the bathroom. It hadn't even occurred to me that I was only wearing a towel, revealing my long legs and a hint of cleavage. None of that registered in the dysfunctional mess of my brain.

I saw him a second before he saw me.

His hair was longer than I remembered it, brown curls resting just over his shoulders. His violet eyes were the same as they had been years ago, glowing slightly in the scarcely lit room. The expression on his face, however, was entirely different from the boy I knew. While back then he had always been smiling, as if he was privy to a joke that the rest of us had yet to hear, his features were now sharp and cold. I would've almost described them as cruel. He was impeccably dressed, as always, in a gray suit jacket and a dark tie. He'd once told me that it was necessary for a businessman like himself to look the part. I had laughed and responded by saying that he was a genie, not an entrepreneur. Of course that resulted in a tickle fight and the loss of my virginity.

Despite the physical changes, the man before me was unmistakable. How many times had I run my hands through those brown locks? Kissed those lips?

I made a sound in the back of my throat, a combination between a gasp and a cry. I had always considered myself strong, but just then, I felt weak. Weak and defeated and vulnerable. I was suddenly sixteen again, head over heels in love with an unattainable man. Sixteen, with the hope I could somehow get a happy ending.

"Lin?" I whispered. His head snapped in my direction.

"Susan?" he said back, sounding just as stunned. His eyes widened, and his expression shattered. In that brief moment when his carefully constructed walls broke, I saw a man in agony. I couldn't look away from his eyes that held me hostage. While all genies had the same violet irises, his were different. There were golden flecks around his pupil, as if he held the sun in those depths. People had always told me that the eyes were a window to the soul, and with him, I believed it. I could see every conflicting emotion—pain, grief, longing—in those beautiful eyes.

"Zara?" Diego asked, eyes volleying from me to Lin and back to me again. I could see his mind spinning, piecing together everything I had ever told him about my past love.

At the sound of Diego's voice, Lin's head whipped in my friend's direction before turning back to me. He finally seemed to notice the state I was in. Namely, a short towel and nothing else. And Diego's state—a short towel and nothing else. His face darkened with an almost incandescent fury.

Before I could say anything, he pounced on Diego.

NINE

Z

I used to have this fantasy when I was younger—to be loved completely and to love someone back. Admittedly, my wistful daydreams usually ended with said guy fighting for me. Physically, of course, because I was a twisted bitch. To see Lin throwing punches for me was sexy as hell. The sixteen-year-old girl in me wanted to swoon.

But to know that those punches were directed at my gay best friend? That kind of put a damper on the whole fantasy.

Lin was glowing, a bright light emitting from his body. His purple eyes flashed dangerously as he leveled another punch at Diego's head. I recognized this as his power acting up. Most of the time, a genie's power only rose to the surface when someone was making a wish. For him to be vibrating so erratically, like an electrical wire strung taut, he must've been immensely furious. Strong or heightened emotions tended to bring out the night-mare characteristics of any individual.

Lin's hands wrapped around Diego's neck, and I immediately ran towards them. I shouldn't have underestimated Diego, though, for my mage friend merely flicked his wrist and sent the genie flying into the wall. He kept his gaze fixated on Lin, using his impressive power to hold him in place.

"Well that was fun," Diego mumbled, using his free hand to rub at the bruises forming on his neck. "Usually, I only allow my boyfriend to choke me." His towel must've come off in the shuffle, giving me a view of his...manhood. It was something I never wanted to see. Not that it wasn't a good dick or anything but...

Lin, still glancing between Diego and me, saw the direction that my eyes flickered and began to glow yet again. His hair moved as if in an invisible breeze at the power running rampant through the air.

"At least you're not hard," I whispered out of the corner of my mouth to Diego. "I don't know how you would've been able to explain that."

"Only two people make me hard, sweets." Diego gave me a crooked smile, eyes still trained on Lin. "My sexy mate and you, of course."

"Of course."

"So please tell me how you know the Crowned Prince of the Genies," Diego said with a heavy sigh. He made a tsking noise and shook his head in disappointment. "I taught you better than that."

"Wait?" I breathed, stunned. "Crowned prince?"

Diego was wrong—Lin wasn't a prince. He was the man that had broken my heart, the teenager I had foolishly fallen in love with before I understood what love was. He was the person that had caused me to build walls around my heart, unbreakable barriers that not even Mali or Diego had fully chipped away. He gave me the irrational fear of falling in love, and not because the aspect of love itself was terrifying. What was terrifying was falling so deeply and desperately in love with someone, only to realize they didn't feel the same way. They say you can't die from a broken heart, but those people have obviously never had their hearts ripped from their bodies and stepped on by the person they loved the most. If I hadn't met S, I would've stopped believing in love and what it could do for you. Lin had destroyed me, and S had been the one to glue the shattered remains of my heart back together again.

And then S had died.

Trust me. Love didn't exist.

"His name is Devlin. Devlin Genie."

I couldn't help but snort at the name. There was nothing remotely funny about the entire situation, yet my miserable brain latched on to the first coherent thought it could think of. Devlin Genie. Believe it or not, the terms genie, vampire, shifter, mermaid, shadow, incubus, and mage were not actually intended to be the names of the species. When the Seven Deadly Sins came to Earth, they gave themselves seven different last names that would eventually become the names of the supernatural species.

The names stuck. What were once last names became a way to refer to an entire species. Their direct descendants had ruled the nightmare and human world for hundreds of years, if not thousands, since nobody could be certain when the nightmares came to be.

To hear that my Lin was the Crowned Prince Devlin? Devlin Genie?

That was fucking hilarious.

"What the hell are you doing here, Lin?" I hissed. Lin's—excuse me, *Devlin's* head swiveled in my direction.

"I could say the same about you," he retorted. "Can you please release me?" This was directed at Diego, spoken through gritted teeth.

"Do you promise to behave?" I answered.

"If he puts some damn clothes on and steps away from you, then yes."

Diego and I exchanged a look before breaking into laughter.

"I'll put my towel back on," Diego amended, still chuckling. "But I'm not moving away from my sweets."

Once again, Devlin growled, actually growled like a damn Neanderthal, before taking a calming breath.

"I promise," he said at last, sounding anything but sincere. Diego dropped his hand, and Devlin fell to the ground. Fortunately, Devlin's power seemed to have lessened from what it had been earlier, but he still threw glares in Diego's direction.

Diego, for his part, unashamedly flexed his stomach muscles. God, I loved him. Everybody needed a friend like Diego in their life.

Devlin and I participated in a silent stare off. As before, a thousand undefinable emotions flickered in his violet eyes before his lashes fluttered against his cheek-bones, like twigs of ebony.

"I'm here to officially thank Z for his service," he said at last. I folded my arms over my chest.

"And I'm here as Z's assistant," I admitted. At that, his eyes flashed to my face. It was no secret that "assistant" often translated to "lover." This time, I could clearly see the emotion darkening his features—jealousy.

What right did he have to be jealous? He was the one who had left.

"Zara..." Diego whispered beside me. He had grabbed his towel off the ground and had somewhat reluctantly wrapped it back around his waist.

"Zara?" Devlin asked in disbelief. "You told me your name was Susan. Was anything you told me the truth?"

I remembered when we met. He'd caught me stealing a loaf of bread from the local bakery.

"What's your name, love?" he'd asked, lips tilting up in amusement, and I'd scrambled to come up with a name that wasn't Z. It was no secret that names like mine were associated with the Alphabet Resistance and, more importantly, the assassins' guild. My eyes trained on the nametag of an employee in the bakery.

"Susan," I read, voice stumbling over that one word.

"Susan," he repeated.

Now, as I stared up at Devlin's arresting face, I couldn't help but laugh humorlessly.

"You have a lot of balls saying something like that, Lin. Or should I say Devlin?"

"So we both kept secrets from each other." Devlin shrugged. "No relationship is perfect. I did what I did to protect you. Being the prince brings about a lot of enemies."

While my mind immediately screamed bullshit, the reasonable voice inside of me pointed out the reason for my own lie as well—protection. He was a nightmare, and I was an assassin. I'd thought him to be a normal genie, and he thought I was a normal girl. Why did it just occur to me how toxic our love was?

Was it even love? Or was it just lie after lie piled on top of each other, turning our relationship into something unrecognizable?

"I don't care why you're here, but you need to leave. It's not safe," Devlin said earnestly. His eyes were locked on mine.

"Diego, will you leave us for a moment?" I asked, turning towards my friend.

"Will you be safe?" he asked.

"I would never hurt her!" Devlin shouted, but Diego ignored him.

"Will you be safe?" he repeated, and I offered him a small smile.

"Seriously, dude?"

Chuckling, Diego hoisted his towel farther up his waist and exited the room. I watched his retreating back, trying to ignore the eyes I could feel penetrating my skin. Devlin always had a way of innately commanding attention from me. Even when we were younger, I wanted nothing more than to stare at him and hang on to every word he said. I was so dumb back then, consumed by this love that defied all logic. A genie and an assassin fell in love... That was the beginning of a bad joke.

"You shouldn't be here," Devlin said again, once he was certain that Diego wasn't lurking in the hallway. He was beginning to sound like a broken record. Shouldn't do this. Shouldn't do that.

When did I ever listen to him? Silly boy should've known me better.

"And you shouldn't be *here*." I waved my hands to emphasize the here I was referring to. His frown only deepened.

He really had changed. Gone was the fun-loving boy who'd told me he wanted to save the world. In his place was a stranger, with hard edges, narrowed eyes, down-turned lips.

"Because your lover, Z, is going to arrive soon? You don't want to be seen with me, right?" he asked tersely.

"Yes," I said. Satisfaction filled me when his face darkened with jealousy. Call me petty or vindictive, but an odd thrill went through me at seeing such an expression on the brooding male.

"He's dangerous. He's a murderer," Devlin said, and I began to laugh.

Yes, *she* most definitely was.

"You don't get to tell me what to do anymore," I said instead. I took a step forward, and Devlin instinctively stepped backwards. His Adam's apple bobbed when he swallowed. "We are not together anymore," I stressed. "Hell, we're not even friends. You made the choice to walk out of my life, not me. You left. *You* fucking left! And now you think..." I trailed off in irritation. The tips of our feet touched, his clad in brown leather and mine bare. My chest was heaving as I pressed a finger against his well-developed stomach. He'd gained more muscle than I remembered. That was glaringly obvious, even with the suit jacket. I yearned to touch every crook in his stomach, the broad width of his shoulders, the hair cascading in soft curls around his oval face. The need to touch him was almost painful. Distance had not lessened my attraction to the genie. It only amplified it. I wanted to kiss the shit out of him, and that thought terrified me.

Instead, I shoved him.

He staggered, though not because I was strong. From the widening of his eyes, I deduced that he was shocked by my aggressive display.

"I hate you," I said. My voice, which I meant to be strident and cruel, trembled. "I hate you so fucking much."

He didn't respond. Instead, he continued to watch me with large, despondent eyes.

I shoved him yet again, and the movement propelled me forward, off my feet. His large hands curved around my waist, and he too fell to the ground.

His breathing was just as heavy as mine. I lay over him, our noses practically touching. I could feel his heartbeat beneath my breasts, pumping in tandem with mine.

"I hate you," I whispered, sitting up so I was now straddling him. My bare pussy clenched with need, even with the layer of clothing separating us. I yearned to be skin to skin with him...and I hated myself for it.

I felt him begin to harden beneath me. The twisted asshole was getting turned on. Granted, so was I, but I was a shameless hussy and he was the supposed Prince of the Genies. I would've thought he had more class.

"Susan...I mean Zara—"

"You don't get to talk," I said, cutting him off. He reached a hand out, as if to touch me, and I grabbed his wrist and placed it behind his head. "You don't get to move either."

Now, the little shit was rock-hard beneath me. Quite distracting, if I did say so myself.

"You hurt me. You left me. Do you get that? Does that make sense in that thick head of yours? *You* left *me*. You never even told me why."

"I told you—"

I pressed a hand over his mouth.

"I said you can't speak." Instinctively, my hips began to rock against his length. He let out a muffled groan, but quickly smothered it when I glared at him. "Now, here is what's going to happen. I'm going to get off of you, and you're going to disappear from my life. You're quite good at that, aren't you? You're not going to speak to me again. You're not going to talk to me again. Hell, you're not even going to think about me." With each statement, I rolled my hips to emphasize my point. Pleasure bloomed low in my stomach, and my eyes closed in bliss.

Just as quickly, they snapped back open to focus on the quivering genie beneath me.

"Do you understand?" When he remained silent, I grabbed a fistful of his hair and pulled his head back. "You answer when I speak to you."

"Yes, I understand," he grumbled.

"Great." Without another word, I climbed to my feet. I knew from his sprawled position on the ground, he got a front-row seat to my lady parts. Too bad for him. Hopefully, he would forever be pained by what he could never have.

I placed one hand on my hip and used the other to gesture towards the doorway.

"Now get the fuck out of my room."

"YOU'RE SUCH A TURD," I teased, swatting at Lin's arm. His curly hair was cut short, a contrast to his usual stylish locks. He'd told me that one of his brothers, Bash, claimed he had looked too feminine with his long hair. I'd profusely argued. Personally, I loved running my hands through his shoulder-length curls, pushing them to the side to kiss the nape of his neck. This Bash person sounded like an asshole.

"You're a nerd," he retorted.

"Why are you even dressed like that?" I asked, throwing back my head to laugh. "You look like a stuffy businessman."

We were sitting on the bed of the hotel where Lin was staying. This was his first solo mission as a genie, granting the wishes of a middle-aged human man. From what Lin had told me, the man had uncovered his family's lamp. Thus, he was given three wishes.

Fortunately for us, the man was indecisive on what he wanted. I found it hilarious when Lin would act out their interactions, lowering his voice dramatically in a poor impersonation of his client. The man, Jerry, couldn't decide if he wanted his final wish to be a wife or a million dollars. He had stupidly wasted his first two wishes on a new car and *a new gaming device—proof that evolution could go in reverse. I also loved the way Lin talked about his genie duties, as if it were a job and he an experienced entrepreneur.*

Lin smiled, leaning forward to kiss me. I allowed myself to melt in his embrace, momentarily forgetting that I was on a mission to rid the world of a murderous mermaid. B would've been expecting me to check in by then, but he, along with the rest of the world, was a distant memory. How could I possibly focus on death when Lin was breathing life into me? Each stroke of his tongue sent me further and further over the edge.

His hand pushed my shirt up, gently cupping my breast through my bra. I groaned at the sensation.

"I want you," he whispered between kisses.

"You have me."

Forever and always.

I AWOKE WITH A GASP. Waning sunlight came through the opened blinds, casting the room in shadows. I must've fallen asleep after my confrontation with Devlin. My body ached at the uncomfortable position I found myself in. The towel, at some point, had fallen off, leaving me butt naked.

In a matter of hours, I'd discovered that I was participating in a fight to the death, had fought against three assassins, had come face-to-face with my ex-boyfriend, and had fallen asleep in my birthday suit. All in all, it wasn't my worst Friday night.

There was a slip of paper folded at the end of my bed. I recognized Mali's delicate script immediately and reached for the card.

Hunter German. Age 33. Vampire. Murdered seventeen children but never convicted. Seventh floor. Fourth door.

I smiled at the card. My rage was consuming me with an almost elemental fury, and I needed an outlet. My world had quickly fallen into shambles around me. I didn't know how to deal with this newfound knowledge about my old lover. I kept replaying every conversation in my head, wondering when and how our love turned into something so toxic and dangerous. A prince and an assassin.

How could I possibly kill Lin? I'd loved him so fiercely at one point. It was inconceivable to be in a world where he no longer existed.

But ridding the world of scum like this Hunter person? That I could do.

I grabbed my necklace off of my bedside drawer and pressed down. Immediately, I was clothed in Z's badass attire.

Just another day in the life of an assassin.

———

I GRAPPLED with the rock protruding from the side of the capital.

The exterior of the building—alternating between rocks and painted wood—provided surprisingly easy handholds for me as I climbed. My arms wobbled as I attempted to pull myself up onto a windowsill.

Shit. I was getting out of shape.

Pressing myself against the wall, I surveyed the room. The window was opened slightly, providing circulation into the small bedroom.

A man and a woman were in the room. The man was handsome, a sort of traditional, sculpted beauty I was beginning to associate with all vampires. The woman was naked, moaning loudly as the vampire pounded into her.

Well...

I wasn't in the mood to watch a porno.

The vampire, Hunter, pressed his lips against her neck, and at first, I thought he was kissing her. It took me a moment to realize that he was biting her. Sucking her blood.

The woman's eyes rolled back into her head, and her body tilted to the side. Tiny gasps of pleasure escaped her parted lips. I'd heard that a vampire's bite was the equivalent to ten orgasms. Of course, I'd never experienced it myself.

I pulled a dagger from its sheath, flicking my gaze between the blissed-out woman and the vampire. Without giving myself too much time to think about it, I threw the dagger through the opened window. It sailed through the air, hitting the vampire's chest directly over his heart. He stopped mid thrust, and the woman turned her head marginally to see her lover. An anguished cry escaped her lips, and I almost felt bad. Almost. And then I remembered the horrendous crimes that Hunter had committed, and my guilt diminished. If this girl was capable of loving such a monster, if she was willing to defend him, then she was a monster too.

Her pupils dilated when they rested on me, her face contorting until it was entirely unrecognizable. Tiny sprouts of hair grew on her body. Her once delicate features sharpened, mouth elongating into what resembled a snout.

A shifter.

I attempted to maneuver myself down to the level below me. I kicked my feet, gaining momentum to pull myself into a lower floor window. The shifter rushed at me, and I used one hand to aim a dagger at her face.

But that movement caused me to lose my balance. The hold I had on the rock slipped, and my feet struggled to find purchase on the sill.

The shifter snapped her teeth at me, but I was already falling.

Down and down and down and down...

TEN

LUPE

I could barely focus on the words in front of me. I tried to concentrate, tried to read the story that once entranced me, but all I could think about was *her*.

The girl without a name.

The girl who was the star of every one of my dreams.

The girl who I couldn't get out of my head.

When I sniffed her, my bear had begun to pace inside the confines of my brain. I could feel him, an almost physical entity, demanding to be let out, to claim what he thought was his. The urge to hold that strange woman, to protect her, was overwhelming.

To see her walk away from me was hell.

I could picture her clearly. Blonde hair, like sunlit spun silk cascading around her shoulders in perfect waves. Her cheekbones, sharp and chiseled. The rose-tint to her cheeks. The white curve of her neck.

She was an angel in human form.

I'd resisted the urge to write a soliloquy commenting

on her ethereal beauty. I wasn't sure how much that would be appreciated. Shifters were known for their muscles and strength, not their eloquent words. I would scare her away if I began sending her poems and flowers.

Besides, I didn't even know her name, nor what type of nightmare she was. Usually, a shifter was able to scent what type of species someone was, but I'd been a little distracted by her ethereal beauty and the floral aroma of her perfume. She was an enigma, a box with lock after lock on it, and I ached to uncover every secret she had.

What I wouldn't give to paint her...

The swoop of her shoulders. The hourglass figure. The—

"You're brooding more than usual. What's up?" My sister, Atta, moved to sit on the couch beside me. We were in an abandoned corner of the library, light slanting through the stained-glass windows. The smell of dust and worn leather assaulted my enhanced senses. Still, I couldn't think of a better, more enticing, smell.

Unless you counted *her* sweet scent, a combination of roses and something almost spicy.

Mate, my bear had growled.

I couldn't help but agree.

I didn't know what I'd expected when I eventually found my soulmate, but it wasn't this. I most certainly hadn't expected this all-consuming need to be by her side and loving her, the way a woman like her deserved to be loved.

But I was terrified. I'd seen firsthand how toxic love could be. It wasn't a blissful emotion. It was the waters that drowned you, the knife that stabbed your heart, the iron clamps around your neck, choking the life from you. Falling in love was dangerous because there was no guarantee that both parties would fall. Besides, who would be willing to accept a mate like me? A shifter who preferred words over actions. A shifter who was over two hundred pounds of pure muscle yet had never been in a fight.

"Where did your mind go?" Atta elbowed me yet again, voice inquisitive. While I looked more like my father, Atta had my mother's characteristics—soft, dewy features and bright red hair.

"I don't want to talk about it," I mumbled, turning a page in my book. The words were barely comprehensible in the mess that was my brain. I wouldn't have even been able to tell you what the name of the book was.

"Well..." Atta gave me a knowing look but dropped the subject. My sister sometimes knew me better than I knew myself. "*I've* been enjoying the Matching immensely." Her eyes twinkled mischievously, and I snorted.

"You competing with Bash?"

She scoffed.

"It's not a competition when I always win. You'll be surprised how many of those women prefer the boobs over the dick. Bash has nothing on me. I saw this one girl that was super hot. Blonde, curvy—"

Before I realized what was happening, I began to growl. All I could think about was someone else, someone besides me, looking at my mate.

And her looking back.

The thought made my nails sharpen until they were

keen claws. The fabric of the chair ripped with my death grip.

Atta blinked, her eyes widening at my uncharacteristic behavior. Understanding dawned on her face suddenly, and her lips parted.

"Oh..."

"Don't even say it," I hissed.

"Holy shit! You found your mate!" She bounced up from the chair, jumping and clapping her hands in glee.

"Shhh..." I whispered, putting a finger to my lips. I could feel my cheeks flaming.

"You found your mate! You found your mate!" she sang, punctuating each word with a shake of her hips. "What's her name? Where is she? What did she do? Tell me everything!"

I didn't know how to answer those questions. I was told that no matter what the species was, a nightmare would know immediately when they came into contact with their mate. Yet the beautiful girl had barely even acknowledged my presence. My heart ached at the memory of her running away from me.

My dad was right—I would never find love. They would always run from me, always leave me. I was a mistake, a malfunction, and my mate surely realized that. Why else would she leave as if she'd had the hounds from hell on her heels?

"I heard that Jax put on quite the show," Atta said, changing the subject. Her eyes continued to study my face, but she smiled softly as she reminisced on her "fiancé's" antics.

Grateful for her ability to gauge my emotions, I asked, "What did he do this time?"

"Besides meeting the girls ass naked? He told them that his blood tingled from fairy spells."

I paused, mouth opening as I prepared to speak, before shutting it once more. Sometimes, I really didn't know what to do about my brother. Though none of us were brothers by blood, we all grew up with each other. Our entire childhoods had revolved around our friendships with one another. Without them, I wouldn't have been the man I was today. They were more my family than my own parents.

"He needs to feed," I groaned out at last, running a large hand through my hair. Jax's decision not to drink blood was slowly breaking him. Already, I had trouble recognizing the person he'd turned into from the man he once was. I understood the reasoning behind his decision, I honestly did, but that didn't mean I agreed with it. What happened to Sasha was an accident and, though tragic, shouldn't define the rest of his life. He had to learn to forgive himself for what had happened.

Atta's nose scrunched up, the only indication that she agreed with me. Though the relationship between Atta and Jax was strictly platonic, I knew that she cared about him. She cared about all of them the way she cared about me—as brothers. The fact that our parents were pushing for a marriage between her and Jax was disgusting.

A boisterous laugh interrupted whatever she was going to say. Frowning, I closed my book and set it on the library table. Life at the capital, I realized, was chaotic. I was never able to have more than a few minutes to myself before the devils ascended.

The devil this time took the form of my mage brother, Bash. He had his arms slung around two, petite brunettes —competitors for the Matching—and his shirt was unbuttoned. Alcohol wafted off of him, unsurprisingly pungent. Both Atta and I wrinkled our noses. Behind the three of them, Killian followed timidly.

"Are you kidding me, Bash?" Atta snapped.

"What?" he drawled lazily, flopping into the seat opposite us. One of the girls perched on the armchair while the other sat beside Atta. I could see the two females exchange meaningful glances.

No doubt, this was one of the girls that Atta had... relations with.

I shuddered. That was the last thing I wanted to think about.

As I glanced from Bash, leisurely stroking the hair of the incubus girl beside him, to Killian, I noticed something that struck me as odd.

Killian was hard. Like, full-on, *dick tenting his pants* type of hard.

"What the fuck, Kill?" Atta screamed, noticing the same thing I had. I mean, it was kind of hard *not* to notice. Rumor had it that all incubi grew a few inches when they reached puberty...and not just in height.

"Oh, that?" Bash waved his hand dismissively in the direction of his friend. "He found his mate."

"Found his...?" Atta looked between me and Kill. Her emerald green eyes sparked with excitement. No doubt, she was already planning a double wedding. Damn sisters.

"I ha-have-enn't-t-t see-en-n-n her yet," Killian said. He anxiously glanced from face to face, noticeably uncomfortable at having this conversation in front of strangers, and the brunette beside Bash began to chuckle unashamedly at Killian's stutter. My beast roared inside of me at her blatant disrespect and rudeness towards my brother. Even Bash's eyes narrowed in the direction of his lover.

"He can sense his mate, though he has yet to see her," Bash cut in, finally turning away from the horrid girl beside him. "Hence the hard-on."

Something flashed in Bash's eyes. Something akin to jealousy.

Despite his repeated claims of not wanting a mate, I knew that he longed to have one. He longed to call a girl his own, to hold her late into the hours and whisper sweet nothings into her ear. He'd admitted that on more than one occasion when he got wasted. Despite this, the bastard was terrified.

Of losing us, his family.

He didn't want some girl to come between us all. I knew for a fact he would bust a nut if he discovered I found my mate as well. From the pursing of Atta's lips, I deduced that she'd come to the same conclusion.

"So little Killian is growing up?" Atta cooed. She flashed the man in question a wicked smile, and Killian blushed. It was the strangest thing to see. A muscled man, not nearly as defined as me but still more developed than an average male, with tattoos evident on every swath of bare skin, was *blushing*. He ducked his head, hiding behind his auburn hair.

Maybe that was why we were friends.

We were both fuckups at being nightmares.

"I hope I never find my mate," Bash began, leaning back in his chair indolently.

Here we go...

Killian met my eyes over Bash's head and sighed heavily. Bash's rants could last anywhere from a minute to an hour.

Atta glanced at me out of the corner of her eye. Her dainty hand was already wrapped around the girl's.

"I'm going to head out," she whispered. "Before I leave, do you have a picture?"

I knew what she was asking. A delicate blush dusted across my own cheekbones. I felt like such an ass for making fun of Killian's blush when I was no better.

Glancing at Bash, still discussing all of the cons of having a mate, I grabbed my notebook off of the table and reluctantly handed it to Atta. She wouldn't stop pestering me until I did.

I knew what she would see when she opened the notebook to the first page.

The beautiful girl.

The girl whose name I had yet to discover.

The girl who'd been shoved into my world...and became the sun that my earth revolved around. Maybe I *should* start writing some poems...

ELEVEN

Z

Pro tip—never scale the side of a building without a parachute.

Seriously. Don't.

Falling? Scary as hell. Knowing that you're going to die? Well...let's just say I wouldn't recommend it.

The world spun as I fell. A kaleidoscope of colors. Shapes. Sounds. They all whirled past me. I saw my life in those brief moments before I would've hit the ground. All of my mistakes and failures were displayed before me, suffocating me. I thought of B. He would be so disappointed in me for failing my mission. I thought of Mali and Diego and how they would mourn me. I thought of T, the assassin who'd been in love with me for years. I even allowed my mind to drift to Devlin. He'd been my first, and I did love him. Even now, my heart squeezed painfully at the thought of my genie.

My genie. The possessiveness I felt towards Lin had always scared me, but now it gave me strength. I didn't forgive him for what he did to me, but I wanted one more memory with him. His hands running over my body. His lips between my breasts. His skilled fingers bringing me to the peak of pleasure.

Did it make me a hussy that I thought of sex with Devlin before I died? Strangely enough, I also thought of the shifter I met earlier. The prince. He'd been hand-some, an immense brute of a man that I normally wouldn't have looked twice at. Why did my final thoughts turn towards him?

What the hell was wrong with me?

You might think that those thoughts took hours to articulate. They actually only lasted approximately three seconds, just long enough for me to see the water rushing towards my face. I braced myself for the impact, for the excruciating pain, but it never came.

Instead, I found myself engulfed in something warm.

Water.

It held me in gentle arms, a physical being, before depositing me into the lake. This exchange lasted only a moment. There was no pain. Just comfort.

I broke the surface of the water, sputtering slightly. The waves lapped at my skin, surprisingly warm despite the frigidly cold air.

Stunned, I glanced from side to side. How had I survived? I was positive I was a few feet away from the lake when I'd initially fallen. I should've been splattered on the concrete, a Z pancake, not in the water.

It was almost as if...

Almost as if the water had caught me.

But that was ridiculous, right?

My thoughts spun, even as I continued to scan the

dark abyss of water. Oceans and lakes had always terri-fied me. They were vast and unknown. Anything could be lurking in their dark depths. Hell, mermaids had lived there for years without anyone knowing. What else hid away beneath the roiling sea?

White foam crested against the nearby shore, and I immediately swam in that direction. The fabric of my assassin outfit stuck to my body like a second skin.

"Are you okay?" a soft voice asked, and I spun towards the sound. Using my arms to tread water, I stared at the blond head poking above the surface. He was too far away for me to be able to distinguish any noticeable characteristics. "I tried to make you land as painlessly as possible."

"Was that you?" I asked. "The water?"

"Yes."

So my savior was a mermaid. I didn't know how I felt about that.

"Thank you. For saving my life."

I felt hesitant about how to deal with him. A mother-fucking mermaid had saved my life. Why? To kill me himself?

"The water heard your cries," he continued, oblivious to my thoughts. "You spoke to me in a way no one has ever spoken to me before."

That explained it.

Mr. Mermaid was insane.

"Well, thank you. Again."

The water rippled as he ducked beneath the surface. He reappeared a moment later directly in front of me.

Golden blond hair clung to his temples. His skin was

tanned and deliciously muscled. His blue eyes, the color of a translucent pool of water, surveyed my face intently. He was beautiful, in the way that art was. It was a traditional beauty that couldn't be referred to as "sexy" or "hot." Those words weren't eloquent enough to describe the man before me.

He reached a hand out, and I flinched away.

"Don't...don't touch me," I managed. His expression shuttered, surprise giving way to unreadability. After a moment, he held up his hands in surrender as if he were a prisoner approaching a police officer. He appeared rightfully wary and cautious, regarding me like one would look at a rabid shifter.

"I'm not going to hurt you."

Despite the sincerity in his voice, years and years of abuse at the hands of nightmares couldn't be ignored that easily.

Pro tip number two—everybody had an agenda. People could offer you false promises, present after present wrapped in bows, but there would always be a catch. That promise? It was actually an exchange for your soul. That present? It was a ticking time bomb. You couldn't trust anyone.

I scrambled backwards, accidentally swallowing a mouthful of water in my haste. His eyebrows crinkled with concern, but he still respected my wishes and remained a safe distance away.

"Why would I save you if I was going to hurt you?" he asked, sounding honestly confused.

A lot of reasons why, I thought sardonically, my anger cresting.

A lot.

God. What was wrong with me? What had life done to me that I automatically assumed that everybody had bad intentions? He'd done nothing to me, and yet I was cowering before him like a child instead of the assassin I knew myself to be.

My legs were aching from treading water for so long. I'd gone swimming once or twice when I was younger, but this was different. If I had to fight while in water, I would merely accept defeat. I was so tired, my body leaden, and the urge to allow the water to consume me was overwhelming.

I was just so tired of fighting.

So tired of everything.

"Don't you hear the water?" the mermaid asked me, voice rising in disbelief. "It's significantly louder now that you're here."

"Um..."

How did one respond to that?

"You look exhausted. May I help you back to shore?"

I considered his words seriously, picking apart what little I knew of him. He wasn't a competitor for the Damning, I would've recognized him from the files B had provided for me, so he must've been an assistant. Innocent. He could've been completely innocent, a pawn in this game we'd both been forced into. I needed to stop fearing every nightmare I came into contact with. I needed to stop assuming they were the enemy when I knew plenty of humans that were ten times worse.

Trust. I had to trust this stranger, this mermaid, and the mere thought of it was terrifying. My thoughts turned to Mali and Diego, my two best friends, who both happened to be nightmares. Their species and sin didn't define who they were as a person.

And if this mermaid was somehow able to pull one over on me...

I still had two knives hooked to my thighs.

Eyes trained on his, I nodded.

Before I could change my mind, he grabbed my arm and began to glide across the water. Each movement allowed me to see the dark blue of his tail, scales reflecting in the sinking sunlight. It was incredibly beautiful, a word I would have never used to describe a nightmare before. But that was what this man was—beautiful.

Instinctively, like a voice was whispering inside my mind, I reached a hand out to stroke one of the shimmery scales. His body froze suddenly, and his breathing turned ragged.

"That is...that is extremely sensitive," he gasped out at last. I removed my hand as if his tail were acid.

"Oh shit. Sorry."

I could feel my face burning. I'd practically touched a stranger's dick. Yup. I wouldn't blame him if he decided to drown me.

Trust.

I had to trust him.

"You didn't know," he said through clenched teeth. His tail twitched in the water, rising up and hardening as if it were...

Nope. No more looking at the tail for you, Z.

"So why are you here?" I asked before I could stop myself. "Most mermaids prefer to use their twelve hours as a man during the day. You know, to interact with people and whatnot."

And to have sex, I thought, but didn't say. Rumor had it that a mermaid couldn't get it on while in their mer forms. A horrible flaw in their creation, if you asked me.

And why was I even thinking about sex?

With a mermaid?

"I don't like for people to see me," he answered uneasily.

"Because you're hot?"

Again, I really needed to develop a filter. I wondered if the potion I had drunk earlier was still in effect.

He chuckled, a surprisingly delicious sound. Or perhaps unsurprisingly, given that he looked like a model.

We reached the shoreline, where a small hut separated the water from the shore. After depositing me on land, my mermaid savior swam inside the diminutive building, out of view from me.

"I need to change into my human form." His voice was muffled through the wall separating us.

I considered briefly pressing my necklace to turn back into Zara. I quickly decided against it. Despite my intuition telling me I could trust this strange man, I would not risk my identity because of a pretty face. Hearts and minds were often liars. It was hard to distinguish between the two.

"Why don't you like your human form?" I pressed. I heard the sound of clothing being shuffled around before he replied.

"You know that mermaids are descended from Envy, correct?" he asked. I couldn't help but snort.

"No shit. Everybody knows that."

Once again, my words were greeted by a toe-curling laugh.

"Did you know that I have three mermaid brothers?" he asked. Pulling myself onto my elbows, I faced the wooden siding of the shack. Though I couldn't see him, I imagined him pulling his clothes on.

Dammit. That thought made me throb.

"How the hell would I know that?" I retorted.

"They were always envious of me. I was the handsomest. The smartest. The funniest." He spoke without preamble, as if he was stating facts and not bragging about his perfection. "So they decided to do something about it."

"I have a feeling this story doesn't have a happy ending," I said softly. My heart ached for some undefinable reason. I didn't know why I felt pity for a mermaid. I should hate him—I *did* hate him—but at the same time, I wanted to soothe him. I wanted to bandage the scars I knew cut deeply. He'd saved my life, and a little voice inside of me wanted to save his.

That little voice was a dumbass.

"No happy ending," he said, chuckling. "At least not yet." He paused for a moment, as if considering his words. "They cut off my tail."

I allowed his words to process. My heart hammered inside of my chest at his declaration.

"But I saw it...your tail, that is. I even stroked it."

Okay. I did not mean that to sound as sexual as it ended up being. I was grateful for the barrier separating us just then. I was sure my face was the color of a ripe tomato.

"My tail grew back," he said after a long moment of silence. "But my legs? They weren't as lucky."

He finally emerged from the shack, and I gasped as I took stock of the beautiful man.

He was confined to a wheelchair. His legs, from his knees down, were completely gone.

Tears welled in my eyes unexplainably. I hated seeing him like this, hated seeing the pain in his eyes, as if he thought he was less of a man. I couldn't understand my own emotions. I had just met him. I should've hated him.

What was happening to me?

The mermaid mistook my silence for something else.

"It's ugly, right? I hate the looks of disgust. The pity." His lip curled. "I don't want anyone to think of me as less than. Less than a man. A lover. A person."

I gasped at him, stunned that I had correctly guessed his inner turmoil.

"You're not," I whispered. "Less than, that is."

"You know... I don't even know why I'm telling you all this. Or showing you. I haven't even told my brothers —my real brothers, not my blood brothers—about the way I feel."

"To be honest, I don't know why I'm listening."

Or why I cared.

"What's your name?" I asked suddenly. His beautiful cerulean blue eyes turned towards me, blinking slowly. They widened with the realization that he hadn't shared that snippet of information with me, nor I with him.

"Dair," he answered at last. The word rolled off his tongue like music.

Dair. A beautiful name. And a slightly familiar name, though I couldn't pinpoint where I'd heard it before.

"What's your name, little assassin?" he asked. My heart thumped at the nickname.

"Z," I answered.

"Z." The way he said my name...it was almost a physical caress. "Can I see your face?"

I almost agreed. Logical reasoning had left my mind, and all I could focus on was him and my need to please him. My hand moved towards the necklace.

One push...

All it would take was one push...

I scrambled to my feet, away from him. He made me feel too much, too deeply, too quickly.

It suddenly occurred to me the reason why I was feeling like that—a spell. He'd used his powers on me, made me trust him. It was the only explanation that made logical sense.

What type of assassin was I to have fallen for such a ruse? A pretty damn stupid one, that was for sure.

Despite my mind demanding me to kill him, my body prohibited it.

"I, um..."

Self-consciousness flickered across his handsome face, followed quickly by despair. I knew it was an act, I knew it, but I wasn't able think straight. There couldn't have possibly been any sincerity in his expression. I had to remember what he was and what he'd obviously done to me.

Monster.

They were all monsters.

And this one in particular had used his allure to make me trust him. What had he planned to do with me? Torture me? Kill me? Rape me?

"I need to leave," I said. "I need to..."

And then I did the thing he expected me to do. The one thing that made me hate myself a little more.

I ran.

TWELVE

Z

Cursing beneath my breath, I entered through the back door of the capital building. My wet shoes sloshed against the linoleum flooring.

I couldn't stop thinking about the strange mermaid I'd met. Dair. Where had I heard that name before?

The realization came to me only seconds later, my hand tightening on the golden rail of the staircase.

Dair Mermaid.

The prince.

The damn prince.

The strength of my epiphany nearly made me stumble. I took a calming breath in an attempt to slow my racing heart. So far, I'd met three princes. Three men that I'd been tasked to kill. Was it fate? Something else entirely? I was suddenly rethinking everything I knew about nightmares and life itself.

I couldn't kill them. Not Dair, who'd saved my life. Not Lin, who'd held my heart in his hands before crushing it. Not even the shifter, Lupe, who both terrified and entranced me.

Had they put a spell on me? Was that why I was suddenly feeling empathy for such monsters? I didn't know how to answer those questions, nor did I want to. Anger rushed through me when I considered how easily I'd trusted Dair with my life. The only explanation was that he'd used his siren allure on me and had broken down my defenses through his magic. And I'd been dumb enough to fall for it. Never again, though. Never again. Maybe a good night of sleep would clear the incoherent mess that was my brain.

Sleep. I needed sleep.

My thoughts were interrupted by a wave of unquenchable lust. My nipples hardened beneath my shirt, and my pussy clenched with need.

Dammit.

An incubus.

This was only reaffirmed when a striking figure descended the staircase above me. He had dark skin and even darker hair. He emanated a type of confidence that one could only dream of having. The smirk on his lips hinted that he knew what he was doing to me and enjoyed it. His power rolled off of him in waves.

I wanted nothing more than to tear off all of my clothes and—

No!

I saw the dagger in his hand a second before he lunged. I rolled out of the way, the keen tip slicing through my mask and grazing my cheek. I winced at the pain but kept my attention on the grinning, seductive assassin before me.

"Not much is known about you, Z," he said, voice like honey. "No one knows what your species is. Hell, no one even knows if you're a male or a female."

He swung the dagger again in a large arc, and I jumped out of the way.

"I don't like mysteries," he hissed. The need to touch myself was almost excruciating. Damn incubus and damn incubus powers. Instead of giving in to my desires, I balled my hands into fists.

The incubus charged, just as I knew he would.

My first order of business was ridding him of his weapon. This was surprisingly easy, given his clumsy, lumbering frame. From the way he moved, I reasoned that he wasn't the type to use stealth as a tool.

I ducked beneath his arm, using my own to wrap around his throat. His movements became erratic as he scrambled for air, his knife swinging wildly in front of him. I used my free hand to knock the dagger to the ground.

He grunted, pushing backwards. My arm lost purchase where it gripped his meaty neck, and he stumbled away from me, gasping for air. Before he could catch his bearings, I grabbed the weapon from the floor and shoved it into his neck.

Blood immediately sprayed from him, drenching my already soaked clothes. The incubus desperately grabbed at his throat as if he could somehow hold the skin together. He dropped to his knees, blood still dripping from the wound, before he fell face first into a pool of his own blood.

Dead.

He was dead.

He was the second man I'd killed in only a matter of hours. Did it make me a psychopath that I couldn't conjure up any pity for these kills? If anything, I felt relief that there was one less nightmare in the world.

"You're not as a strong as the others. But you have speed. I would recommend using that to your advantage," a silky smooth voice said. I grabbed the dagger out of the dead incubus' neck, ignoring the blood dripping off of the blade in red rivulets, and aimed it in the direction of the intruder's voice.

All I saw was a dark silhouette.

A shadow.

"Are you here to kill me?" I asked tersely, lowering my voice in a poor impersonation of a man.

"Why would I kill you?" The man sounded honestly curious, if not amused, by my question. I watched the shadow move from one wall to the next.

"Because this is a game. It's kill or be killed."

I repeated my life motto as if I weren't scared, as if my heart weren't beating rapidly at death being so close to me.

"It may be a game, but…" Warm breath tickled my ear, and I spun to the side expectantly. "I'm not playing."

Nobody was there.

"Who are you?" I asked, spinning in a circle. I kept my dagger raised in preparation.

A chuckle emitted from above me, near the rail of the

staircase, and I glanced up. All I saw was the flash of black before the shadow moved once again.

"I'm a shadow," he answered.

"I asked who you are, not what you are," I snapped. What I really wanted to know, however, was whether he was friend or foe.

"They call me Ryland," he said, voice coming from a windowsill five levels above. It echoed throughout the room.

"But is that your name?" I pressed.

"What even is a name?" he mused. "It's just a title, is it not?"

"But..."

His chuckle receded as he moved farther and farther away.

A shadow.

I'd met a shadow, and he hadn't killed me. I'd met a mermaid, and he hadn't killed me.

I rubbed at my forehead, ignoring the blood that smeared across my skin, before lowering both hands back to my sides. I needed sleep.

I needed sleep, and, more importantly, I needed clarity.

Without bothering to turn back towards the dead incubus, I walked upstairs.

Everything would make sense with sleep.

"LIN?" I asked, pushing open the door to the hotel room. How many times had I come here? One hundred? One

thousand? "Lin? Baby?"

My eyes searched the room expectantly. The bed, freshly made. The lack of clothes that usually littered the floor. The closed suitcase on the small table.

My frown deepened when I noticed Lin standing beside the suitcase. His expression was carefully blanked, almost impassive, but his eyes were anguished.

"Lin, what's wrong?" I asked, running towards him, hands outstretched. He stepped away from me as if my touch were toxic. The feeling that something was wrong only amplified at his rejection, at his dismissal of me.

Lin was a shell of the man I remembered and loved.

"What's wrong?" I repeated, chewing on my nail anxiously. It was a horrible habit that I was determined to break.

"I need to leave," he whispered. He wouldn't meet my gaze.

"Okay?" I couldn't understand why he was behaving so strangely. He'd left numerous times before, but he'd always found his way back to me. He'd told me that I was a magnet he couldn't ignore. He'd told me that we would always find our way back to each other, no matter the time or distance. "When are you coming back?"

His Adam's apple bobbed as he swallowed. He still refused to meet my questioning gaze.

"Lin?" I said slowly. "When are you coming back?"

"I'm not coming back."

I frowned, sure I had heard him wrong. We belonged together—two broken souls that had miraculously found each other in the unpredictable chaos of life.

"What do you mean?"

"This..." He gestured between the two of us. "It isn't working."

My world stopped. My blood turned to ice.

That was the moment when he destroyed me. When he took what little heart I had left after my parents' and A's deaths and trampled it.

"You don't mean that," I whispered. He was wrong. He wasn't thinking clearly. We were meant to be together, that was what he'd always told me.

"I do. We're not..." His face pinched as if he'd swallowed something sour. "We're not good together."

A part of me wanted to beg. I wanted him to fight for me. For us. Why wasn't he fighting? Had he ever loved me the way I'd loved him? It had never occurred to me before that our love was one-sided, but I couldn't help but replay every conversation we'd ever had and every touch between us.

I'd been so stupid.

"Walk away," I said. "Walk away and don't look back."

"Susan..." He trailed off helplessly.

My voice rose to a scream.

"Walk away! Walk away!"

And he did.

I WOKE up to somebody shaking my shoulder. In my dazed, sleepy state, I assumed I was still dreaming. What else could possibly explain the figure standing beside my bed?

A vampire.

"Whatyadoing?" I muttered. I knew I should've been frightened by the strange man towering over me, but I couldn't muster an ounce of fear or terror. There was so much vulnerability in his unguarded expression. So much tenderness.

I wondered, briefly, if my fight or flight response was broken again.

What a strange, realistic dream.

He had light brown hair, cut short. Even in the darkness, I could see that his handsome face looked as if it was carved from marble.

"My blood tingles. But it stops when I'm with you. The voices stop."

Fucking hell.

I'd had my fair share of weird dreams in my twenty years of life, but this one took the cake.

"Can I sleep with you? I want—no, I *need* the voices to stop."

"Only if you shut the fuck up and let me sleep," I murmured drowsily. I lifted the quilt back from the bed and patted the spot beside me.

The smile that lit up his face was brilliant. He eagerly climbed into my bed and rubbed his nose against my neck. His hand pushed up my shirt, touching the bare skin of my stomach, as if he couldn't bear to have that layer of clothing separating us. I smiled in contentment.

"The voices are finally quiet," he murmured.

"Let's go to sleep," I replied, darkness already beginning to claim me.

And we slept.

THIRTEEN

JAX

I'd watched her with the incubus, her lithe and graceful body easily able to overtake the assassin.

The voices had finally stopped when I'd laid eyes upon her. They no longer screamed at me or reminded me of what I had done.

I just needed silence.

Because I knew I was mad, but madness was only in the eye of the beholder. Mad. What *was* mad? Was it the implication that the mind wasn't able? And how did mad differ from disabled under this notion of abled?

I brushed her hair behind her ear. She'd allowed me to stay, allowed me to silence the strident voices inside of me.

Silence.

The voices had nothing more to say.

FOURTEEN

DAIR

"Get up, you fat bastard. I need to talk to you." I shoved at Lupe's arm. My brother let out a loud grunt, a combination between a snore and a yell, before bolting straight upright in bed, eyes flashing with a predator-like intensity as they flew to my face. "Easy there," I murmured, attempting to placate his bear.

"What are you doing here? It's three o'clock in the fucking morning."

Closing his eyes yet again, he settled back into the bed. It only took a second before his loud snores filled the room.

I shoved him again.

"I need to ask you something."

"And it couldn't wait?" he murmured sleepily.

My fingers anxiously fiddled with the edge of his quilt. I focused on the repetitive movement, on the soft material sliding between my thumb and pointer finger like silk.

"How do mermaids know when they find their mate?" I whispered. The words tasted funny in my mouth. Never before had I believed that the word "mate" would leave my lips.

"Mermaid? Mate?" the giant mumbled again. It was obvious from his heavily-lidded eyes that he was still half asleep. It was a wonder he could even speak coherently at all. "From what I've read, the water will tell you. I don't know for certain, though." As if he'd just comprehended what I had asked, he sat straight upright in bed again. His sleepy eyes widened as they rested on my face.

"Mate?" he asked, stunned.

I shrugged sheepishly, but my mouth curved up instinctively.

Z.

What an odd name for an even odder female.

I knew next to nothing about her. Where did she come from? What did she look like?

My heart clenched painfully when I thought about how I'd found her. She'd been falling to her death. And death would've claimed her too, if I hadn't interfered. It became apparent the second I laid eyes on her that she was a competitor for the Damning. My mate, the assassin. A part of me felt proud. I'd never wanted a damsel in distress type of mate. Another part of me was utterly terrified. There were one hundred competitors in the Damning and only one winner. What were the chances that she would be it? That she would survive?

After I came to that conclusion, I immediately began running through every scenario in my mind. We could leave, the two of us, but that would mean forsaking both of our duties. Not that I would mind leaving behind my depressive life...

My eyes flickered to my legs...or what was left of them. Pathetic. Utterly pathetic. No wonder she ran from me. Her mate, the male who was supposed to be the other half of her, was nothing but a broken man. How could she expect me to make her whole when I had yet to find my own missing pieces? I couldn't protect her.

Failure.

I was a failure, just as my father and blood brothers had told me time and time again. I could smile flirtatiously, charm however many women I wanted, but I would never find true love. Nobody was capable of looking past my deformities.

My father had told me a story once of a mermaid who'd met his mate, a girl who would eventually become the first shadow. She was the sweetest, most vibrant person anyone had ever met, and she seemed to shine brightly, as if wreathed in light. For all her inward beauty, her face was marred by a hideous scar. The mermaid, insanely jealous of the perfection around him, grew increasingly disgusted with his fate. Although his mate was beloved by all for the kindness she radiated, he became more and more enraged by what he thought she lacked—outward beauty. One night, as his mate slept heavily drugged, the mermaid took his knife and skinned her. In his mind, having no skin was better than having blemished skin. Although she was heartbroken, her pride prohibited her from exposing his cruelty. Instead, she resolved to cloak herself in shadows to save him from embarrassment. Thus, the first shadow was born.

That was just a legend, of course. We all knew that the shadows were descended from the sin of pride, but my father had a tendency to spin his stories like a spider spun a web. His own father was a terrific storyteller. In return, he felt the need to be an even better one.

I thought that all as I met Lupe's penetrating stare.

"I'm not certain," I said, though those words felt like a lie. I'd known the second I felt her essence, a touch as soft as a moth's wing, that she was my mate. She was made to be mine, just as I was made to be hers. They'd told me that it was fate, our mates, like two threads twined together. The bond was inseparable. Irresistible.

And yet...

And yet she had resisted.

There had even been fear in her eyes when she regarded me. Fear...and something almost haunted. Despite her youthful face, her eyes were ancient.

Why would she fear me, her mate? It didn't seem like something that would be possible.

All supernatural creatures had one fated mate. I pitied the humans in that respect. Wandering the world without the other half of your soul seemed to be its own form of torture.

"I'm probably mistaken," I said, chewing on my lip. "Never mind. It was stupid."

I immediately began to wheel myself towards the door. It was stupid to have come here in the first place. What had been my reasoning? For knowledge?

Or to brag?

"Wait," Lupe said, and I paused, turning my head to

see the large man sitting up straighter. "I found her too. My mate, that is. I found her."

His expression took on a wistful, dream-like quality. A small smile made his harsh features appear softer.

"You have?" I asked in disbelief, not because I didn't think Lupe was capable or even worthy of having a mate, but because I knew how his father would react if he were to discover such information. A mate would be used as leverage against Lupe, a tool dangled precariously in front of his face, just out of reach.

As you could probably imagine, our dads got along well.

"What's she like?" I spun my chair to face him fully.

God, I felt like a teenager again. Girls may have believed that they were the only ones who engaged in gossip, but they were sorely mistaken. Us guys? Ten times worse.

"She's beautiful." Lupe's eyes glazed over, no doubt envisioning her in his mind. "It's almost as if she is a beacon of light in the middle of a storm. With her, I know I have a way home. She's my guide, my home, my *hope*. The way she looked at me...she didn't see me as a mistake or even a shifter. She saw me as a person. The world can burn to ashes for all the shits I give, just as long as she escapes the flames."

Lupe always had a way with words. If he weren't a prince, weren't a shifter, he no doubt would've been a writer or even an artist. He didn't fit the stereotypical mold that all shifters seemed to fall into. He wasn't a brute driven by his rage, and he wasn't cruel. If anything, he was the kindest man I'd ever met.

"She sounds amazing," I said, basking in our shared happiness.

"I don't know her that well. I don't even know her name, though I'm sure someone said it at one point." He chuckled. "I was a little distracted."

"Tell me about it." That girl made me into a drooling, googly-eyed fool. It had only been a minute, and she already had me wrapped around her diminutive finger.

"And yours? What is she like?" Lupe pressed.

How to answer such a question? The answer to some might have come easily. Kind, perhaps. Pretty. Fierce. But my girl?

I didn't know how to even start.

I opened my mouth to confess that she was a competitor for the Damning but quickly snapped it shut. It wasn't as if I didn't trust Lupe with such important information, I trusted him with my life, but I didn't know what other ears were in this room.

There were trained assassins and murderers roaming these halls. Our words weren't our own with them here.

"She's interesting," I admitted at last.

And I don't know what she looks like. Nor do I know anything about her. Yeah. There's that.

"Was it that girl I saw you talking to?" a quiet voice asked from the shadows, and I flinched. Lupe jumped from his bed, hands raised threateningly. The newcomer chuckled darkly.

"Dammit, Ryland. Wear a bell or something next time," I snapped. The shadow that was Ryland appeared at the foot of the bed. His features were indistinct, due to the darkness obscuring him from view. He was almost always clothed in shadows.

"Did you hear the rumors?" he asked. The silhouette disappeared from the bed, only to materialize on the windowsill.

"What rumors?" Lupe asked. "And how long have you been here?"

"Long enough," Ryland said slyly. He paused, allowing that to sink in. Damn shadows. "But you're not the only princes who have found your mates."

"What?" I asked. "Who?"

I wondered if it was Bash and snorted softly at how preposterous that would be. His mate had something else coming if she expected sunshine and rainbows. Bash was afraid of getting hurt, which wasn't so much a justification as it was an excuse. The walls he built up around himself stemmed from years and years of neglect, abuse, and pain. He would not settle down easily, nor would he let a girl tame him. But when he did end up falling, he would fall hard. Bash never did anything half-assed, and I imagined his love would be just as fierce.

"Jax," Ryland said simply, responding to the question I'd nearly forgotten I had asked.

"Jax?" Lupe and I screeched in unison. Jax? Jax, of all people, had found his mate? I didn't know if that was comical or sad. I supposed it depended on whether or not he could become whole again. After the incident with Sasha...

That had fucked Jax up. Maybe his mate would finally be able to piece his broken shards back together again. When people said rock bottom, they weren't kidding. You completely shattered once you hit the ground. After that initial fall, you had two choices—try to climb back up but leave a little bit of yourself behind in the process, or wait until you were saved. Jax? He chose neither. He tethered himself to the edge, halfway up the hole but with no real destination in mind.

"Remember? He said that his blood was tingling..." Ryland trailed off, voice traveling from the window to somewhere behind me.

"I didn't even think about it," Lupe muttered. When I glanced at him with a raised eyebrow, he elaborated. "A vampire's body begins to tingle when they are near their mate. It's like an itch that's only soothed when you come into contact with your other half. To be frank...your blood begins to tingle."

"Shit," I cursed, half in awe and half in shock.

"And don't forget about Kill," added Ryland.

"Kill? He found his mate too?"

Both Lupe and Ryland began to chuckle. I couldn't help but laugh as well. Killian, no doubt, was terrified about how to handle that...situation. I may have been slightly inexperienced when it came to sex, but I might as well have been a prostitute compared to him.

"I heard him talking to it like a dog," Ryland mused. The "it" referred to Killian's dick. "He asked if he could pet it."

Typical Killian.

"What's next?" Lupe asked. "Asking it if it would like to go on a walk?"

"I think it would have a life of its own if it gets set free. Like a compass, it will propel him towards his mate."

We all laughed at Killian's expense. Just as quickly, my laughter subsided. There was somewhere I had to be before I could crawl back into my ocean cave, away from pitying eyes and a mate that had run from me.

"I'm going to the library," I lied easily. My brothers barely blinked at my declaration. They were used to my nocturnal tendencies. Sleep during the day, live during the night.

If you could call my pathetic existence living.

"Don't turn into Lupe," Ryland quipped, and Lupe chucked a book at the shadow's head. Of course, he missed. It was nearly impossible to catch a shadow unless the shadow wanted to be caught.

Smiling at my brothers' antics, I wheeled out of Lupe's bedroom and down the dark hallway. None of the lights were on, plunging the building into an inky darkness. This was only broken apart by splotches of starlight from the small windows. There was no moon tonight, a fact that made me moderately uncomfortable. Mermaids always preferred the full moon.

My thoughts drifted to what I knew was about to transpire, as it had occurred every day for years. Why did I put myself through this? Why did I endure it time and time again? The answer came to me easily as I envisioned my mother's kind face. I dealt with it so she wouldn't have to.

I rolled myself inside a room nearly identical to Lupe's in appearance.

Four figures stood beside the bed.

"You're late," my oldest brother, Tavvy, snapped. I'd always hated that term—brother. He wasn't my brother, despite our blood declaring us otherwise. The bonds authentically made between two individuals somehow went deeper than flimsy familial ties. He was my brother by birth and blood, not by choice.

My father's teeth gleamed in the dim lighting as he smiled at me. I merely glowered in response.

"Let's get this over with. Tavvy. Father." I nodded at my big brother and father before turning towards the two other men in the room, my younger brothers. "Idol and Manchester."

They nodded in greeting, identical apathetic expressions on their faces.

Without waiting for instruction, I pulled myself out of my chair and onto the bed. Once I was firmly on the mattress, I turned towards my father expectantly.

He silently handed me a glass vial, and I tipped the contents back, barely wincing at the bitter taste.

"Delicious," I murmured dryly.

Immediately, my body began to tingle, as it always did. Warmth started low in my stomach, spreading to my thighs. I bit my lip to keep from crying out as my body grew—that was the only word I could use to describe it. My legs lengthened, becoming whole once again.

I became a whole.

It was a powerful spell that could only be created by the blood of the mage king and the mermaid king. A reformative spell, one that people would pay billions to possess.

I wiggled my toes, as I always did after downing the potion. If only for a moment, I could pretend to be a walking, capable man. A man that might've even been worthy of having a mate.

Just as quickly, the dream shattered around me like a ball being thrown at a mirror.

My father grabbed a keen machete, his preferred weapon, and my brothers all grabbed knives and daggers from their waistbands.

I'd learned not to scream when they came at me, slashing at my skin. I'd learned that the pain only amplified when I outright cried. After all, pain was a manifestation of my imagination. If I didn't allow it to consume me, it wouldn't.

So as my family—my blood relatives—cut through skin and tendons and bone to remove the legs I had just grown, I drifted away.

It was safer that way.

FIFTEEN

Z

I woke up feeling more rested than I had in months, if not years. I found this especially shocking, given my circumstances. What type of assassin did it make me that I was able to sleep like the dead throughout the night?

A pretty shitty one, if you asked me.

I stretched my taut muscles, pulling my arms above my head and listening to the satisfying crack. I hadn't even realized how tired I was, how heavy and leaden my body felt after a grueling day. Falling to your potential death and getting sexually frustrated to the point of unbearable pain most definitely counted as grueling.

And I'd had the strangest dream...

I snapped my head towards the empty side of the bed beside me, nearly laughing at how ridiculous I was for believing *he* would actually be there. Did I really think that a guy had climbed into bed with me? Had *cuddled* with me? My libido must've been in overdrive due to my confrontation with Devlin and then the handsome mermaid. Even the shifter had affected me more than I cared to admit. All of those delicious muscles on display. The swoop of his dark hair.

And now this new guy, this figment of my imagination.

I envisioned him in my mind. His hair had been a light brown and wildly disheveled, as if he'd run his hands through it one too many times. His lips had been plush and kissable. Cupid bow lips. And his body had perfect dips and crevices leading towards a delectable...penis.

Wait a minute...

Why had I imagined a naked man coming into my room? What the hell was wrong with me? A lot, apparently.

Almost involuntarily, my hand crept towards the empty space beside me. The bedspread was warm, as if someone had been there recently.

My brows furrowed.

For starters, there was no reason that someone would have snuck into my room to do anything other than kill me. Secondly, I sure as hell wouldn't have invited someone in willingly, right?

Right?

My head throbbed, but I managed to push aside my blankets and amble to the living room. Diego had set up wards around my suite when we first arrived. Anyone with ill intentions would be unable to enter. Even then, the wards kept a record of when, and if, they were broken. It was surprisingly basic magic, at least according to Diego, and combined both a mage's natural skill and technology. The rectangular device resting on the wall beside the door sparkled with the telltale sign of Diego's magic. It was a light sheen, an emerald green that somehow varied from the monotonous greens of all the other mages. A color as unique as the mage himself.

Using my thumbprint, I logged myself into the database. I didn't know whether I felt silly or frightened or—and this was the worst—*aroused*. I kept picturing the strange, beautiful man, and instead of fear, I felt my stomach churn with desire. That was most definitely not a normal reaction one should experience when dealing with an absolute stranger.

My breath left my lungs when I saw the red dot on the screen blinking erratically. It almost seemed to taunt me, that pinprick dot.

At one thirty-three AM, someone had broken into my room.

I didn't know how I felt about that. Obviously, the person hadn't intended to do me harm. I'd been half asleep, and he hadn't so much as touched me inappropriately, save the cuddles. And *I* had been the one to instigate such contact, the greedy bitch I was. He'd felt so warm, so right, that I couldn't resist the need to get closer. I'd wanted to disappear inside of his soft embrace and drown in his musky scent. His hard, sculpted features had hinted at him being a vampire, yet I'd felt no fear when I was with him.

Was it because I'd been half asleep?

Had I been drugged?

What had been the fucking point of him entering my room in the first place?

I jumped, reaching for the dagger I always kept tucked beneath my clothes, when a knock sounded on the door.

"Knock! Knock!" an annoyingly chipper voice said. I groaned, turning off the alarm and opening my bedroom door. Mali stood in the entryway, face flushed. Her right hand rubbed sporadically at her neck, while her left hand crawled underneath her blouse to scratch at her stomach.

"You all right?" I asked, raising an eyebrow. She huffed.

"Just a little itchy." As she spoke, she rubbed her body against my doorframe. Sensual moans escaped her mouth, and I resisted the urge to slam the door in her face. That was the last thing I wanted to deal with this fucking early in the morning.

"Stop. Please," I deadpanned. She glared at me, as if angry I'd interrupted her itching pleasure, before pushing past me to enter my room. "And come in," I added to her retreating back. She threw herself onto the bed, once again scratching at her arms.

"What's the plan today? Plan? We need a plan? P as in princess. Why did I say princess? I meant poop. P as in poop. L as in love. As in princess and love. And A as in anal. N as in—"

"Dude." I gave her a look, and she jumped from the bed, pacing the room yet again.

"I'm feeling very...cagey. I need to move. Move and run. Where do I run to...? And ohmygawd, I fucking itch."

"You okay?" I asked, slightly concerned. I mean, only slightly. If your best friend wasn't a little batshit crazy, was she really your best friend? "You seem slightly agitated."

She directed another blistering glare my way.

"You don't say," she drawled sarcastically. She resumed her itching once more. Before I could inquire further, another knock broke through the silence like the crack of a whip. Diego poked his head into the room, eyes widening slightly when he took in Mali's withering form. He quickly smoothed his expression over.

"How are my favorite sexy ladies doing today?" he asked, stepping towards me to ruffle my hair. I swatted at his hand in annoyance.

"Don't touch me."

"Most people *love* it when I touch them." He wiggled his eyebrows suggestively.

"I'll make sure to let HH know that," I said wickedly, and he blanched at the use of his mate's name. HH was a small man, almost insignificant in appearance, but I knew him to be a deadly fighter and a skilled sharp shooter. And from Diego's stories, he was also insanely jealous.

A useful tool to have in my arsenal.

"Don't you dare," he warned, but his eyes softened at the thought of his mate. It must've been difficult to be separated from him, though it wasn't uncommon in our line of business. It was a risk to send two lovers on the same mission. Emotions got in the way, and mistakes were made. It was a wonder Mali and Diego, my two closest friends, were able to accompany me here. I reasoned it was because B knew I would always put the mission first.

Kill or be killed.

I chose to kill.

Every. Single. Time.

Diego glanced at Mali once more.

"What's her problem?" he asked me.

Mali managed to grunt out, "Itchy."

"I believe it's sexual frustration," I said teasingly, and Mali's face paled. "Holy shit! It is sexual frustration, isn't it?"

She pursed her lips and gave a quick shake of her head. Despite her denial, I could read my best friend easily. The bitch was hiding something from me, and it was my sacred duty to pester her until she caved and told me.

"Is my little Mali craving the D?" Diego teased. "Or is it the V?"

"You're one to talk," Mali hissed. "I know that you once masturbated with a hot dog. And I also know that it got stuck up your butt."

I had to give Diego credit. He didn't even blink.

"I wanted to know what it felt like," he insisted. "Before HH attempted it."

"Are you comparing your mate's dick to a hot dog?" I teased, and this time, a blush darkened his cheeks. "I mean, I suppose you could say that you—"

"Don't say it!" Diego pointed an accusatory finger at me.

"That you—"

"Z!"

"Did it doggy style."

I broke into laughter, Mali following soon after.

"Laugh it up, bitches," Diego said, crossing his muscular arms over his chest. "Laugh it up."

"Okay. Okay. Enough messing around. I actually came here for a reason." Mali seemed to momentarily forget her itch as uneasiness crossed her features. The despondency in her once jubilant eyes instantly put me on alert.

"What's wrong?"

"I got notice that you'll be required to attend a dinner tonight. As Z. All of the competitors are required to attend."

Fuck.

"Fuck," Diego unintentionally echoed.

I knew exactly why the game makers did this—to get us all into one area, one room, to ensure the maximum amount of bloodshed. And blood would be shed, that I was certain of. The only question was if it would be mine.

"It's going to be a bloodbath," I mused out loud, picking apart what little information I knew. On one hand, it would allow me to gauge a rough estimate of who remained and what their skills were. It would also stand to reason that those still alive were either the best of the best or mediocre fighters. The worst had already been taken out, and those deemed as the best assassins would've been the first targeted.

"And the dinner is mandatory?" I added, and Mali nodded.

"The vampire council dick himself delivered the news to all of the assistants."

I couldn't help but snort. What a coward. He

couldn't even face us, the people he was killing off through his twisted game, to inform us himself. The important, scary vampire was scared of some assassins? Comical.

"Well then..." I tapped a finger against my chin. I really didn't have an option. There was this elusive concept, free will, and it had never occurred to me before how much of it I was lacking. I'd never had a say in my line of work, and that wasn't going to change with time. I wouldn't consider my life as an assassin a prison, but it definitely wasn't sunshine and rainbows. If I were to win the Damning, I would be trading one prison for another, either in the form of servitude to a crown I could never support or in an actual prison. Surprisingly, this realization did not bring me any fear. If anything, I felt oddly calm with the hand I'd been dealt.

After all, it was what I'd prepared for.

"We'll convene in a couple of hours to finalize the plans for this dinner," I decided on at last. Mali immediately opened her mouth to protest, but I shushed her with one eloquent look. "It's what needs to be done."

And I knew she wouldn't argue with me after that. She'd seen, firsthand, how horrendous nightmares could be. Her entire family had been slaughtered by her own species. The ones that were supposed to protect her had instead destroyed her and all she held dear. If she had to choose between saving one life, mine, or saving hundreds of others by ridding the world of a serial killer, she would choose the latter. I couldn't fault her on that, though I often wondered if I would make the same decision.

"On a lighter note..." Diego began, changing the topic in a way only he could. "How did it go with Devlin?"

"Devlin?" Mali injected. She raised a dark eyebrow.

When I remained silent, she turned towards Diego for answers.

"Apparently, Devlin used to go by the name Lin."

I wondered if it was a mage thing or a Diego thing to stir up shit. Either way, I mentally planned his murder by way of a rusty spoon.

"Holy shit!" Mali screamed. "Your ex-boyfriend is the Prince of Genies!"

"Shut up!" I hissed.

"You fucking rubbed the prince's magical lamp! And I'm not talking about an actual lamp!"

I groaned, placing my head in my hands.

"I know what you meant," I mumbled. Mali, of course, wasn't done. After another earsplitting screech, she went on a rant that included more genie sex puns than I thought could even exist. Diego merely smirked at me, mouthing, "Revenge for the doggy style comment."

"Bitch," I mouthed back. He dramatically grabbed at his heart.

After a particularly detailed comment that included the words "three wishes" and "pussy pleasure," I cut Mali off.

"I have stuff I need to do. Go bathe in blood to soothe your itch."

As expected, Mali was immediately distracted.

"Vampires do *not* bathe in blood," she said indignantly.

"But they want to," Diego pointed out. "It's a fetish

they all have." Mali stared him down, expression contorting from excitement at the revelation of my ex-lover to stone-cold bitch. Mali could be scary when she wanted to be.

"Say that again. I fucking dare you."

Diego, never one to back down from a challenge, winked.

"They want to bathe in blood because vampires are kinky shits. Love ya!"

Before Mali could respond, he ran from the room. Mali immediately ran after him, cursing beneath her breath. Apparently, my love life, or lack thereof, was forgotten.

I watched my friends go, amused and filled with something akin to love. I didn't know what I would do if I had to decide between them and the mission. As much as I would like to say I would choose the mission each and every time, I knew that was a lie. I was selfish. Was it really so wrong of me to want to hold on to the few relationships I had left?

Shaking my head, I grabbed a robe out of my closet and stepped into the hallway. I would have to find Mali before she castrated Diego. The last thing I wanted to deal with was HH mourning the loss of his mate's dick.

My blonde hair was wild this morning, and I debated whether or not I should brush it. Deciding against it—I didn't have anyone I wanted to impress—I hurried in the direction I'd seen my two friends disappear down.

"Where are you leading me, boy? You know you can't just take off like that. Do you want to go this way?"

It was a man's voice, low and sultry. Goosebumps

immediately pebbled on my arms. There was something about that husky voice, something that made me want to run in his direction.

An incubus, I decided immediately.

It wasn't the same pull I'd felt with the numerous other incubi I'd encountered throughout my life. It wasn't purely sexual, though there was plenty of that too. It was almost like an innate need within me that urged me forward, urged me to set eyes upon his handsome face.

And handsome he was. Sexy.

Auburn hair, longer on the top and shorter on the sides, grazed his eyes. His body was a canvas of ink and muscle, each one of his tattoos so intricately designed that I wanted to stare at them for hours. Admittedly, he looked like a player—the type of guy that would fuck you senseless and then leave you in the morning. I imagined he had a new girl every night, each one submitting to him fully.

For some undefinable reason, that thought bothered me. It fucking *bothered* me to think of this stranger, this nightmare, with any girl other than...well, me. I blamed it on the incubus allure he emanated in waves.

"This way, boy? Where are you taking me?"

I frowned when I saw no one in the immediate proximity. Who was he talking to? That confusion morphed into amusement when I saw his eyes flicker down to his rock-hard dick.

Was he talking to his dick?

And what a dick it was.

Even with his pants on, I could see it would be long

and thick. I immediately imagined that erect dick pounding into me, consuming me, becoming *one* with me.

I shook my head rapidly to clear the direction my thoughts were heading.

Nope. Not going there.

The man's eyes glanced up towards me and widened. Thousands of emotions flashed in his gaze during that five-second span of time—hope, relief, awe, and then finally, fear.

The sexy man opened his mouth, and I prepared myself for the perfect words all incubi seemed to have. How else could they manage to get lover after lover into their beds? They had a way with words, a way to innately demand your attention.

But then he spoke.

"Your h-h-hair looks l-like spag-g-ghetti."

Before I could reply, he hurried away.

What the actual fuck?

SIXTEEN

Z

Did he just say…?

I replayed his words for the umpteenth time in my head. Yup. He had most definitely compared my hair to spaghetti.

Well, fuck him!

On a bed, preferably. With whips and chains and—

Bad Z. Bad. Bad. Bad. He'd insulted me, right? That had been an insult, of that I was almost certain. Like, fifty percent sure.

And he was one to judge! It wasn't as if he'd rolled out of bed looking perfect.

With his perfect hair and his perfect dick. And I wonder if he had red hair leading down to his—

Stop it, Z!

I mentally slapped myself.

My body fought a vigorous battle against my head. Before I realized what I was doing, I ran in the direction the incubus had gone. The annoying voice in my mind, a voice getting louder and more demanding as the seconds dragged on, told me to talk to him. Just talk to him.

Why I wanted to have a conversation with a nightmare that compared my hair to food was beyond my comprehension, yet I found myself eagerly scanning the halls. Finally, I spotted his shock of red hair, an auburn color with golden and dark red streaks heightening the flecks of gold in his eyes. He glanced at me, horrified, and immediately turned to head down a separate hallway.

Fortunately for me, incubi did not have the speed of a vampire, and I found myself easily catching up with him.

"You said my hair looks like spaghetti," I blurted. Because, really, I couldn't seem to focus on anything else. The man blushed, an adorable shade of red that contrasted greatly with the tattoos climbing up his neck.

"I d-did-dn't-t mean to," he stuttered. "It j-just-t-t came out."

For some reason, I wanted to put this man at ease. I hated seeing him so upset, so embarrassed. The voice inside my head grew louder, urging me to do whatever was necessary to take his pain away.

"Oh it's fine." I waved my hand dismissively before pointing to my mess of curls. "Totally spaghetti hair. And I suppose you could say that your hair is spaghetti with marinara sauce on it."

Okay, so I would've been the first to admit that my attempt at making an awkward situation normal backfired. When he stared at me, blinking rapidly, it was all I could do not to curl into a ball and die a slow and painful death.

"Marinara sauce," he repeated slowly.

"Well, it's not butter sauce."

Ohmygawd. What the fuck is wrong with you, Z?

He surprised me by laughing, throwing his head back and all. His body shook.

Now it was my turn to stare at him like an imbecile.

It was official—he was crazy. Granted, I was crazy as well, but he was a different brand of psycho. And dammit if I didn't feel all warm and tingly at the thought of us being psychos together.

"I don't even know why I'm laughing. I'll stop," he managed to say, get this, between peals of laughter. Of course that only set him off again. This time, I found myself joining in. His laughter was positively contagious. Finally, he took a shuddering breath and took a tentative step closer to me.

"God, I'm sorry. I don't understand what I'm talking half the time. I meant speaking. *Saying.* I don't understand what I'm *saying* half the time. I'm horrible with words. I just never expected to meet you. Ever. And you're so..." I couldn't help but note that he had an adorable stutter. Somehow, that fact demoted him from intimidating to approachable. He gestured towards me helplessly at his final line, which only proceeded to confuse me further. What was he even talking about? Why would we ever meet? Was he expecting to meet? "You're so perfect, and I thought your hair was blonde. And curly. And you have nice shoulders."

"Thank you?" I self-consciously rubbed at said shoulders, peeking through where my robe had slid down. I would've been the first to admit that yes, they were nice shoulders.

I must've misjudged him. He wasn't utterly horrible at communicating—

"You look like a giant toe," he blurted.

Well.

Okay, then.

The blush I was beginning to associate with this strange incubus blossomed across his cheekbones. I didn't know whether or not to be intrigued by this man who'd both called me a giant toe and compared my hair to pasta, or frightened by him. I decided I was intrigued, if not slightly entranced. There was something about him, a vulnerability perhaps, that went beyond the sexual appeal found in all incubi. His awkwardness was sort of adorable and was not what I expected from a guy that looked the way he did.

"My name is Killian," he said at last.

"Zara," I replied smoothly.

He smiled, and it was a positively brilliant smile, like bloated storm clouds finally moving away from the sun after days of thunderstorms. He was so beautiful that it pained me, a sort of ethereal beauty and sexiness that put others to shame. I knew that all incubi were attractive, but he was something otherworldly.

And an added bonus? I didn't immediately want to kill him. That could change, though, once I deciphered which side he was on. For all I knew, he was a fellow assassin or an assistant looking to gather information on Z. I didn't recognize his name or face from the files though, but incubi were masters at disguises.

Despite my suspicions, I didn't detect anything other than sincerity in his words. There were no malicious undertones, no threats. I trusted my intuition with my life, and just then, it told me to trust this nightmare just like it had told me yesterday to trust the mermaid. I should've been terrified of him. He could, in a matter of seconds, turn me into a withering mess of nerves and sexual tension. He could make me orgasm with the snap of his fingers.

While an incubus' power may have seemed less than the power of the other nightmares, it was still immensely dangerous, perhaps even more so. There was something frightening about the loss of control incubi evoked within you. Your body suddenly wasn't your own, and your emotions didn't correspond with your desires.

That aspect, the loss of free will, was terrifying.

And slightly familiar to me.

The incubus, Killian, rubbed a hand through his hair. The dark red, almost garnet-colored strands stood on end. His mouth opened—

And abruptly snapped closed as a dagger flew through the air, catching him in the shoulder.

I gasped, spinning around with my hands raised, despite the fact that I was supposed to be Zara the assistant, not Z the assassin.

Nobody was allowed to harm Killian.

I didn't know where that thought came from, only that it was true. I imagined I would've felt something similar if the person had been Mali or Diego.

The shadow materialized mere feet away from me, axe raised as he prepared to deliver the killing blow to Killian's prone form.

"For Aaliyah," he whispered.

Before I realized what was happening, before I stopped to think about anything other than saving Killian, I pounced on the shadow, my own dagger raised.

I wasn't thinking coherently at the time. All I could focus on was the blood seeping through Killian's fingers, at his wide eyes staring up at the assassin, at his face turning paler and paler as the blood cascaded down his stomach. I recognized the assassin, vaguely, as a contestant in the Damning. I couldn't recall his name nor why he'd been chosen. For all I knew, he could've been like me—a good man at heart sent to kill the horrors that ruled our world.

At one point, I might've even helped him end the incubus's life. But I wasn't thinking clearly, wasn't able to see beyond the red sheen of anger that coated my vision.

The shadow would pay for harming what was mine.

Blood sprayed on the white carpeting. My dagger sunk deeper and deeper into the Shadow's jugular, his gargled screams muted by the blood filling his mouth. His eyes, full of shock and despair, gazed at me helplessly. He clawed at my arms and face, his nails ripping at my skin. Still, I didn't release him. As I felt his energy deplete and his body go limp, I prayed that I would be forgiven. We were one and the same, after all, though we apparently fought the nightmares for different reasons. But he had hurt Killian...an incubus that I barely even knew yet felt protective towards. This was purely my one chance at retribution.

Now that the threat was eliminated, I scrambled to my knees beside Killian. He was gaping at me, eyes volleying between the dagger protruding from the shadow's neck and my blood soaked clothes.

"Are you okay?" I whispered harshly, removing his hands from the wound to assess it myself.

"How did you...? You killed him!"

I didn't dare meet his eyes. For reasons unknown to me, I couldn't bear to see the disgust and judgement I knew would be evident in his gaze.

"Incubi heal with sexual energy, correct?" I asked, ignoring his question. "Who can I grab for you?"

The words were difficult to get past my suddenly dried throat. The thought of anyone touching him made me sick to my stomach. And slightly murderous.

"I'll be fine," he muttered.

"You're not fine! Who can I grab to help speed up the healing?"

Finally, *finally*, I dared to glance up at him. His eyes were fixated on me, but instead of the disgust I had expected, there was only fascination in his gaze. He stared at me as if I were a fine piece of silk he longed to purchase. He stared at me as if I, in my blood soaked clothes and with my spaghetti hair, was the most beautiful girl he'd ever set eyes upon. My heart thundered against my rib cage.

"I could..." My voice croaked, this time for an entirely different reason. "I could help you."

I was offering myself to an incubus?

What the hell was the matter with me?

I didn't know the answer to that, but I did know with absolute certainty that I longed to heal him, both physically and emotionally. It was similar to what I felt with Lin and even what I felt with Dair.

"You don't..." His cheeks burned brightly, even as he grimaced with pain. "You don't have to."

"Just tell me what I need to do."

I felt suddenly shy, and I imagined my face was just as red as his. There was a dead body only a couple feet away, and we were discussing... Well, I wasn't entirely certain what we were discussing.

"Would kissing you help?" I asked timidly, and his Adam's apple bobbed as he swallowed.

"Yes."

I kept my eyes locked on his as I leaned forward, and he tilted his head down. Our lips met in the sweetest, most innocent kiss imaginable. His lips tentatively moved against mine.

Unsure.

Inexperienced.

"Is this okay?" I asked against his lips.

His answer was a grunt.

"Yes."

Sensing hesitancy on his part, I slid my tongue between his lips. His body tensed beneath mine before he returned the kiss, meeting me stroke for stroke. His hand slid over my back and into my hair, the touch as light as a moth's wing. He held me as if I were breakable glass, as if he were terrified I would shatter to pieces at the mere application of pressure.

I grabbed one of his hands and held it just above my breast, giving him permission to touch me there if he so desired. He let out a moan of pure bliss, hesitantly groping my heavy mound. I mewled like a cat when his fingers pinched my nipple beneath my shirt.

Note to self—don't wear bras anymore.

My panties were soaked, and I wanted his hand down *there*. Or his tongue. Or his dick, which I could feel pressing against my stomach.

He pulled away from me with a blistering speed. His eyes were wild.

"I...I'm healed now."

He scrambled to his feet, his arousal plainly evident through his pants.

"I n-neeed-d-d to go."

And then he left.

The bastard fucking left me alone with a wet pussy and a dead body. Maybe I should've just let him die.

SEVENTEEN

BASH

The two girls were arguing over the effectiveness of a particular plant in healing. Arguing over a fucking plant.

I placed my head in my hands, unable to decide if I was amused or annoyed. It was only a night ago when I'd taken both girls to my bed...at the same time. While they'd seemed to enjoy it, I found myself wishing it was over. I didn't know what was wrong with me. My magic had been running haywire since the Matching had commenced. One second, I'd be minding my own business, and the next, tiny flowers would be growing or sparks would emit from my fingertips. I had tried to talk to my father about it, but he'd lazily waved me away.

It was too time-consuming for him to have a five-minute conversation with his only child, apparently. I considered talking to my brothers about my predicament, but I didn't want to hear what they had to say. I was irrationally pissed at my brothers. No amount of booze could soothe the anger I felt.

Dair, with his droopy, wistful expression.

Devlin with the fucking half-smile on his face.

Lupe and his damn soliloquies.

Ryland and his stalker tendencies.

Jax's tingly blood.

Killian's damn boner.

All of my brothers had found their mates. Was I supposed to feel happy for them? Proud? All I felt was an incandescent fury at the cruel world and a smothering depression at my own misfortune.

Frowning, I took another swig from my beer bottle. I was already slightly buzzed, despite it being still early in the morning.

The Matching was in full swing. Women from all across the world were being groomed to be our future wives. If we didn't find our mates in a year, these horrid, superficial girls would become our futures.

Correction, if *I* didn't find my mate in a year, one of these horrid, superficial girls would become *my* future.

I'd followed them out to the garden, where Mrs. G was discussing the usage of plants in medicine, hence the reason for the argument between Lover One and Lover Two.

I glanced at the two girls once more, brows furrowing in confusion. They were attractive, I'd give them that, but they didn't cause me to melt into a puddle of lust. I'd tried taking both of them. Hell, I had even tried having them take each other while I watched.

Nada.

Not even a little jump from my flaccid dick.

Was I embarrassed that I couldn't get off while two

beautiful women attempted to pleasure me? Maybe. If anything, I was confused and slightly concerned.

I didn't know what I would do with myself if my dick was broken. I needed it almost as much as I needed food and water. A world without my dick was not a world I wanted to live in.

And then I thought of the *other* reason. The reason I knew my brothers would bring up if I discussed my problem with them.

I could hear them now.

"Most mages," Lupe would say, an imperious set to his chin. He would clear his throat before beginning once again. "Most mages would be incapable of being with anyone other than their mate. That would also explain your unpredictable powers. She's here. In the capital." It would also explain my dreams, though no one knew about them. Hopefully, I could keep it that way.

Killian would probably gripe that he wasn't the only one with an broken dick. Personally, I'd rather have my cock hard all the time than the limp fucking noodle it was now.

Jax would say some weird-ass shit that had nothing to do with anything.

And the others? They would give me a knowing smirk, as if they themselves weren't whipped by females they barely knew.

I didn't want a mate. Never had and never would. Why would I want to be tied down for the rest of my life? That sounded about as appealing to me as jabbing my eye out with a rusty needle would've been. I didn't believe in love, and love was the foundation for mates. Lust and infatuation, maybe, but love? Supernaturals believed that our mates originated before we were even created. A soul was split into two in the early stages of development, and then were separated when we came to Earth. For our entire existence, we would look for the other half of us, the person that would make us complete. Half the time, we never even knew that we were supposed to be looking. We never even knew that we were empty until that person came into our lives like a freight train.

Bull. Shit.

Love didn't exist.

And mates? They were an absence of free will and choice.

Frowning once more, I took another swig of alcohol. I'd just woken up, and I was already dying to go back to sleep again. My eyelids drooped, and my head lolled against my shoulders. At least after I dreamed, I would be able to find some release.

"WHY ARE YOU HERE?" she asked, tone husky. My dick hardened, pleased by the heat evident in her eyes. She looked so beautiful sprawled out on my bed. Perfect.

And mine.

"Why did the cock cross the road?" I asked instead, basking in the giggle that followed my question. She'd never struck me as the giggling type of female. It still did funny things to me when I heard such a magical sound.

"Why did it cross the road?" she asked, finally caving.

I held my dick in one hand as my eyes surveyed her

perfect body. She still wore a flimsy robe, and her blonde hair cascaded over her shoulders like golden silk. She was so beautiful that my heart physically ached when I looked at her.

"To get to the backside," I said, grabbing her tiny waist and spinning her around. She squealed, the sound making my already hard cock twitch. The movement forced her robe up, revealing her golden ass to me.

We'd talked about this a few times. I knew for a fact she had done it with the others...and liked it. I also knew that my girl was a kinky shit. She'd love it if I were to call one of the guys back into the room. One in the front, and one in the back. We may not have swung that way with each other, but we all agreed that seeing the lust in her eyes was worth it.

Maybe next time, I'd allow one of them to join us. For now? She was mine.

Every last piece of her.

I WOKE WITH A GASP, heart hammering in my chest. The garden was empty, save for a few critters exploring the grounds.

What the fuck?

This wasn't the first time I'd dreamed of her, this mysterious girl. One time, we'd been making love. I'd held her so tenderly in my hands, as if she was my entire world, and she'd stared back at me with something I would almost describe as love.

Almost. If I didn't know how unloveable of a bastard

I was, I'd say it *was* that emotion. But it couldn't be. I didn't love, and I didn't expect anyone to ever love me in return.

In some of my dreams, we were doing nothing but talking and laughing. Others, I was pounding into her.

And always, I would wake up with a raging boner that could only be soothed by my good old friend, Mr. Hand. I would imagine her perfect lips wrapped around my cock and explode.

Today was no different, though I felt slightly awkward jacking off in the middle of a garden on a stone bench. Still, I welcomed the release, and I came with a loud cry.

Once that...*situation* was handled—get it? *Hand*led? —I tucked my now flaccid dick back into my pants and headed inside. Father was probably looking for me by now. He may have been the king, but he was a lazy son of a bitch. Responsibility had settled heavily on my shoulders at a very young age. It was nearly staggering, the weight he put on me, and I wanted nothing more than to drown beneath it.

"Where the fuck have you been?" a strident voice demanded the second I stepped foot into the capital. Devlin hurried towards me, eyes wild and mouth pursed. His violet eyes locked on mine.

"Hello to you too," I drawled lazily. Sue me for being a cynical bastard, but I wasn't in the mood to talk with any of my brothers, particularly Devlin. He was an asshole on the best of days, his protective instincts even worse than Lupe's, but lately, he'd been something else entirely—moody and brooding and dickish. He was quicker to snap than previously, and he always looked moderately constipated. I knew he was angry at the world, and I couldn't entirely fault him on that. He'd once admitted to me, after I'd gotten him wasted on fairy wine, that he'd found his mate but had been forced to leave her. Apparently, she'd fallen in love with a human shortly after he'd left.

Another reason why I didn't want a mate. Bitches were never loyal.

The bond was supposed to be unbreakable, and the two individuals connected by such a string were supposedly inseparable. To know that it could be so easily broken, or at least ignored, gutted me and shattered the wistful fantasies I'd held since I was a child. Younger me had been a hopeless romantic…and a dumbass.

"Killian's been stabbed," Devlin said through clenched teeth. I could tell his anger wasn't directed at me but the situation. At his words, I felt my body grow cold.

"Is he…?" I couldn't bear to finish that question. If something were to happen to my brother, my best friend, I would murder everyone in this godforsaken building.

"He's fine. He was able to heal."

My thoughts went from worrying over Killian to surprise at what Devlin had told me. There was only one way an incubus could heal—sexual energy. Either Killian had visited the brothel yet again, or my little boy had finally turned into a man. If this was what it felt like to be a proud father, maybe I would rethink my decision not to have kids.

Not with a mate, of course, but I could easily find a willing woman to plant my seed into.

"Where is he?" I asked harshly. Now that my initial panic had ebbed, I wanted to kill someone. Painfully. Nobody harmed my family and lived to tell the tale. I already had to deal with seeing Dair's blood relatives after what they did to his legs. To see Killian's assailant as well? That would destroy me.

Killian was inside his bedroom, perched on the bed. His shirt was off, and Lupe was worrying over the incubus with his brow creased. The rest of my brothers were noticeably absent, though I wasn't sure if it was because they had already been told the news of Killian's attack or because they were busy. In Jax's case, he probably couldn't be found. And in Ryland's...

One glance towards the corner confirmed he was, in fact, silhouetted against the white wall of the room.

"Are you sure you're okay?" Lupe asked Killian. The big man always seemed to panic over the littlest of things. If he were to discover I had been drinking again, he would blow a nut.

Set one house on fire, and suddenly, you were an alcoholic. Geez.

Lupe sniffed when I entered the room, and his eyes flared dangerously. Despite smelling the alcohol wafting off of me, he chose not to comment. Smart move on his part.

"Tell Bash what you told us," Devlin said briskly, falling into the leadership role he'd always occupied since we were children.

"As I've said one hundred times..." Killian began,

trailing off to throw his shirt back on. "The assassin attacked me. I think he was hired to take me out."

"And what was the name he said?" Devlin pressed, glancing at me. His mouth was a thin line.

"Aaliyah," the incubus answered reluctantly. "He said he was doing this for Aaliyah."

Both Devlin and Lupe turned to look at me, identical expression of condemnation on their faces.

"What?" I asked, raising my hands placatingly. "Why are you looking at me?"

Devlin's pinched the bridge of his nose.

"Do you know who this Aaliyah person could be?"

I stared at him like an imbecile, wondering if this was something I *should've* known. Their expressions were expectant.

And then it clicked, even in my drunken haze. They assumed Aaliyah was a girl I had fucked. A girl whose heart I had shattered along with countless of others. A girl so obsessed with me that she would send killers after my family. I felt myself bristling at the implication that I was somehow behind Killian's stabbing.

"I don't know any Aaliyahs," I hissed, though I wasn't entirely certain if that was true or not. I was just furious at the accusation in their gazes, at the judgment. These two weren't damn saints either. "How do you know it's not that ho of a mate you had? Susan?"

I knew I'd hit a sore spot when Devlin's power rose, eyes flashing in the dim lighting. Lupe quickly grabbed the genie before he could lunge at me.

I knew I was being an asshole, but I didn't care anymore. I honestly didn't care about anything.

Don't get me wrong. I wasn't suicidal or anything, but if a train were to barrel down on me, I wouldn't complain. It just didn't matter to me whether I lived or died.

"Calm down," Lupe hissed at Devlin. I continued to meet the genie's stare defiantly, the power he emanated stirring my hair. I would not be the first to back down.

"Don't talk about her like that," Devlin managed to say through clenched teeth. "You don't know anything."

Before I could retort, Devlin's eyes flashed once more before dimming. He was always the first to anger, but also the first to reel his anger in.

"We have more important things to worry about than Bash's jealousy," Devlin snapped, turning his back to me and facing Killian. I opened my mouth once more to argue against the jealousy claim, but a warning look from Lupe had me snapping it closed. The shifter shook his head subtly.

He was right—now was not the time to argue.

"So you really expect us to believe that you fought and killed an assassin?" Devlin asked Killian in disbelief. "You?"

Killian's cheeks turned a dark red, but he kept his chin up and gaze locked on Devlin's.

"Yes."

"And you just so happened to heal yourself afterwards?" Again, no one could miss the skepticism evident in Devlin's voice.

"Yes. There must've been lovers nearby."

I couldn't help but snort.

My brother was lying his fucking ass off. For one, he was the *trip and fall onto a knife* type of guy, not a kickass defender. Secondly, I knew that incubi only healed from injuries with direct...*contact*, so to speak.

I wondered who he was protecting. One of the people who'd harmed him? Was he being threatened? Did it have something to do with that damn mate of his?

I decided, right then and there, that if his mate had something to do with his attempted murder, I would kill her myself. He could hate me for it, but in the long run, he would thank me.

Nobody was allowed to harm my family.

EIGHTEEN

Z

I could've almost imagined he was sleeping. That was, if sleeping men had blood staining the whites of their necks and creating a puddle around their bodies.

I tilted my head to the side, unable to tear my gaze away from the shadow. I'd killed him. Me. Zara the assistant. I wasn't sure what to do. Turn back into Z? Claim self-defense? Would this kill count towards my overall goal of five? I understood that these questions were not the sanest to have while staring at a dead body, but it was all I could focus coherently on.

That, and the tingling of my lips.

I pictured the incubus once more. Auburn hair. High, prominent cheekbones. Smooth lips, thin at the top and full on the bottom. How his tongue had felt mingling with mine...

I shook my head once, angrily. The bastard had left me. I had saved his life—*twice*, I might add—and he'd run like a little bitch. If I were to see him again, I'd stab him myself.

Or kiss the shit out of him. The verdict was still out on that one.

Turning away from the grotesque body, I headed in the direction of my room. I would wash myself, find Mali and Diego, and then figure out what to do. Before I could do any of that, however, something sailed through the air and hit me in the back of the head. I let out a cry, more surprised than anything else, and spun towards the offending object.

It was...a book?

Someone had thrown a book at my head. A damn book. It occurred to me that if it had been something heavier or sharper, it would've killed me. That thought made my hands clammy.

Death.

I really wasn't ready to die.

But it wasn't a knife or an axe or even a brick. It was a book titled *Lovers on the Mountaintop* and featured five half-naked men around one woman. I pitied her. Sure, I knew some people took multiple lovers, but I couldn't ever imagine doing it myself. For one, what did you even do with that many dicks? There were only so many holes available on a human body. And that girl must've had one hell of a sex drive to please all of them, as I would've been in a wheelchair by the end of the night. Balls. Balls everywhere.

I squinted down the hallway, searching for anyone who had felt the need to chuck a book at my head. Was it an accident? Was this some perverted way to murder a person?

A lilting laugh cut through the silence. It was low and husky and did funny things to my damn libido that was already thinking about balls and penises. It was also familiar, though it took me a second to place where I'd heard it before.

A figure appeared on the wall beside me, a black silhouette against the white tiling. A shadow. Ryland, if I remembered correctly.

"Why the hell did you throw a book at my head?" I asked. Really, I was quite offended. Did he really think I could be killed by a smutty romance novel? And I wasn't even dressed as Z, but as Zara. One thing was for certain —Ryland was a twisted motherfucker.

"Your response time is slow," he answered smoothly. The shadow materialized inches from my face. It was the strangest sensation to look at him but not actually *see* him. I could decipher the outline of broad shoulders cloaked in ink and strands of hair poking in every direction, but his features remained indistinct. "If that was a knife, then you would've been dead."

"What are you talking about?" I asked, popping my hip to the side and twirling a piece of blonde hair around my finger. I hoped I looked ditzy—the part of an assistant and a lover. I had to remind myself continually that I wasn't Z, that the mask was gone, and I was an entirely different person. Surprisingly, I couldn't decide which version was the real me and which one I liked the best. That was the funny thing about wearing masks. They were capable of changing your personality so effortlessly that you lost sight of who you really were.

I had worn my mask for years.

"Don't play stupid." I felt his breath against my ear, and goosebumps erupted on my sensitive flesh. "I know exactly who you are...Z."

The way he said my name...it sounded like molten honey. It rolled from his tongue in a way that was sickeningly delicious. And then it struck me what he'd said, what he'd admitted to.

Z.

He knew.

He knew.

He fucking knew.

I scrambled to think of something to say, something to contradict what he seemed to know with absolute certainty.

"Are you talking about my lover?" I asked coyly. I even managed to giggle, punctuating each word. "I'm Zara, not Z."

"You're both." This time, his voice came from behind me, stirring the hairs on my neck. I jumped, hands fisted. I debated once more if I should lie. Deny. That was my go-to move. I could deny profusely, twist stories in accordance to my will, until I almost believed them to be true. Did anyone truly know a person? We all spun our webs, lies and deceit twisting words to fit the perception we had of ourselves.

Lie.

Deny.

It was my motto.

But I knew it wouldn't work right now. It was apparent that this shadow was privy to more information than I was comfortable with him having. It also was immensely important for me to know what he would do with such valuable information.

"Fine," I said briskly. "What do you want?"

I again wondered who he was and what his goal was. If he was an assassin, he sucked at his job. I briefly considered the prospect of him being an assistant, perhaps even a spy for one of the competitors.

"Your response time is slow," he repeated. "And you struggle against shadows. You rely so much on your sight that you fail to realize you have other senses."

I spun towards the voice, stunned.

"What?" I sputtered. "Are you giving me advice?"

He ignored my question, gliding across the floor to stand millimeters away from me. Once again, I had the strangest urge to see past his front to the man beneath.

"Close your eyes," he whispered.

"No!"

"All you have to do is find me, and your secret will be safe."

This asshole was blackmailing me. I couldn't understand his reasoning though. Why go through all this trouble in the first place? Why hit me with a book, insult my skills, relinquish the knowledge that he knew of my true identity, and then make me close my eyes? It made zero sense. *He* made zero sense. I supposed that could've been his point—throw his competition off before stabbing them in the back. If that was his MO, he was damn good at it.

"Is this some kind of kinky sex game?" I asked, my bravado pathetically fake. I didn't like the lack of control he was forcing upon me. No, that he was *demanding* from me. Not only by holding my secret hostage, but also because of the trust he wanted me to give him. I didn't trust easily, and I could list only a few people still alive that I would listen to.

And yet...

I thought I was losing my mind. That was the only logical explanation for why my eyelashes feathered against my cheekbones and darkness obscured my vision. Once again, I relied on my sixth sense, one of the senses he felt I lacked, and trusted him irrevocably and probably irrationally. He could kill me right then and there. A stab in my neck, a blow to my head, a knife to my heart.

And the twisted part of me would allow it.

I wouldn't have been able to tell you what possessed me, why I behaved the way I did. I killed people for a living, I'd lost everyone I had ever truly loved, and the trust I gave was few and far between. Why him? Why this stranger? What made me trust him against my better judgement?

I thought of Devlin just then. He'd never given me the world, yet he was capable of making me feel like I was the only woman in it. I didn't know why I felt something similar with this stranger. It could've been a spell cast by a mage, but either way, I was helpless against it.

"Why are you helping me?" I whispered, my eyes still squeezed tightly closed.

"Because I don't want you to die," came his answer from farther down the hallway.

"Why don't you want me to die?" I felt like a child, parroting his answers back to him in the form of a question.

"Don't you feel that?" he asked instead. "The shadows are so much thicker when you're around. They call to me. *You* call to me."

I was reminded of something that Dair had said. The water had spoken to him about me in the same way the shadows apparently talked to Ryland. I didn't know what drugs they were taking, only that the demented part of me wanted a bite. They spoke as if the shadows and the water were actual people with thoughts and feelings. I wondered if there was a connotation behind the words that I was missing.

"Open your ears. Hear me—my breathing, my footsteps. Quiet your mind, and focus on me. Focus."

I kept my eyes shut, instinctively doing as instructed. At first, I heard nothing but my own pounding heart. There was no rhythm to the erratic beat. It was just noise, loud and surprisingly calming.

I quieted my thoughts and turned my attention outwards.

There—to my left.

I heard soft breathing and the gentle tapping of a nail against the banister. I turned in that direction immediately.

"Very good." His voice now came inches from my lips. My own parted automatically. "Now, what do you smell?"

I breathed in deeply.

"Pine trees," I answered immediately. "You remind me of being outdoors. Of Christmas."

"Feel me," he whispered, and my hand, of its own accord, reached out to touch the shadow in front of me. They articulated the width of his shoulders, each dip and crook of his stomach, the hard muscles of his bicep. The moment my searching fingers would've touched his face, he stepped away from me.

"Focus on all of your senses, hearing especially. You may not always see a shadow in a fight, so you have to learn how to rely on sound. See if you can find me."

I strained my ears and sniffed the air. There was the softest sound of clothing being rustled a few feet in front of me. One inhale confirmed the pine scent I was beginning to associate with Ryland, the strange shadow.

Feigning a punch to the right, I grabbed my dagger with the opposite hand and held it inches from where I suspected his neck to be.

"Very good," he said softly, not at all worried about the keen blade inches from his jugular. He'd obviously seen me kill a shadow only a short while earlier, yet he was giving me the same trust he expected of me. It was a two-way street. Before you could demand trust, you had to reciprocate it.

"Thank you." My breathing was embarrassingly loud. Hand trembling, I retracted the knife from where it could easily slash his neck.

"Your incubus is taking credit for your kill," he continued, the change of topic momentarily taking me off guard. "Why is he protecting you?"

I didn't know how to answer such a question, nor did

I wish to. Why would the incubus protect me and my identity? How did Ryland even know that?

"Maybe because I'm special," I murmured, finally daring to open up my eyes. For just a brief second, I saw his face. I didn't know if it was because he was so engrossed in our conversation that he forgot to hold the shadows around him, or if he just assumed I would keep my eyes closed.

All I could do was gape at him, shocked by what I was seeing.

His expression shattered, the coy smirk giving way to unreadability. Before I could inquire about what I'd seen, the shadows returned, once again obscuring his features from view. I could feel his eyes penetrating my scalp, and I opened my mouth helplessly. I didn't know what I wanted to say, but it didn't seem to matter. The shadow disappeared in a cloud of smoke.

I closed my eyes and focused, listening to his footsteps as he hurried down the hall.

What type of person was I? He was the second man to have run from me in a very short time span. I thought through hundreds of statements I could've said, but each one seemed superficial in the grand scheme of things. I didn't know if words were even necessary for what I saw.

Sometimes, silence was louder than thousands of false condolences.

But what I'd seen...

I didn't know how to even put it into words.

I heard the loud footsteps a second before a girl appeared around the corner.

"Holy shit! Are you okay?"

I tensed, surveying the female in front of me. She had orange hair that curled down her back. Her shoulders were broad and muscular, and her face was lightly freckled. Her green eyes were anxiously scanning my blood-stained clothes in what appeared to be horror.

"Yup," I said cheerily. "I was helping my assassin, Z, clean up a body."

Did that make me sound psycho? Probably. In my defense, I was struggling to come up with a reasonable explanation for why I was coated in blood, wearing nothing but a robe, in the hallway.

Oh, no big deal. I just murdered a shadow to protect an incubus because I'm actually Z the assassin and not Zara the assistant.

Yeah. *That* would've gone over well.

"Z?" She quirked a brow at me. "You're his assistant?"

Once again, it was nearly impossible to miss the connotation behind that seemingly innocent word. I could see the wheels turning in her head, coming to the same conclusion that countless others already had. Slut. Whore.

I hated those terms, even if they weren't true. There was nothing wrong with a woman enjoying lots of sex. Men did it all the time, so why should women have different standards?

"Lupe is not going to like this," she muttered.

"Huh?"

Ignoring me, she smiled widely, revealing two rows of perfectly white teeth.

"My name is Atta, and I'm the Princess of the Shifters."

Princess.

Shifters.

Shifters.

Holy shit.

My mind drifted to S. A Shifter had killed him, had taken the man I loved away from me. This girl, this Atta, was standing mere inches from me.

I wanted to kill her.

I wanted to take my knife, stab it into her black heart, and rid the world of another nightmare. How dare she smile so serenely at me when her species had taken everything from me? It was her father that had designed and implemented hundreds of human concentration camps. If she was anything like that monster of a man, she deserved to die.

I could barely breathe as I stared at her. Red coated my vision. Still, Atta continued on, utterly oblivious to the direction my thoughts had headed.

"I would like to invite you to the dinner tonight," she said in a singsong voice. "My brother will be there." At this, her eyes watched me carefully, as if gauging my reaction.

Murderer.

Monster.

Shifter.

Those words were one and the same to me.

"Z will also be there, of course, because it is a dinner designed for competitors of the Damning and the Matching." Her voice stumbled over my real name.

Murderer.

Monster.

Shifter.

I still had the knife in my hand from my confrontation with Ryland. It would only take a second to stick it in her chest. One second.

"So are you interested?"

I slowly raised my hand...

Only to have it pulled back down and behind my back. Mali wrapped her arm around me, flashing Atta a bright smile.

"She would love to! Isn't that right, Zara?"

My best friend was barely breathing. Her eyes were fixated on Atta, expression indecipherable. Atta stared back, but her attention was narrowed on Mali's arm around me. The air practically seemed to shimmer with tension. It was enough to pull me out of my murderous daze.

Mali looked away first, brows crinkled with confusion. She tugged at my arm and pulled me in the direction of my room.

"She'll be there!" Mali said with forced cheerfulness. I dared to glance back at Atta, the shifter, only to find her staring after us with an unreadable expression. It almost appeared to be hope and longing, but for what I wouldn't have been able to tell you. Either way, she was lucky Mali had arrived when she did, or else I probably would've killed her.

NINETEEN

Z

"No way in hell," I hissed the second I stepped into my room. "No way. No."

Mali folded her arms, expression calculating as she watched me from the doorway. All I could see was red. I was positively livid—at the shifter, at the world, even at my best friend.

"How the hell am I supposed to go to the dinner tonight as Zara when I'm supposed to be going as Z?" I hissed, shoving a hand through my blonde hair. I had yet to shower, and I was sure I smelled something awful. "Why did you agree for me to go?"

"Because I panicked!" Mali threw her hands into the air in exasperation. "When the crowned princess asks you to go to dinner, you fucking go to dinner!"

Her lip turned down as she spoke, her nose scrunching up as if she'd eaten something sour. I wondered if Mali knew this shifter princess. That was the only reason I could think to explain the tightening of her eyes and the pursing of her lips.

"So what do you suppose we do?" I asked sarcastically. I was Z...but I was also Zara. I didn't know how she expected me to be two different people at the same time. Not even a mage could solve this problem.

"It's easy." She moved farther into the spacious room and parted the heavy curtain. All I could see was her profile as she surveyed something through the window. "Diego will be Z."

"Diego?" I asked, sure she was joking. Diego was a lot of things, but a badass assassin wasn't one of them. He relied on HH to take care of him almost religiously. He blamed his chronic laziness on his Sloth genes. I blamed it on the man himself. "Diego stabbed himself accidentally with a toothpick and was in the hospital for a week."

Mali grunted. "I know, but—"

"He once farted and set a building on fire. *A fucking fart.* Who does that?"

"It was the mating call—"

"And don't even get me started on the peanut butter incident."

"I feel verbally abused, Zarakins," Diego purred, stepping out of my bathroom. He was, once again, wrapped in only a towel.

"Did you use my shower *again*?" I asked through gritted teeth. "And don't call me that."

"Baby girl, relax. It's just a dinner."

At that, I let out a bark of laughter.

"Just a dinner? There will be the most sick, twisted, psychotic men in existence at this dinner. They kill people, innocent people, and *like* it. They kill children, rape women, blow up schools. And I'm willing to bet you money that they *will* attack at this dinner. Poison the drinks, perhaps? A knife to the throat? Brute force?" The more I spoke, the more I felt my resolve strengthening. I would never again put the people I loved at risk. It had already happened once with S. Guilt churned in my stomach like lead, weighing me down until I was practically falling through the floor.

Guilt wasn't just an emotion, but a way of being. It was the thing that prohibited you from getting out of bed in the morning. It was the vise around your wrists that held you captive. It was the inability to see light in the darkness of the world.

If something were to happen to Diego or Mali, it would destroy me. S' death had been a knife to my heart, but their deaths would be the equivalent of someone twisting the handle. I didn't know if I could, or even wanted to, survive it.

"Out of the question," I said, moving to my desk. A few of my favorite knives were spread out, each one looking keen and terrifying in the natural light from the opened window.

"Z...." When I didn't turn towards Diego, he grabbed my shoulders and gave them a shake. "Look at me."

I stubbornly refused, eyes glued to the collection of penetratingly sharp weapons. Diego's gentle hand grabbed my chin, forcing my head up.

"You feel like you have the weight of the world on your shoulders, but let me help you. Let me hold a fraction of what you've been carrying. I know it's been hard since S, but you're not alone anymore. You'll never be alone with us. Trust me. Trust Mali. Trust yourself. I'm not completely inept at fighting, and I truly don't believe anything is going to happen tonight. If it does, you'll be right there. You can protect me, protect us all, like you always do."

His words resonated within me, and I wanted desperately to believe him. I'd been alone for so long. Everyone had abandoned me—my parents, Lin, and S. It had never occurred to me that my fears were selfish until that moment. I was afraid of a lot of things, the biggest one being abandonment. People came into your life only to leave you, a revolving door of false promises and fake assurances. Every story I had ended that way, but I'd never been capable of writing it myself. I was a player that someone else controlled, a shell of a woman drifting through life. It wasn't as if I expected a happy ending, but was it too much to ask for people to stay with me?

"I..." I trailed off, unsure how to express what I felt. Diego's eyes were earnest as he held my own captive.

"Trust us to handle it," he said softly. "Trust us."

A knock on the door interrupted whatever I was going to say. Both Diego and I jumped, his hands instantly leaving my shoulders. Mali blanched at the sound, muscles tensing as if she expected a monster to be on the other side of the door. A monster...or a nightmare.

Throwing both Diego and Mali a warning look, I hesitantly pulled open the heavy door. Mali instantly relaxed when she saw who was there, and Diego's eyes popped out of his head.

The incubus from before stood in the doorway, his muscular body blocking the hallway from view. My tongue turned into sandpaper in my mouth as I took in his exquisite body. The tattoos wrapping around his muscular forearms, the shock of red hair, the surprisingly kind eyes...

I had to physically pinch myself to stop ogling him like a perverted schoolgirl. Once my initial lust waned, I was left with an elemental fury directed at this very sexy man.

"What the hell, Killian? Why did you just leave me?"

After we'd kissed.

After I'd saved your life.

After your hands had pulled at my hair, our mouths merging together. We'd been one at that moment.

And I hated it. Hated him.

Frankly, I was a spiteful cynic. Sue me.

"I'm sorry," he sputtered. "I just panicked."

I wasn't stupid. I realized he had a stutter. However, it was barely noticeable to me. I reasoned it was because my father had had a stutter as well, though my memories of him were blurry at best. I could still hear his voice, though, as it broke through the confines of my mind where I held the remnants of my parents and S.

"You panicked?" I asked coldly, crossing my arms over my chest and resting my hip against the doorframe. Killian gulped.

"I'm not the most experienced," he managed to say at last. Despite how laughable that statement was—I mean, look at him—there was nothing but sincerity in his voice. His thick lashes fluttered against his cheeks, and I realized that he was waiting for me to judge him. To laugh at him. To turn him away.

I didn't know how I knew that, only that I did. My

heart warred with my mind over how to handle this precarious situation we'd found ourselves in. Why did I have the strangest urge to invite him inside? To soothe his fears? I went from hating all nightmares besides Mali and Diego to actively wanting to hug one. What was wrong with me?

"I'd like to make it up to you," he said at last. His eyes were warm as they grazed my face, their path leaving behind a trail of heat. I felt my cheeks flame at his scrutiny.

"Is she blushing?" I heard Diego whisper to Mali, and fortunately, she had the brains to punch him.

"You want to make it up to me?" I repeated coyly, straightening my back. I willed my cheeks to return to their normal color. "How do you suppose you'll do that?"

"Lunch, maybe? One of my friends has a car here. I could ask him for the keys...or we could eat here. Whichever you prefer."

Did he just...did he just ask me out?

An incubus?

And was I actually thinking about saying yes?

"Get that ass," I heard Diego mutter. Once again, he was punched by Mali.

"Fine," I said at last, shocking even myself. I heard Mali's sharp intake of breath and Diego's rather dramatic gasp. They acted as if I was agreeing to partake in a ritualistic sacrifice, not go out to lunch with an incubus. Geez.

Killian blinked at me, as if stunned I'd agreed.

Same, man. Same.

I told myself I was only meeting with him to gauge

how much he knew about my true identity. He was a stranger, a nightmare, and I would more than happily end him once I got all of the information I needed. If he knew too much, I wouldn't hesitate to kill him.

"An incubus with a stutter," Diego commented as I stepped around him, reaching for my purse. Unbeknownst to the incubus, I had numerous knives and daggers hidden within the pink fabric. If he were to try anything, I would end him in seconds.

A girl had to be prepared.

"Don't," I warned Diego, slightly defensive. Irrationally defensive, if I was being completely honest with myself. I didn't know why it bothered me to hear Diego make fun of Killian, only that it did.

Turning away from my mage best friend, I flashed Killian a cautious smile. I had to be careful with a man like him. Someone who looked that good could only bring trouble. I wasn't worried about protecting my heart, since he could never have it the way I'd once given it away, but one glance, and I was ready to relinquish my body to him. I was a quivering puddle of lust whenever he opened those big, pouty lips. When he smiled? It was like a cloud moving away from the sun.

"Let's go," I said, stepping around him and into the hall. Killian immediately followed behind, bouncing on the balls of his feet. I didn't know if it was an anxious tick or if he just possessed an abundant amount of energy. Either way, I found his exuberance infectious.

"So..." I trailed off, unsure of what I wanted to say. How could I possibly ask him everything I wanted to? If he didn't know that I was actually Z, I didn't want to give it away. If he did, what would it take him to remain quiet? Questions pounded inside of my skull, in tandem to my rapidly beating heart. One thing was for certain—Killian was dangerous.

"I ran into a wall yesterday," he blurted, cheeks turning scarlet at his unintentional confession. Despite how strange that statement was, I found myself amused, if not moderately curious.

"How did that happen?"

He shrugged. "Walking."

"I thought incubi were supposed to be graceful?" I couldn't stop the laughter that slipped out. His lips twitched at the sound.

"I'm not like the other incubi," he admitted, as if that answer should've been obvious.

"What do you mean?"

"Well, I have a stutter for one."

I raised an eyebrow at him, as if eloquently asking why that mattered. Once again, his cheeks flamed.

"And I'm also not the most...articulate...around other people."

"You just used the word 'articulate,'" I pointed out. "That's a pretty big word for someone who struggles with speaking."

I didn't know why I was entertaining the idea of having a conversation with Killian. It wasn't as if I was automatically anti-nightmare, but those who lived in the capital were inherently evil. This was the same group of people that supported human segregation and work camps. They were disgusting, but at the same time, I couldn't deny that the shy smile on Killian's handsome face and his anxious chuckle made my heart hammer.

"Kill! I've been looking for you everywhere!"

We both spun towards the intruding voice, and my jaw practically dropped to the ground. It was a female who'd spoken, and one look confirmed that she was an incubus.

I'd never been attracted to females before, but hot damn. Her incubus allure was strong, nearly staggering, and only made me think that she was of a noble family to have a power that strong. She was almost ethereal in beauty, with caramel highlighted hair and large blue eyes.

Those eyes were currently locked on Killian, lust darkening her features.

My hands clenched into fists at her blatant ogling of him. The possessiveness and jealousy came from nowhere. And yet...

I wanted to claw her eyes out.

"Hi, Tessa," Killian stuttered, offering her a warm smile.

"I just wanted to see you," she purred. Actually purred. I didn't know whether to punch her or vomit. Or both. I had a *why choose* type of mentality.

"See me?" Killian quirked his eyebrow adorably. He seemed honestly confused by the various sexual innuendos behind that one statement.

"It's a shame that you weren't one of my mates," she cooed, her lip pushing out into a pout. Grown women shouldn't pout. Ever. It was disgusting and demeaning to all women everywhere. "But that doesn't mean we can't still have some fun."

She reached out with a perfectly manicured hand and touched his bicep. I saw red at that diminutive gesture. Killian gave her an awkward smile, sidestepping her greedy hand. That bicep she was touching? It was mine.

"Shame," Killian said with a forced smile. His eyes flickered anxiously to me, gauging my reaction. I wasn't sure what he saw, but his lips crooked upwards at the expression on my face. "Tessa, this is my...*friend*, Zara."

Tessa reluctantly turned to face me. She couldn't even bother to hide the distaste from her face.

"She's human," she pointed out. Rather obviously, if you asked me. She wasn't the sharpest tool in the shed.

"Yes." Killian's voice was suddenly tight. "She is."

"You can't possibly believe that this will last?" she continued, ignoring the penetrating glare he directed her way. Tessa's expression was almost pitying as she stared at me. I, however, struggled to understand what "this" she was referring to. "What are you going to do when you find your mate, Kill?"

I knew that every male nightmare had one fated mate. Females, on the other hand, could have up to two. I once heard of a female shifter having three mates, but anything higher than that was unheard of. The female population was significantly lower than the male population, especially since the nightmares came into power. Humans liked to believe that it was God's way of punishing the monsters.

I'd thought that Devlin and S were my mates, though I wasn't sure if humans were even capable of having some. I'd loved them both in two entirely different ways.

S was my heart and Devlin was my strength, but they'd both left me, albeit unwillingly in S's case. Mates were supposed to be infinite, and yet we'd been torn apart as if our bond was nothing at all.

I shook my head, focusing once more on Tessa.

"You're sadly mistaken," I said, unable to hide the laughter in my voice. "I just met Killian like an hour ago. We're not...*anything*."

Killian's face briefly flashed with hurt at my words, but he schooled his expression quickly. It was replaced by careful indifference.

"Practically strangers," he said, tone clipped. I glanced sideways at him, stunned by his change in behavior. Tessa eyed the two of us.

"Whatever. I'm going to visit Bash. I heard that he's having lots of fun."

Woah. I did not want to know what type of fun she was referring to. My type of fun was stabbing a nightmare in the neck. Her type? It probably involved penises. Lots and lots of penises.

"Great! We're looking for Bash too. I need to borrow his car keys." Killian's smile was once again radiant on his face. He changed personalities quicker than I changed knives.

"Ahh...I'm pretty sure that isn't a good idea," I mumbled, thinking of what a man like Bash would do for fun, just as Tessa said, "Whatever. It's not like I actually wanted to get stuck with a retard like you."

Time stopped. The world stopped. Everything tilted sideways, balancing precariously on the edge, and my vision was obscured by a red sheen.

How. Dare. She?

I lunged forward, she squealed, and Killian grabbed my arm.

"Are you kidding me?" I asked, spinning towards him. Why wouldn't he let me stab the bitch?

"She's a high-ranking noble," Killian hurriedly said, confirming what I'd already suspected. "If you harm her, you'll be thrown in prison for the rest of your life, if not killed."

"She *insulted* you," I hissed. My reaction was irrational, but it consumed me. Red. Red everywhere. Red like rivulets of blood.

Killian placed his hands on my shoulders, lowering his head until his forehead touched mine. His breath caressed my face, and I trembled in his embrace.

"It's okay. I'm okay. Her words don't matter. Only you matter. Only you."

His words didn't make sense in my incoherent mind, yet they calmed me instantly. In the little cocoon of our own making, only we existed. Only us.

"Holy shit!" Tessa's voice brought me out of my daze. "The crown prince and a human? Holy fucking shit."

Prince? Killian?

And why was Tessa so shocked?

Killian's face was positively livid as he leveled a glare in her direction. She blanched under the intensity of his scrutiny.

"Not a word to anyone. You got that? If anyone gets word of this, I will know it was you who told and you will *not* like the consequences. Do you understand me?"

When Tessa didn't answer straight away, he took a threatening step forward. "Do you understand?"

She nodded. I was almost afraid her head was going to fall off.

I gaped at Killian wordlessly. The change from a shy, timid boy to a prowling tiger was shocking. And sexy, if I was being honest with myself. There was something extremely appealing about Killian threatening her.

Without another word, she turned on her heel and strutted towards where this Bash person apparently was. I wasn't even aware that "strutting" was an actual thing, but that was the only word I could use to describe her long strides and the subtle shake to her hips. I glanced towards Killian, suddenly afraid that he would be staring after her very large butt on display, but he was looking at me. His lips curled up into a gentle smile.

"Ready?" he asked, offering me his arm. I hesitantly linked mine with his.

"Who's Bash?" I questioned as we walked down a long, unfamiliar hallway. There were numerous paintings adorning the wall, each one representing the Seven Deadly Sins. I stumbled over my feet at the painting depicting Greed. In it, a purple genie floated out of a lamp, a mockery of the old movies. Gold was everywhere —on the walls, the floor, even in the form of intricately crafted jewelry for the genie. Still, the genie had a scowl on his face as he stared at his possessions. Always wanting more. Never happy with what he had.

I scoffed as I thought of Lin, of Devlin.

All genies were the same, apparently.

Before I could study the painting further, Killian began to speak.

"Bash is my best friend. My brother. We grew up together."

I wondered what creature Bash was, but I didn't want to come across as rude by asking. Was asking what species he was taboo?

Killian, however, must've seen the question on my face, since he added, "He's a mage."

Ah. A lazy son of a bitch.

The name Bash sounded familiar, but I quickly shook my head to keep my brain from making the connection it wanted to. What were the odds that I would meet another prince? The mage prince? I didn't believe in coincidences. If Bash proved to be a prince, I would stand to believe that it was fate.

To do what, however, remained unclear. To kill them all, perhaps? That didn't seem right, especially after meeting Dair and Killian and coming to the realization that Lin was a prince as well.

Tessa stopped in front of a heavy, wooden door. Turning around to glare at us haughtily, she pushed it open, and we all stumbled inside.

The sight I saw... There were no words.

It was a mesh of limbs and bodies and hair and holes. In front of me, two girls were making out while a man screwed one from behind. Her breasts bounced as he pounded into her. Another couple was a tangle of limbs and breasts and penises. I saw one man giving another a blowjob. Two guys were pleasuring the same girl, one in each hole. And two girls were grinding against each other, sucking on one another's breasts. I had to give them credit—that took considerable flexibility.

"So many holes," Killian whispered, stunned. "What do you even do with that many holes?" Face flaming, he spun towards the doorway.

I watched a naked Tessa strut—again with the damn strutting—towards a handsome man sitting on a leather chair. He looked like a king on a throne, overlooking his filthy peasants.

He was a beautiful man. Finely sculpted cheekbones, arresting green eyes, a mop of blond hair. His body was lightly muscled with a scatter of blond hair leading down to his dick. His limp dick. Despite having one woman sucking on his neck and the other fondling his balls, the appendage continued to hang there in all its glory. He was glaring at his dick, as if it had personally offended him.

He finally turned fully towards me, and his eyes captured mine. I was held in his gaze, one tortured soul calling to the next.

Mine.

The thought came to me with an almost blistering speed. Pinpricks of desire ghosted over my skin.

He pushed both girls away and scrambled to his feet. His once flaccid dick was now rock-hard and twitching. I licked my lips as I stared at the throbbing vein. What I wouldn't give to lick and suck—

No! I mentally berated myself for my lust filled thoughts.

"Everyone out." Though his voice was quiet, it seemed to innately demand attention. Every person stopped in mid activity. Tessa actually had the nerve to pout. "Everyone out now!"

The blast of power that accompanied that statement sent goosebumps down my arms. Despite how terrifying the amount of power he wielded was, I felt safe in his presence. I knew that he would never harm me. I knew that as surely as I knew my name.

As surely as I knew that he was made to be mine, along with—

Nope. It's just the lust speaking, Z. Snap out of it.

"What the hell, Bash?" Killian asked, aghast.

"What are you doing here?" the man—Bash, I assumed—yelled, his gaze flickering from Killian's back to my face. I tried really hard to focus on his words. I honestly did.

But his *thing* was nearly poking my stomach from how close he was, long and proud.

"Ahh..."

"What were you even doing, Bash?" Killian continued, finally turning around. He kept his eyes carefully averted and put his arm around my shoulders to pull me closer against his side. Bash's eyes locked on that movement and narrowed.

"What did it look like I was doing? The fucking tango?"

"No need to be a *dick* about it," I quipped. "I know this is a *hard* situation. We really should've *orgy*-nized our schedules better."

Killian, beside me, began to chuckle. Bash's eyes narrowed further, as if they could physically penetrate my skin. Or my clothes.

"And you?" He spun towards Killian, jabbing an accusatory finger into the incubus's chest. "Why would you bring her here? How did you even know who she was?"

Killian brows furrowed in confusion.

"We talked about this." He glanced shyly at me and then lowered his voice to a whisper. "The whole dick issue."

"Don't fucking talk about my dick," Bash hissed.

"*Your* dick?"

"I'll have you know—"

"Look," I said, cutting Bash off. "You apparently were *balls deep* in something when we arrived. We wouldn't have *cum* if we knew you were busy. We'll just be heading in the opposite *erection*."

Bash glared down at me.

"Don't expect flowers or shit like that. Don't expect me to actually care about you and your fucking tight ass."

Um...okay?

Bash began shaking his head erratically, simultaneously backing out of the room. He didn't seem to care that he was still as hard as a rock, nor that he was going out into public butt naked.

"Nope. That is a whole lot of nopes. Nope. Nope. Nope. Nope."

He was still chanting "nope" as the door slammed shut on his face.

TWENTY

Z

We didn't speak as Killian led me out a backdoor, down a steep, stone staircase, and underneath the drooping canopy of the nearest cluster of trees.

Back at home, the forests had been leafless, their branches mere skeletons. The beauty at the capital was in complete contradiction to the despondency of my hometown. There was no comparison. Everything was extravagant, from the polished windows to the white pillars to the various arcades. There was an opulence here that a town like mine, a town that existed in poverty, couldn't recreate no matter how hard they tried. It was disgusting that these nightmares lived in such wealth while the rest of us struggled to make ends meet. Even the gardens looked as if they were plucked straight from a storybook.

I was in awe as I surveyed row after row of perfectly planted tulips mixed in with roses. Bushes lined the siding of the building, each one sprouting a flower I couldn't quite identify. I couldn't deny how beautiful the garden was, nor how safe I felt beneath the shield of leaves.

Killian sat beneath the boughs. Evidently, the initial plan to leave the capital was no longer in play. He patted the spot of grass beside him, now dry from the morning dew. I sat crossed-legged beside him and leaned my back against the rough bark of the nearest tree.

"I'm sorry about...him," Killian said at last. His long fingers absently pulled at the grass, one green strand after another. The movement was oddly mesmerizing as he placed the blade of grass between his thumb and pointer finger. His attention was focused on his leg, the grass, the trees. Anywhere besides my questioning eyes. "I don't know why he was behaving like that. Bash has always been an asshole, but he's never been so..." He trailed off, unable to find a word that adequately described the blond-haired mage.

"It's fine. It was actually sort of entertaining. I mean, my first orgy, and I wasn't even participating in it." I'd tried to make light of the situation, tried to make a joke out of what we'd seen, but the blush coloring Killian's cheeks clued me in that I may not have said the correct thing. Apparently, the sexy incubus was embarrassed when it came to talk of sex. Changing the subject, I rubbed my stomach and asked, "What's for lunch? I'm starving."

Smiling gratefully, Killian waved his hand. A young human servant hurried towards us.

"Yes, Your Highness?" the servant asked, reverence evident in his voice. While most humans had been taught to fear nightmares, most of all royalty, this man looked at Killian with what I could only describe as respect.

"Would you mind grabbing the picnic basket out of the fridge in the kitchen, Brad?" Killian asked. His eyes flashed towards me, and he smiled shyly. "I forgot."

"Right away."

Without another word, the servant, Brad, hurried towards a door that I assumed led in the direction of the kitchen. I watched him go, awe mixing with confusion.

"You know his name," I said at last.

Killian blinked at me in surprise.

"Of course I know his name." He almost appeared insulted, and I hurried to explain.

"Most night—" I stopped myself before I could say nightmare. "I mean, supernatural creatures don't bother to learn the names of the help. Of the humans. It's a way to dehumanize them and place them low in this constructed social hierarchy."

I shrugged, long since accepting the role I was expected to play in life. In their minds, I wasn't worthy of having a name, of being anything besides a slave, a servant, and a pawn.

Killian's eyes darkened with anger, and at first, I feared I'd overstepped with my rather rude comment. It took me a moment to realize the anger wasn't directed at me, but at the situation.

"The way humans are treated is ridiculous," he said at last, teeth grinding together.

Despite already knowing the answer, I tentatively asked, "And you don't treat people like that?"

He released a heavy sigh, his hand creeping up to rub

at his temples. When he finally met my gaze, there was such melancholy in his eyes that my heart stuttered to an abrupt stop before restarting with a vengeance.

"Not every nightmare is evil, just like not every human is good. There are facets in every aspect of nature —good and bad, light and dark. There are some people who are actively seeking to rid the world of humans for good." His lip curled dangerously at that statement. "But there are others fighting for equal rights between super-naturals and humans. Do you know how my mother died?"

The question was so sudden that all I could do was blink up at him like an imbecile. I managed an inarticulate, "Huh?"

"My mother was the soulmate of my father. She was an incubus, like him, but she'd never had sex before marrying my father. Hell, she'd never engaged in any sexual activities besides what was necessary for her survival. My father, on the other hand, had a different lover every night, even after meeting and falling in love with my mother. Often, these lovers were humans. He preferred them that way, since he was able to drain them completely."

His eyes turned distant, lost in a memory only he could see.

"When I was five years old, I got a nanny. She was only twenty, and she was a human servant." At this, a small smile graced his features. It was apparent he cared deeply for this woman. "She was my second mother. My older sister. She was with us for years."

His hand clenched on his leg, and I instinctively

reached over to pull apart his fingers. Tiny, crescent indents remained in his skin from his keen nails.

"When I was ten, I began to go through puberty. I didn't know what was happening. All I knew was that my body was changing and growing, and no one understood." I gripped his hand tighter. Somehow, I knew that this story wouldn't have a happy ending. For anyone. "I made the mistake of telling my father, and he sent...he sent my nanny to my room. He told me that I had to sleep with her."

My heart ached for the little boy who'd had his childhood torn from him in such a way. An incandescent fury burned a hole in my stomach at the thought of his father. Forcing his son to sleep with a woman he considered his mother? It was beyond disgusting.

"She refused, of course, but my dad didn't like that. He raped her right in front of me, draining her body dry." A single teardrop cascaded down his face. I used my free hand to capture it before it could reach his lips.

"I am so sorry," I whispered, despite knowing how inadequate those words were. I always hated when people apologized to me. It wasn't their fault that my parents and S died. Sorry was just a word we used when we didn't know what else to say.

"My mother..." Killian started, eyes misting with tears. My body moved closer against his, and I gently rested my head on his shoulder—a stranger's shoulder.

And yet...

And yet it felt like a piece of my soul becoming whole once more.

"My mother killed herself shortly after. She couldn't

live with the knowledge of what her husband had done, and she couldn't live with the fact that she still loved him. Sometimes, we crave the darkness when the light is too much for us to handle. She left me alone with that monster. That was how I developed my stutter. After her death, he beat me nearly to death. One of his blows landed on my throat. No amount of sexual energy or healing spells could fix the damage. We don't understand why, but we concluded that he'd placed a spell on me to prohibit such healing."

It was official—I was going to skin his dad alive and then feed him to the gators.

My thoughts were interrupted by approaching footsteps. The servant from earlier appeared with a blanket and picnic basket. After exchanging quick pleasantries with Killian, he spread out the blanket, placed the basket on top, and hurried away.

Killian handed me a turkey and cheese sandwich, the crust neatly trimmed off. A lump formed in my throat at the sight. My mother always used to cut off the crust when she packed me my lunches.

"Does it bother you?" Killian asked, after a couple minutes of comfortable silence had passed.

"Does what bother me?"

"My stutter."

"No," I answered honestly. "I barely even notice it. My dad had a stutter as well, though his only came out when he was nervous."

I remembered he once had to give a speech at my kindergarten graduation. He could barely get the first word out. My mother climbed up on the stage, took his hand, and gave him the strength to finish. It was one of my last memories of them.

"You said 'had'..." Killian trailed off, allowing me to choose whether or not I would answer. The man had bared his soul to me, had made himself vulnerable in front of a stranger. Though it went against every fiber of my being, I owed it to him to give him the same level of trust. For so long, I'd kept shields around my heart. They were impenetrable barriers that nobody dared break. At that moment, a tiny crack appeared.

"They were killed," I said bluntly. "By nightmares."

There was no guilt on his face, only sadness. It struck me as odd that he didn't classify himself as a nightmare, that he separated himself from that title and identity. There was also empathy etched across his handsome features. I realized long ago that there was a distinct difference between empathy and sympathy. You never really understood what someone was going through unless you had been through it yourself. We had both lost people, and that bond connected us in a way only shared grief could.

"And then I made the stupid mistake of falling in love. Twice." I snorted at how ridiculous I'd been. "The first man left me." And had torn my heart to pieces in the process. "The second one was killed. By a rogue shifter."

And it should've been me. If I hadn't gotten involved...

If I hadn't insisted...

If I hadn't...

I couldn't allow my thoughts to continue down that dark path. Guilt would consume me.

To keep from divulging anything else, I took another bite of my sandwich.

"Yum," I mumbled around a mouthful of food. Killian hesitantly traced a pattern on my arm. The touch made my stomach flutter and goosebumps appear on my skin.

"So we both had fucked-up lives?" he asked softly.

Up and down his finger went.

Up and down.

Up and down.

"I know the only reason you agreed to go to lunch with me was to figure out how much I knew about your identity," Killian said casually, and I tensed beneath his stroking fingers.

Up and down.

Up and down.

"I don't care that you're an assassin. I don't care that you're competing in the Damning. I don't care that you kill nightmares for a living. I care about the girl I see now. And what I see is someone funny and smart and so incredibly beautiful."

"You don't even know me," I whispered, my heart in my throat. Tears sprang to my eyes unbidden.

"I know." He sighed heavily. "Trust me, I know."

We were amicably silent for another moment, each finishing up the last of the sandwiches and basking in our own thoughts. I didn't know how I felt about his revelation. It was immensely dangerous for him to know who I was, both for me and for him.

"What's this?" he asked, pulling away from me. I immediately missed the warmth he emitted and hated myself for my neediness. I told myself I'd just met this man, that it was irrational and utterly illogical to have feelings for him. But my traitorous body refused to listen.

It took me a moment to realize that Killian was grabbing something out of my purse. For a horrible, nauseating second, I thought he'd noticed the knives I had packed away. That fear turned into confusion when he pulled out a small paperback book.

I recognized it immediately as the book Ryland had thrown at my head.

Lovers on the Mountaintop.

"Is *this* what the scary assassin reads?" Killian teased, quirking a brow in amusement. I felt my cheeks flame.

How did that even get into my purse?

The answer came easily—Ryland.

Flipping it opened, Killian peered down at the novel.

"'She massaged his balls, and he rubbed her lady part. She came like a wave cresting against the shore...the shore of pleasure.'"

Killian paused and flipped to a new page.

"'Her hot molten lady cave quivered.'"

Frowning, he turned towards one of the last pages.

"'His huge cock filled up her ass crack. It was as if she was taking the meanest shit in her life.' What the hell am I even reading?"

Killian dropped the book as if it were on fire.

"It's erotica," I said with a giggle. When Killian continued to look down at it with horror, I timidly asked, "Have you ever been with a girl before, Kill?"

His eyes flickered to my face, and he noticeably gulped.

"I didn't want to be like *him*. Like my father."

"So how do you survive if you don't have sex?" I was genuinely curious. From what I knew, incubi needed sex to live until they found their fated mate. And from what I knew of Killian, he had yet to find her.

"Sexual energy," he said at last. "I go to brothels and sit in the hallways."

Before I could rethink my words, I whispered, "Do you want to?"

"Want to what?" It sounded as if he weren't breathing.

"Touch a female."

Now I was positive he was holding his breath. I could feel his incredible power rise up in tandem to his own lust. His eyes flared with desire.

"I want to touch you more than anything," he rasped out at last.

"Okay."

Without breaking eye contact, I pulled my shirt over my head. He sharply inhaled, eyes roaming the exposed skin of my stomach. The air was slightly chilly with only my bra and pants on, but I'd never felt so warm before. His gaze set my skin on fire.

Slowly, as if giving me the chance to change my mind, his fingers touched the sides of my stomach. They were as light as a butterfly's wing, gently tracing my protruding rib cage.

"You're so beautiful," he murmured, leaning closer. The movement propelled me backwards until I was lying on the grass with him over me. Normally, I would've hated being in that type of position. I was at the mercy of another individual, but I only felt empowered with Killian staring down at me as if I were a goddess personified. "So beautiful."

I reached for the clasp on my pants, wiggling them down my hips. Killian helped me pull them all the way off.

His hands started at my toes and slowly made their way up. Over my calves. My thighs.

They paused there, lightly drawing invisible designs on the sensitive skin, before moving upwards. They skimmed my hips, his fingers sliding beneath the elastic of my underpants and touching the bare skin there. I moaned at the contact, tiny spurts of his power rushing straight to my core.

He pulled away suddenly, eyes hooded and fixated on my heaving chest. Nodding to give him permission to touch me further, I unclasped my bra strap.

Killian leaned over me once again, and I felt his dick press against my mound, only his pants and my underwear separating us. I yearned to memorize his broad, tattooed shoulders through touch alone, yet I resisted. This was about him. Only him.

His hand cupped one of my breasts, testing the size, while the other tentatively drew a circle around the mound. His finger went upwards until it was hovering over my peaked nipple. Eyes locked on mine, his finger grazed the tip.

I let out another mewl from his simple, innocent touch. I wanted him to consume me, to eat me alive, to make me his.

As if he could read my mind, he lowered his mouth to

my aching breast and darted his tongue out to lick my nipple. His expression turned contemplative as he watched me—the desire I knew was in my eyes, my opened mouth as I struggled to breathe, my incoherent pleas. The smile that lit up his face was smug satisfaction and so positively male that I couldn't resist moaning yet again. He dropped his head back to my breast, his teeth grazing my peak. He rolled my other nipple between his thumb and forefinger, the same way he had with the grass earlier.

Before I could beg him to continue, he began kissing down my breasts. Down my stomach. Once he reached my panties, he paused, hot breath warming my aching core. Over the thin material of my underwear, his tongue darted out and licked a long line over the seams.

"Yum. You taste delicious," he murmured. All I could do was whimper for him to continue. Using one hand to press my underwear to the side, his skilled tongue finally met my wet slit. The pleasure was immeasurable. I was a trembling pile of putty under his inexperienced, albeit obviously skilled, hands and tongue.

"Again."

His tongue leisurely licked me yet again. Savoring me. Tasting me.

It wasn't enough. Call me a greedy bitch, but I wanted him to devour me. I wanted to get lost in his body and forget my own name. I wanted us to merge as one, so I had trouble deciphering where he ended and I began.

I wanted—

An arrow soared through the air, landing millimeters away from my head. I froze, and Killian staggered backwards in horror. Another arrow descended, and it would've hit me if Killian hadn't pulled me out of its path with an almost blistering speed. I pressed my naked body against his, panting.

"Shit," I cursed, glancing towards the roof of the capital. I could make out a silhouette in the golden glow from the high sun.

We were under attack.

TWENTY-ONE

JAX

The incessant stomping of feet reverberated down the hallway. Coming. They were coming. Coming for me.

Stomp. Stomp. Stomp.

The grandfather clock ticked simultaneous with the footsteps.

Tick. Tick. Tick.

And the voices...

I pressed my hands over my ears, a futile but desperate attempt to drown out the sounds. I didn't want to hear them. I didn't want to hear anything. For the umpteenth time, I debated detaching my ears from my head.

Too loud.

The voices, the footsteps, the *tick tick tick* of the clock. My head pounded at the onslaught of noise, my senses overstimulated.

Your fault...

Monster...

Drink...

So thirsty...

"Stop!" I screamed at the voices. Why couldn't anyone else hear them? Why wouldn't they just leave me alone? I moved farther down the carpeted hallway, anxiously glancing from door to door. I hated doors. Anything or anyone could be lurking behind them. Doors were meant to be open, and yet they were always closed.

Stomp. Stomp. Stomp.

Tick. Tick. Tick.

Thirsty.

I needed to go. I needed to find *her*. The voices always stopped when she was near, as if her mere presence calmed them. They were unruly beasts, and she was their skilled trainer. They obeyed her as if she were innately able to dive inside my mind and command their respect.

Stomp. Stomp. Stomp.

Tick. Tick. Tick.

I scratched erratically at my arm, barely caring when skin fell to the ground. I hadn't even realized I'd scrubbed my skin raw. Blood ran in rivulets down my arm.

Blood.

My blood.

Still, I picked at the skin, as if that could somehow lessen the persistent itch.

Stomp. Stomp. Stomp.

Tick. Tick. Tick.

Itch. Itch. Itch.

My life was a strange combination of all three. I

didn't glide through life like some—I stomped. My mind? A ticking time bomb. My body? An itchy, painful—

I lost my train of thought. That wasn't necessarily surprising.

Where was she?

I had to find her. I couldn't bear another moment away from her and her calming presence.

Turning down yet another hallway, I paused mid step. There, at the end of the hallway, was a familiar figure. Her hair was cut short, just above her shoulders. Her emerald green eyes shone behind wire-framed glasses. Skin ghastly pale, she took a tentative step towards me. I instinctively moved away. From her. From myself.

I wanted to run away from myself.

Stupid Jax, and his stupid decisions.

So stupid. See? I was even speaking in third person now. Lupe had told me it was a way to detach myself from the situation. I didn't deserve to be an "I" when she wasn't even a "she" anymore. Could dead people still be a "she," or was she now an "it"? I didn't deserve to live. It would be better for everyone if I were to become lost in the abyss of my own mind.

Stupid.

So stupid.

"Sasha?" I breathed, unable to tear my gaze away from the twelve-year-old girl.

"Why did you do this to me?" she asked softly. Her feet shuffled across the cranberry red carpeting. The dark color nearly obscured the blood dripping from an opened wound on her neck.

Stomp. Stomp. Stomp.

Tick. Tick. Tick.

Itch. Itch. Itch.

Drip. Drip. Drip.

"You're not here." I squeezed my eyes shut, automatically counting backwards from ten. It was a trick that Lupe had taught me to do whenever I saw her.

Ten. Nine. Eight.

"Look at me." Her voice came from directly in front of me. A voice that had haunted both my waking moments and my nightmares. "Look at me."

Seven. Six.

I snapped my eyelids open.

Five. Four.

Her face was contorting, transforming, before my very eyes. The pale skin melted from her face like ice on a warm summer day. She coughed, and something fell into her hand. It was only as she moved to hold the strange object in the light that I saw it was a tooth.

Three. Two.

Cough. Cough. Cough.

Tooth. Tooth. Tooth.

Blood continued to cascade down her body, staining the white of her gown. All I could do was look at her in mesmerized horror, helpless to save her. Always helpless.

One.

"Stop!" I screamed as her bones caved in on themselves like old, yellowing paper. "Stop!"

My itching intensified, and I rubbed at the sensitive skin with a renewed vigor. I wanted my skin to fall off. I want to bleed.

My legs were unable to support my body, and I collapsed on the ground.

There was only one thing that could help me, one person, but she wouldn't come. Nobody ever came for me.

Alone. All alone.

Unloved. Unwanted.

As I stared at the spot where Sasha had been, I realized that I deserved it.

The clock in the hallway continued to tick away.

Tick. Tick. Tick.

TWENTY-TWO

Z

There were only two things that pissed me off. The first was not being able to finish a delicious orgasm by the hands or mouth of a very skilled incubus—obviously. The second was being shot at moments before said orgasm would've happened. *That* was just pushing my limits.

Grabbing my purse, I pulled out two throwing knives.

"Fucking hell," I mumbled under my breath. Still naked, I ambled to my feet and faced the intruder. From this distance, I couldn't tell what nightmare he was. My guess would've been a vampire, since he moved with an agility and speed that surpassed an average person. That would make things difficult. Not impossible. Just difficult.

Lifting my arm, I prepared to throw the knife at the shadowed figure. The second I would've released it, he ducked behind a pillar.

"Damn," I cursed.

He moved too fast for my eye to follow, a mere blur highlighted against the pale blue sky. His body moved from his hiding place to a windowsill one level below. Then another. And then another.

It took me a moment to realize he was coming down here. I glanced at Killian, who was currently gaping up at the figure, and that momentary lapse in concentration cost me. The vampire lunged at me with his fangs extended, and we both fell to the ground in a tangle of legs and arms. Killian scrambled to his feet, running forward as if he was going to take on the vampire himself. That thought only made me angrier. Killian was too kind, too pure, to deal with the violence in this world. I yearned to spare him from any more of it.

"I got this!" I yelled beneath the heavy bastard's body. His teeth snapped inches from my neck, but I was able to hold him away. Damn him. Stupid, orgasm ruining, bloodsucking vamp.

The vampire's eyes suddenly glazed over, flashing white in the second it took them to close.

What the fuck?

He let out a blissful moan, rolling off of my body until he was lying on his back. As I looked on in terror, his hand unzipped his pants and he began to fondle himself.

What. The. Fuck?

I glanced at Killian, who had somehow snuck up behind me. His worried eyes trailed over my still naked body, checking me for any injuries.

"Are you okay?" he asked, slightly panicked. Before I could assure him I was fine, he reached for my shirt and gently helped me get it back on. The tenderness he displayed was astonishing. I've never had anyone care for me before, let alone help me get dressed.

Even Lin and S had known better than to treat me like fine glass. But Killian? He looked at me as if I was precious, as if he wanted to give me the world.

"I'm sorry I didn't do anything earlier. I promise I'll do better next time. I won't let you down again."

I didn't know why I felt the need to comfort him. I didn't do cuddles and shit. Yet my arms moved of their own accord until they wound themselves around his neck, my fingers playing with the silky hair at the nape of his neck. He froze, stunned by my initiation of contact, before he moved to engulf my tiny waist in his strong arms. It was immensely soothing to be in his arms. I didn't feel like an assassin just then, but a girl. Like we were just a girl and a boy, each desperate to hold on to something, to *someone*.

"It's okay," I whispered into his ear. "I'm okay. Let me be strong for you."

I held him for a second longer before releasing him, somewhat reluctantly. I couldn't forget about the vampire that had attempted to kill me.

Or was he going after Killian?

It occurred to me that I was acting as Zara, not Z. Either this man knew of my true identity...or the target had been the incubus prince.

Crouching down beside the vampire, I watched his hand touch the pre-cum at the tip of his dick. His breathing was heavy as he jerked himself off.

"What's your name?" I asked the vampire, offering a seductive smile. He glared at me, but that glare morphed into unadulterated lust as Killian's magic consumed him.

"Ted," he gasped.

"Ted." I rolled the name over my tongue, an almost husky sound, and the vampire let out another moan. "Ted...why were you going after my friend over there?" I jerked my head in Killian's direction, who was watching the entire scene unfold without comment. I could feel his power, however, emitting from his body in soft waves. Fortunately, it wasn't directed at me. With how sexually frustrated I was, I would probably explode in only a second. Not the most intimidating interrogation method. "Why did you go after Prince Killian?"

The vampire, Ted, noticeably bit his lip to keep from talking. I began to walk my fingers up his stomach, and my touch only seemed to intensify his pleasure. His grunts escaped erratically now, and sweat beaded on his forehead. Fortunately, I knew that he would only be able to come when the incubus allowed him to. Until then, it would be nothing but painful pleasure.

"Do you want to come?" I whispered against the shell of his ear. He let out an inarticulate gasp in response. "All you have to do is tell me who you work for and why."

He stubbornly shook his head, but I could see the considerable strain that diminutive movement caused him. Behind me, I could hear skin slapping skin as he worked himself into a frenzy. I was glad I was looking the other way—I really wasn't in the mood to vomit.

"Tell me."

The next noise he made was a painful cry. I almost felt bad for him. Almost. If he hadn't tried to kill me, I might've told Killian to end his torment.

You know what they say—karma's a bitch.

"Tell me."

A groan.

"Tell me."

This time, he let out a pathetic whimper.

"Tell me."

"Aaliyah," he gasped.

I frowned, remembering that name from before when the shadow had attacked Killian and me in the hallway.

"Who's Aaliyah?" I questioned. "And what does she want with Killian?"

Ted opened his mouth, but just as quickly snapped it closed. White foam formed on his lips, dripping down his chin. His eyes rolled back into his head, and his body convulsed on the grass.

"Shit," I cursed, recognizing a spell when I saw one. Whoever this Aaliyah person was, she'd obviously been prepared. I didn't know what had triggered the spell, but I had a pretty good guess it had something to do with my line of questioning.

The vampire was dying.

Without another thought, I lifted the dagger still gripped tightly in my hand and shoved it into his heart. I didn't know if it was an act of mercy to end his suffering or selfishness to take credit for the kill. Perhaps it was a morbid combination of both.

The second his body went slack, Killian pulled me into his arms and buried his face in my hair.

"You still okay?" he asked softly. His large hand cupped my cheek tenderly.

"Are you?" I countered. I knew this couldn't be easy for him—seeing death, being around death, taking part in it. I was surprised he was still capable of touching me after what I kept doing in front of him. Whenever we were together, I left behind a trail of bodies.

"You saved my life, Zara. Twice. I was being honest before when I said I don't care. I don't see you as an assassin. I see you as *you*."

I didn't know how to respond to that. A part of me wanted to collapse in his arms and hug him to me. The other part of me wanted to run as fast as I could in the opposite direction. I settled for awkwardly patting the hand still cupping my cheek.

See? Compromise.

"I should probably inform the others of what happened," Killian said. By "others," I assumed he meant the six princes.

"I'll walk you to where you have to go," I said immediately, reaching down to pull on my underwear and pants. Killian watched me dress with heated eyes. Once again, the lust between us was almost palpable, despite a dead body lying only inches away. I really hoped this didn't turn into a habit of ours.

"I can walk by myself," Killian said quietly. Defensively. His cheeks turned red beneath his garnet hair. Realizing how my words had been construed, as if he were incapable of protecting himself, I squeezed his hand.

"I know that. But obviously, this Aaliyah chick has it out for you. Let me just walk you to your room."

"I can't say I would mind spending more time with you," Killian relented, flashing me a dimpled smile. I instinctively smiled back. It was only as we entered the capital once again that all amusement got wiped from my face. I was protecting a nightmare. I was protecting a nightmare when I should've been killing him. The thought sent my heart into overdrive. Did it make me a traitor to my race that I couldn't imagine ever killing him? Even if he murdered a human?

At that moment, I hated myself. I felt weak and vulnerable. Physically, I held strength beyond my years, but mentally, I was a quivering mess of lost love and endless sorrow. While before I felt indecision over what to do about Killian, now I only felt resolve. I could never hurt this strange incubus prince, and I would kill anyone who tried. The strength of my conviction frightened me.

As I led Killian to his bedroom, I pondered over what this meant for me. I was confused and frightened by my change in mentality. Had I been spelled?

But when Killian asked if he could see me again and I said yes, there was nothing but genuine happiness in his smile and eyes. He stared at me as if I'd offered him the world.

He was wrong about me though. I couldn't give him the world. Instead, I could only offer him dead bodies.

I HURRIED BACK to my room, slamming the door to emphasize my anger.

How could I have been so stupid?

Developing a stupid crush on a prince?

And not just one prince.

My anger crested before receding deep into the

depths of my brain. I had other things I needed to focus on, and an all-consuming self-hatred wasn't one of them.

Who was Aaliyah, and why did she want Killian dead? I would have to find a way to communicate with B. Perhaps he had answers.

Was she a human resistance leader that happened to employ nightmares to do her bidding? Simply a jealous female upset that he hadn't paid attention to her? Someone else entirely? There were so many questions that I knew wouldn't get answered.

Rubbing a hand through my hair in frustration, I settled for taking a long shower. The hot, steamy water calmed my tense muscles. I still had to restrain myself from running to Killian's side, but I somehow managed. He wouldn't approve of a babysitter.

Yet.

In time, I would wear him down.

After my shower, I settled for practicing a few moves with my knife. Ironically, a knife hadn't been my preferred choice of weapon back at home. I much preferred my bow and arrow or even my sword to such a small device. It was almost comical that all of my kills in the capital had been with a knife.

Time passed slowly. I glanced periodically at the clock, willing the hand to move a little faster. A wistful part of me wanted Killian to stop by my room, Z's room, but he never came. Soon, it was about time for me to get ready for the dinner.

Mali had left a note stating that a dress had been delivered, and I opened the closet expectantly. Glaring back at me was a beautiful purple dress.

Purple.

A damn purple dress.

Devlin's color.

I didn't have to be a genius to know that the genie himself had sent it.

Grumbling, I slammed my closet door shut and stomped out of my bedroom. After a few failed turns and numerous threats directed towards the staff, I stopped outside a room that had been indicated as Devlin's.

Without preamble, I pounded my fist on the door. Admittedly, I imagined that the wood was Devlin's face. It was quite satisfying to imagine beating the shit out of him.

It only took a moment for him to answer, and my tongue turned to cotton in my mouth. He was so beautiful, so handsome, with his oval-shaped head, tanned skin, and shock of dark hair. I was immediately bombarded by memories of us together—him spinning me around and kissing my nose, us lying in bed together, his stupid jokes. Being with him had felt like flying. It was the greatest form of elation anyone could have. However, what went up must come down, and that was what had happened.

"Zara," he said, shocked. He was wearing his customary business suit today, completed with a purple tie that heightened the violet of his eyes.

All of my anger over the dress melted away. In a span of seconds, I was a sixteen-year-old lovestruck girl whose heart had just been shattered.

"Why did you leave?" I whispered.

How could you leave? I wanted to add. He'd been my world, and I never could've left him. Leaving him would've been the equivalent of losing my soul. My other half. My best friend.

He swallowed, his normally impassive eyes pained.

"Come inside." He stepped aside to allow me entrance, and I entered his sparsely furnished room. There was a bed against the wall, neatly made, with a nightstand adjacent to it. On it was a framed photo and a stack of books. Save for a black leather couch and a flatscreen television, the room was devoid of any memorabilia.

It was the nightstand I walked to first. You could tell a lot about a person by the books they read. Tentatively trailing my fingers down the spines, I read the titles.

Nightmare and Human Relations.

The Mate Bond.

Politics of a Genie.

"I want to be a just and fair leader," Devlin said from behind me, allowing me to continue my perusal of his belongings. I glanced at him over my shoulder.

"You have always been a good liar. That skill would make you an even better politician."

My searching fingers touched the gold-rimmed edge of the frame. I wondered who Devlin cared enough about to keep as a picture beside his bed. Himself, probably.

But the person staring back at me wasn't him, though it was someone I recognized. My hair had been shorter then, just past my shoulders, and had hung in loose blonde curls. Chocolate ice cream was smeared across my face as I laughed into the camera, my young, innocent eyes unaware of the torment we would inevitably face. I remembered when this picture was taken. Devlin had snuck me an ice cream cone from a nightmare only store. It was unlike anything I'd ever tasted before, and a moan had unintentionally escaped my lips. Devlin had begun kissing me, but I'd swatted him away with a laugh. In retaliation, he'd shoved his own cone of ice cream into my face and then insisted that we take a picture to show our future kids.

It was one of my favorite memories.

"Lin..." I whispered, stunned. Garnering courage, I finally turned to meet his eyes. In them, I saw a vast loneliness and helplessness. I also saw an overwhelming amount of love. "Devlin."

"I left because my father discovered who you were to me. I left because he threatened to hurt you if I didn't leave. I left because I would've rather been away from you than see you dead or even hurt. I left even though it broke my heart to do so. I *didn't* leave because I stopped loving you. I have never stopped loving you, and I will never stop."

He paused, staring at something over my shoulder. I wondered where his mind had gone. There was so much despondency in his normally apathetic expression—the mask he wore so easily had been ripped into two.

"Have I ever told you about the first time I learned how to be a genie? The time I shadowed my dad at work?" He didn't wait for me to respond. "The rules are simple—the person who finds the genie's lamp gets three wishes. They can ask for anything besides unlimited wishes. The first one I witnessed was of a young man. He was hopelessly in love with a girl, but he was shy and awkward. He wished first to be beautiful. Second, to be talented, and third, to have the girl's heart. I watched the sly smile morph my father's face into something that was unrecognizable. And then he granted the man's wishes. The man *did* become beautiful and talented. My father didn't fuck with him on those wishes. But the girl's heart? I watched my dad carve the heart physically out of her body and deliver it to him. The young man killed himself shortly after. Don't you see? We're evil. He would've hurt you, my father, and I would've been helpless to save you. I had to make a choice between our happiness and your life, but it was no contest. I would always choose you, even if you hate me because of it."

Too much. Too soon.

Stop.

Keep talking.

"Lin..."

"Those years I was away from you were the worst of my life. Sure, I was able to survive, but I wasn't *living*. I was a machine going through the motions."

He jerkily took a step forward, arms extended, and I allowed him to place his hands on my shoulders. For years, I'd wanted him to say exactly that. For years, I'd dreamed of this moment.

"You can't love me," I whispered, my vision blurring. "You don't *know* me anymore."

"But I do," he said sadly. His finger captured one of my tears. "I never left you, baby girl. I watched over you. Always." He swallowed yet again, his Adam's apple bobbing. "I watched you fall in love again."

"And then he died." There was no inflection in my voice. I was merely stating a fact.

Devlin's eyes turned haunted.

"I was called away for a conference in Vampire," he said, referring to the kingdom that was, obviously, ruled by the vampires. "When I got back... I am so sorry, Zara."

Squeezing my eyelids shut to will the tears away, I gripped the belt loops of his dress pants. I didn't want to talk about S. I didn't want to talk about feelings or emotions. And I most definitely didn't want to hear him apologize.

"Get on the bed," I said. When Devlin stared down at me in confusion, I made my voice strident. "I said, get on the bed."

Eyes wide, he immediately fell onto the bed, wrinkling the blankets in the process.

"Zara—"

"Don't talk." I moved to straddle him, one knee on each side of his waist. His chest heaved beneath me, and his eyes flickered from my face to my chest and then back as if he didn't know where he was supposed to look. Thankfully, he kept his mouth shut.

Keeping my gaze locked on his, I removed his tie.

"You like this, don't you?" I whispered, leaning down to graze my teeth across his neck. He lifted his chin obediently, and I alternated between little nips and slow, sensual kisses. His hands grabbed at my waist, pulling me even closer.

"Bad, Devlin," I cooed, biting down on his neck. He let out a grunt of pain that quickly turned into a moan of pleasure. "You know the rules. You can only touch me when I give you permission."

I moved his hands until they were against the headboard and then used his tie to keep them in place. He struggled half-heartedly against the bondage, but I knew he could easily break free if he actually wanted to. Devlin had always been a kinky little shit.

Skimming my nose down his neck, I slowly undid the buttons on his shirt, one after another. Each swath of skin revealed received a kiss or a lick. I rolled my tongue over his nipple, and he bucked his hips against me. I could feel his erection straining against his pants, begging to be set free.

After a moment, I did just that, smiling victoriously when his glorious cock appeared in my hand. I used my fingers to spread his pre-cum across his throbbing length, and he groaned appreciatively. I wondered if he still tasted the same.

Cupping his balls, I licked up the length of his shaft. Salty.

Yes. He most definitely tasted the same.

"Tell me, Lin," I said, wrapping my hand around the base of his cock. Using his cum for lubrication, I worked him in a steady rhythm. He was a writhing mess beneath my hands. "Have you been with another girl since me? Has another girl touched your cock?"

I pulled on his shaft, and he twisted sideways, his bare ass now on display. The position was probably dreadfully uncomfortable with his hands still tied, but he didn't complain.

"You have permission to answer," I said.

"No," he gasped. "No one."

The greedy bitch in me smiled in satisfaction.

"Good. Because *this*..." I tightened my grip on him.

"And *this*..." Using my free hand, I slapped his ass cheek. He hissed, but I soothingly rubbed out the pain. "They belong to me. Got that?"

"Always."

Smiling contently, I jerked him once again onto his back and released his shaft. He immediately groaned in disappointment, but one glare from me shut him up. Pulling off my top—I hadn't worn a bra—I watched his face light up as he took in my bare upper body. My nipples were practically beaded diamonds at this point. Lifting my hips, I shimmied out of my pants and panties until I was utterly naked before him. I didn't feel embarrassed or even vulnerable. I felt empowered as his eyes ravaged me. His arms feebly pulled at the restraints, but I gave him a disapproving frown.

He could look, but he couldn't touch. Not today.

My pussy clenched with need as I lined his shaft up with my wet folds and sank down. Having him inside of me again...it was like two becoming one. It was as if a part of me I hadn't known I needed was returning to me.

It was a tight fit, but it only took me a moment to adjust to his impressive length. I placed my hands on his chest to keep myself steady, and then I slowly began to rock my hips. The pleasure was instantaneous, a finale to my denied sexual encounter with Killian. What started as soft and slow turned into a rough, passionate frenzy. Setting the pace, I rocked against him, my ass slapping against his thighs. My breasts bounced in his face, just out of his reach. At one point, he took one of my throbbing nipples into his mouth, and I allowed him to. It only amplified my pleasure.

The pleasure was coming faster now, like endless waves cresting against the shoreline. I didn't know how much longer I was going to last. Tiny gasps escaped my lips, and then I came with a scream. I couldn't recall ever feeling such bliss before, as if every nerve in my body had come to life. Devlin released my aching nipple as he came with a cry of his own, his seed releasing inside of me.

For a moment, we remained connected, panting. I finally detangled myself from him, using the edge of his blanket to clean myself off.

Once I was sure all traces of our activity were gone, I grabbed my clothes off the floor and began to slowly redress.

"Where are you going?" Devlin asked huskily.

"Away."

His brows furrowed in confusion.

Patting his knee, I said, "See you at dinner tonight."

It was only as I was leaving that I heard his hoarse voice.

"God, I fucking love you, woman."

"I know."

TWENTY-THREE

DEVLIN

For the first time in years, I felt sated. Tiny licks of fire hummed through my veins, an aftereffect of my time with Susan.

Zara.

Z.

She didn't think I was aware of her real name, but you couldn't stalk a girl for years and not discover it. Z the assassin.

Z...my mate.

Eyes still heavy with lust, I stared at the door where she had disappeared through. I wasn't naïve enough to believe she would stay after everything I'd put her through, but the tiny, wistful voice inside my head had hoped. Did it make me a pussy that I wanted to cuddle with her? That I wanted to feel her in my arms, warm and real, her presence as vibrant as a fire?

Her absence from my life had been like wandering the desert. I wasn't quite dead, but my body ached dreadfully as it struggled to quench its thirst. She was the rain pelting my face.

She would never be the light, her darkness was too consuming, but she would always be a necessity. She was the air I breathed, the water I drank, my home in the storm.

But the idiot was repeatedly putting her life on the line to achieve a warped sense of justice. I couldn't fault her for that. Losing her other mate, her human mate, would make any sane person go a little crazy. It was a wonder she could still behave coherently at all. If I were to ever find the person who'd killed S...

I took a deep, calming breath. He was supposed to be my brother, this man, and his life had been snuffed out too soon, leaving my girl alone.

But Z...

I closed my eyes, watching her face behind my closed eyelids as she rode me. I would never get tired of seeing the heat in her eyes, the lust in her sultry grin. Her large breasts had been on display, the pink nipples so enticing. The feel of her around me. Her golden hair cascading around her shoulders in soft, yet wild, curls. She was the only female I knew that could roll out of bed looking as perfect as those who spent hours in front of a mirror. It was an effortless beauty that was almost ethereal. And it was mine.

She was mine.

"Devlin! We need to talk...and why the hell am I staring at *another* dick?" The voice was familiar, though I'd never heard such horror in it before. It suddenly occurred to me that I was still tied to the bed, naked, with my cock once again rock-hard at the mere thought of my perfect mate. At the thought of her tits bouncing in my face, her warm pussy clenching around my length, her wild eyes—

Killian stepped farther into the room, mouth agape.

"Wait? *Another* dick? How many dicks have you been seeing?" Lupe asked. The big man had silently moved into my room, his footsteps shockingly light. He leaned against my eggshell-colored wall, meaty arms crossed over his broad chest.

Killian's face turned green at the memory.

"I don't want to talk about it."

Bash pushed Killian aside, wheeling Dair in as well. Apparently, it was a fucking party in my bedroom. I quite literally wanted to kill them all right then and there, consequences be damned.

"It's not gay if you don't look," my mage brother pointed out to Killian.

Lupe rubbed at his temples.

"We came for an actual reason," the mountain of a shifter assured me, flashing a glare in Bash's direction. Bash glared right back, eyes narrowing into thin slits. He seemed to be in an especially bad mood, though that wasn't necessarily a surprise. Bash always seemed to be in a mood.

"Can you put some clothes on?" Dair asked kindly. He was the only one that didn't seem at all perturbed by my nudity. Mermaids and shifters were similar in that aspect. When they changed from one form to the next, they lost all of their clothes. Dair, through his mandatory twelve-hour stint as a human, was almost as indifferent as Jax when it came to nudity. Lupe, on the other hand, was extremely self-conscious when it came to his body. I was his best friend, and I had yet to ever see him with his shirt off. Rumor was, last time he had sex, he turned off all the lights and kept half of his clothes on.

Lupe was a strange man.

I couldn't help but think that Z would like him, despite him being a shifter. She would like all of my brothers. The thought sent a giddy smile across my face.

Was there anything better than your girl getting along with your family?

"Oh my god. It twitched. Why is it twitching?" Killian whispered, horrified. Cussing, I quickly broke free of my constraints tying me to the bed and pulled on my boxers. Ways to kill a mood? Have your brother talk about your twitching cock.

Crisis averted, I sat on the bed and leveled a glare at all four of them. I didn't have to be a genius to know that Ryland was lurking in one of the many shadows in my room. And Jax?

It was comical to even believe he would be sane enough to be here and partake in the conversation. He was probably running down the hallways naked. Again.

"Why are you guys here?" I asked snidely, jumping to my feet. I ran a hand through my brown hair in agitation. Damn them. If they would've come one minute earlier, when Z had been riding me, I might've killed them. The mere thought of them seeing her like that...

My hands clenched and unclenched by my sides.

Deep breaths. Rein it in, Devlin. Rein it in.

I felt my power swell before diminishing behind a blockade of my own making. It always took considerable effort to tame the beast that was my genie. I was still filled with an almost elemental fury when I thought of my girl with that one mage, Diego. I knew for a fact that he wasn't her mate. If I discovered that she'd been with him...

Control your anger. Control.

"I'm sorry to interrupt your fun," Bash said, eyeing my rumpled bedsheets with distaste. "Have you finally given up on your mate?"

I gritted my teeth together to keep from screaming at him. He wouldn't know since he'd never met his mate, but it would've been impossible for me to be with another woman. Z was my soul, the better half of me, and the thought of touching someone else made me physically ill. It wasn't just the bond causing me to feel that way. It may have been the force that brought people together, but it wasn't the glue that kept them as one.

I loved her.

I always had.

I didn't know how to say all that to Bash. To tell him that it would've felt like ripping my arm from my body to even think of cheating on her. That I would sooner hurt myself than I could harm her. Until he had a mate of his own, he would never understand.

Just like Z wouldn't understand if I were to tell her that S was her mate as well. I knew it the second I'd seen them together. It was a secret I would take to my grave. How would she react if she knew that one of her mates had been killed? How would she react if she discovered that I could've prevented it?

Something on my face must've given me away, as Bash cursed loudly and brought both his hands to his blond locks, pulling at them.

"Fucking shit. She's here, isn't she? Your mate is here. Dammit." He kicked at my couch. "Everybody has their fucking mate now. Fan-fucking-tastic. Who needs free will anyways? Not us, apparently. Not fucking us."

I glanced at Lupe, eyebrow raised, but he subtly shook his head.

Don't ask, the eloquent gesture seemed to say, and I obediently clamped my mouth shut. It would only make matters worse to retort.

Lupe cleared his throat, cutting Bash off mid rant. All eyes turned towards the shifter expectantly.

"I scoured through my books looking for any information about this Aaliyah person. Obviously, she's targeting Killian, but the question is why?"

No shit, I wanted to say. Did they really barge into my bedroom to reiterate what I already knew? Death would occur if that was the case...preferably with a variety of weapons.

Damn. Z was rubbing off on me already. Soon, we would get his and hers matching knife sets. My little psychopath.

"Did you find anything?" I asked tersely.

"No."

Of fucking course.

"But..." Lupe continued, noting my barely concealed rage. "While I didn't find anything about Aaliyah, I did find something on the dead bodies of the men that had gone after Killian."

Lupe reached into his pocket and grabbed a piece of paper. I leaned forward to take a closer look.

It was an unfamiliar symbol, tiny black lines morphing into thicker red ones to create a demented circle. It was unlike anything I'd ever seen before. Frowning, I surveyed the drawings closer.

"This was on both bodies?" I asked in clarification.

Lupe nodded solemnly.

"Tattooed on their backs, just beneath their right shoulders."

I glanced at it once more, positive I'd never seen such an intricate pattern before. However, I knew someone who might've.

"My mate," I began, "might have an idea where this is from. I'll talk to her tonight at the dinner."

"Mine too," Killian added.

Dair nodded. "Same."

From somewhere in the shadows, Ryland began to laugh. It was the first genuine laugh I'd heard from him in years. My eyes widened in surprise at hearing the jovial noise.

"What are you laughing at?" Bash asked darkly, whipping his head in the direction the noise had come from. I could dimly make out the silhouette of my shadow brother.

"You guys are all a bunch of dumbasses," Ryland said simply after his laughter had subsided.

"Excuse me?" Dair asked softly. Again, he was the only one who didn't seem upset by Ryland, just confused and slightly curious. I wondered if it was a mermaid thing to be constantly in a state of bliss and nirvana all the time, or just a Dair thing.

"You'll see in time," Ryland said around another laugh. "Fucking dumbasses."

TWENTY-FOUR

Z

I walked into my room, body humming with the remnants of pleasure from my encounter with Devlin, only to see...me. Assassin me. Posing in front of a mirror.

"You're a sexy bitch, aren't you?" the me said, shooting finger guns at the reflection. "Sexy bitch with curves in all the right places."

"Diego," I began, pinching the bridge of my nose. "What the hell do you think you're doing?"

He jumped, startled by my voice. Even without seeing his face, I knew he would be smiling sheepishly.

"Getting into character."

"And that involves strutting and finger guns?" I asked, quirking an eyebrow. Now that his embarrassment had faded, Diego was left with his usual surplus of sass. He put his hand on his hip and cocked it to the side.

"I need to practice shooting people. Duh."

"I don't even... No words."

"No surprise. I usually make females speechless," he

said smugly, turning back to the mirror. He struck another pose, this one involving a leg kick and more crotch than I ever wanted to see.

"You're a freak," I muttered, but I couldn't help but gnaw on my lower lip in worry. Were we really doing this? Was I really going to put his life on the line? The mere thought of it made my stomach twist and contract painfully.

"I'm going to be okay," Diego said softly, noting the fear on my face. He'd always been observant, especially after S's death. He knew I was struggling before *I* even knew it. "*We're* going to be okay."

While his confidence was contagious, doubt still niggled me, the ever persistent bastard. Doubt and guilt.

The guilt, I realized, was irrational. Nothing had even happened yet, but I was still preparing myself for the worst-case scenario. It was the easiest way to get through life—expect and accept the worst.

Reaching around me, Diego swatted my ass.

"Now, why don't you go get your pretty butt in that sexy dress."

I stuck my tongue out at him but obediently walked into my bedroom, where the dress was still draped across my dresser. After my rendezvous with Devlin, I didn't feel as dirty putting on the purple number as I once would've. I hadn't forgiven him for what he'd put me through, but I didn't hate him. How could I when I understood all too well the enticing pulls of self-sacrifice? We were one and the same, him and I.

Clicking my tongue, I shimmied out of my clothes and into the dress. Mali would insist on makeup and elaborate hairstyles, but I much preferred my natural look.

My eyes widened as I took in my reflection in the bedroom mirror. My hair hung in disheveled blonde curls around my face. The dress itself was tight on my chest, reaching up to clasp around my neck, before flaring outwards in a silky, purple skirt. Even I had to admit, despite being the cynic I was, that the dress was gorgeous. It accentuated my considerable cleavage and my toned stomach. Smirking at myself in the mirror, I grabbed a necklace off of the dresser and a golden charm bracelet. Both items were gifted to me by Diego for my birthday a couple of months back. The necklace was designed to protect me against any harmful spells, and the bracelet was supposed to vibrate when danger was near. Both pieces of jewelry had a "one and done" spell on them. If there was any day to use them, today would be that day.

After a moment of hesitation, I sheathed two knives on both thighs. It wasn't the most convenient location, but it would have to do. I surveyed myself one last time in the mirror, pinching my cheeks in an attempt to bring color to them. It was only then that I saw the lumpy outline beneath my quilt—a very human looking outline.

My dagger was in my hand before I could even blink, my steps tentative as I made my way to the sleeping figure.

Who the hell was in my bed? Was it Mali?

Dagger raised slightly, I pulled back the blanket.

I was greeted by the sight of closed eyes and a contented smile. It was a man—a familiar man. It took me a moment to place where I had seen the shock of brown hair and high, chiseled cheekbones before.

The vampire from my dreams.

Only, right now, he appeared to be very, very real. His eyelashes feathered against his cheeks, looking like twigs of ebony. Even in sleep, his face was vulnerable and serene. He had no idea that a skilled assassin held a knife inches from his slumbering frame. It would be so easy to stick the knife into his heart, to end his life.

But I couldn't do it. It wasn't just because he was sleeping, though I hated hurting people that couldn't fight back, but because an innate voice within me rebelled at the idea of hurting him. I squeezed my eyelids shut, hoping that he was only a figment of my imagination, but one glance confirmed that he was, in fact, real. He let out a sigh of pleasure, burying his face further into my pillow with a sharp inhale.

Dammit. Damn him. Damn myself for having a damn conscience.

My heart warmed as I watched him. Almost instinctively, I moved to push a strand of hair behind his ear. I wondered if it would feel as soft as it looked.

It did.

He stirred at my touch but didn't wake. Despite this, I could've sworn I heard him mumble beneath his breath, "Mine."

Yours.

With one last glance at the mysterious figure, I hurried out of my bedroom, being extra careful to shut the door quietly.

What the hell was wrong with me? Not only was I

allowing him to sleep in my room, but I was making his experience more comfortable? What was next? Foot massages?

Mali had arrived at some point during my strange encounter with the vampire and was deep in conversation with Diego. They both froze when they caught sight of me, Diego whistling appreciatively and Mali blinking rapidly

"Damn, Z. You look hot." Mali sounded honestly stunned, as if I'd somehow transformed into an entirely different person.

"Bitch, I was born flawless," I responded, smirking.

"If I were into girls, I would so tap that ass," Diego teased. Dramatically tossing my hair over my shoulder, I winked at both of them.

"My sexual prowess is out of this world."

"Take me to your spaceship," flirted Diego, and I snorted at how bad of a pickup line that was.

"Oh and by the way..." I grabbed my purse off of the desk, checking to make sure my knives were still inside. A girl could never be too prepared. "Which one of you guys let the vampire sleep in my bed?"

The expressions on their faces were priceless.

Diego pointed to Mali at the same time she pointed at him. Rolling my eyes, I muttered, "Children." Diego's attempt to persuade me that he was all man was interrupted by a knock on the door.

Mali's nostrils flared, and her face paled drastically. Diego stood up straighter, a poor impersonation in my mind to resemble me. Nobody could do me and my badassery like me, but then again, I was kind of biased.

"Stay behind me," I whispered to Diego. If it was someone at the door attempting to harm Z, they would have to go through me and the many razor blades I kept hidden in my hair. Steeling myself, I opened the door with a ready, albeit fake, smile.

The smile disappeared from my face when I took note of the two shifters standing in the doorway. The shifter prince and princess. Lupe and Atta. My eyes instantly roamed the impressive physique of the big man in front of me. I hated shifters, hated them with a passion and intensity that went beyond anything normal, and yet I could only feel wave after wave of lust as I stared at him. The broad shoulders, clearly defined beneath his black suit jacket. The dusting of hair on his rounded jaw. The golden flecks in his eyes, highlighting the lighter strands his dark head of hair.

I felt anger at my body for betraying me so easily. He was the son of the man responsible for human work camps all across the globe. He was inherently evil.

But his warm smile was anything *but* evil.

Mali appeared at my side, eyes locked on Atta.

"What are you guys doing here?" she asked darkly, and I blanched at the venom in my best friend's voice. What had this girl done to make Mali so furious?

I crossed my arms over my chest, and Lupe's attention immediately drifted to my breasts straining against the purple fabric. I heated under his scrutiny, imagining his long tongue swirling over my nipples. His large hands cupping my ass as he hoisted me against a wall. Those plush lips ravaging me.

And then I pictured Lupe on one side of me and

Devlin on the other. Both of their lips touching every bare inch of my skin. My face flushed at the fantasy, and I quickly shook my head.

Damn hormones.

"We thought we would walk you to the dinner tonight," Atta said cheerfully, eyes still fixated on Mali.

Diego moved up behind us, bedecked in Z's attire, and both Lupe and Atta narrowed their eyes at him. I could've sworn I saw jealousy burn in Lupe's gaze. That jealousy only amplified when Diego placed a hand on my shoulder and gave it an encouraging squeeze.

I couldn't help but snort at Diego's attempt to comfort me. He thought I was silent because of my hatred for shifters, not because I was debating whether or not I wanted to jump one right then and there. If only he knew what a twisted bitch I actually was.

"I need to go help set up," Mali blurted, shouldering me out of her way. Without another word, she hurried in the direction I knew the kitchen to be.

That lying bitch. I would torture the information out of her if I had to.

Atta watched her go, lips turning downwards in what looked like disappointment. The truth hit me like a stack of bricks, and I staggered in my heels, instinctively grabbing Lupe's impressive bicep to keep myself steady.

"Holy shit! Are you guys mates?" I hissed at Atta, nodding in the direction Mali had disappeared down. The blush reddening the shifter princess's face was the only indication I needed.

Wow. That was...unexpected.

I knew that Mali had dabbled with females in the

past, but to discover her mate was one must've been a shock. That little bitch hadn't even bothered to tell me! It would explain her itchiness and irritation. What it didn't explain, however, was the distaste in her eyes whenever she stared at Atta.

I wondered if my own opinions of shifters had somehow tainted Mali's feelings for Atta, turning her lust into fear and disgust. Guilt pierced my chest at the thought.

There was a distinct difference between good and evil. I couldn't help but recall Killian's explanation of the various facets in nature. I knew I was being unfair towards both Atta and Lupe. They weren't the same shifters that had harmed me and killed S. I couldn't group an entire species into one box because of my history with a few evil ones. That made me just as bad as *them*—the monsters I was attempting to stop.

Taking a shuddering breath, I flashed Atta a soft smile.

"I'm Zara. Mali's best friend. A pleasure to meet you." My hand couldn't help but tremble as I extended it for her to shake. It had just occurred to me that this was the first time I had willingly touched a shifter. Shock flickered across her features briefly. Just as quickly, a radiant smile blossomed on her face, and she shook my hand.

"Atta. I am so happy to meet you. You are absolutely gorgeous. Is that weird to say? That's weird, isn't it?"

"Atta, stop talking. Please," Lupe said. He ruffled his sister's flaming hair, and she swatted at his hand half-heartedly. Turning towards me, Lupe's expression turned appraising. "I don't believe we have been properly intro-duced. I'm Lupe."

"Zara."

This time, when I extended my hand, he bent down to press his lips against my knuckles. My skin tingled at the contact, especially when his large tongue moved to lick at his lips. What I wouldn't give to have that tongue on my clit...

Face burning at my own perverted thoughts, I began to walk in the direction of the dining room. What was wrong with me? I glanced at Lupe cautiously, wondering if he had somehow found a mage or genie to put a spell on me. I wasn't a trusting person normally, least of all with nightmares. My friendships with Diego and Mali took years to groom and mold into what they were now. However, I felt no fear when I stared up at Lupe's handsome face. That, by itself, was strange. I felt comfort when I was around the large shifter. Comfort and security, as if he were someone I was intimately familiar with. My own emotions confused me.

Diego hurried to keep pace with me, giggling beneath his breath. I resisted the urge to slap him. The last thing I needed was to be known as the giggling assassin.

Seriously. Who fucking giggled anymore?

I frowned, stopping mid stride, when I noted an added weight to my purse. Opening it slightly, my eyes bulged out of my head when I spotted the two novels mixed in with my collection of knives and daggers. They were most definitely not in my bag before.

The Seven Kings and I: an Erotica Novel.

An Idiot's Guide on how to Handle a Polyamorous Relationship.

"What the hell are you hinting at, Ryland?" I mumbled under my breath.

"What was that?" Lupe asked, coming to stand beside me. My body instantly became aware of his presence, as pinpricks of desire sprouted from my feet to the roots of my hair. Desire...not fear.

Face flaming, I snapped my purse closed and offered Lupe a singularly beautiful smile.

"Nothing."

Somewhere in the shadows, I could've sworn I heard Ryland's familiar husky laugh.

And then I remembered that brief moment I'd seen his face...

Schooling my features, I began to walk yet again towards the dining hall. As soon as this dinner was over, I was going to take a nice, long shower.

And kill Diego.

That bastard was currently shaking his ass at every painting adorning the walls. Did he not realize I had an image to uphold?

"Zara!" Devlin appeared from around the corner, and my mouth watered as I took stock of him. His hair was brushed back into a low ponytail, and his violet tie was identical in color to my dress.

It was the same tie, I noted with smug satisfaction, that I'd used to bind his hands to the headboard. My pussy clenched at the heat in his eyes. He, too, was remembering our time together only hours earlier.

"You look beautiful," he murmured, eyes tracing my

features. They started at my feet and slowly made their way up. I could feel the caress from his gaze on my breasts.

Lupe cleared his throat, eyes narrowing in irritation.

"What are you doing here?" he hissed. Devlin blinked as if he'd only just realized that I was standing beside the giant shifter.

"What am I doing here? What are you doing here?"

Diego and Atta's heads volleyed between Devlin and Lupe. I heard Diego mumble, "Where's the popcorn when you need it?"

The two men stared each other down. The air crackled with electricity as each man exerted his will on the other. Frankly, it was the sexiest stare off in my life.

"Just kiss and make up already," I quipped. That drew their attention away from each other and onto me, identical expressions of horror contorting their faces. I couldn't help but chuckle.

Damn. There goes that fantasy.

For now.

Still eyeing one another suspiciously, Devlin walked on one side of me, while Lupe took the other. I couldn't decipher the reason behind their pissing match. I half expected them to whip out their dicks and measure them. Not that I would complain.

And if the dicks happened to touch...

Bad, Z. Bad.

We stepped through a golden archway and into the ballroom I'd been in before, when I accidentally participated in the Matching. Only now, row after row of tables lined the ballroom floor. Participants for the Damning intermingled with beautiful women in fine dresses—the Matching competitors. I spotted Bash's light blond hair as he leaned forward to whisper in a girl's ear. His back stiffened when I entered, as if he'd somehow felt my presence, but he didn't turn around to face me.

"I'm going to look for Mali in the kitchens," I heard Atta whisper to Lupe. Her words went through one ear and out the other.

Sitting at a separate table were two familiar faces— Killian, looking as sexy as ever with his tattoos and garnet red hair, and Dair, the beautiful prince I remembered him to be, looking like a fairy tale hero come to life with his golden hair and blue eyes.

Killian smiled timidly at me, but Dair's brows were furrowed as he studied Diego. Just as quickly, his expression smoothed over and his eyes locked on mine. They widened, slowly surveying my body.

Devlin growled beneath his breath.

"What the hell are they doing?"

"Why do you even care?" Lupe asked darkly.

And me?

Pieces began to click together, one after another. Their behavior around me. Ryland's cryptic comments. My own reaction towards them. All of them

All I could think was, *Fuck*.

TWENTY-FIVE

Z

Surely this was some kind of joke. Surely the world wouldn't be so cruel as to have my mates be the exact people, the exact nightmares, I'd been tasked to kill.

My body warred with my head, various solutions to my predicament taking shape. Everything had a logical explanation. I didn't believe in fate or mates or any of that shit. How could I when the only two people I'd ever loved had been torn away from me? Mates were supposedly eternal, but love itself was a thin shard of ice that could easily crumble under added weight. Love and mates were mutually exclusive, I realized, though I wasn't even certain if I believed in the superstition that one person was made to be with you. It sounded like a whole lot of bullshit to me.

My reaction towards them was just a natural, biological response to gorgeous men, I told myself. They were beautiful, sexy, and funny. How could I not have an intense attraction towards them? It was hormones. It was a spell.

Even my attempts at deflection couldn't completely eradicate the truth.

These men—the brooding genie, the shy incubus, the kind mermaid, the weird shifter, the angry mage, the mysterious shadow, and even the strange vampire—were my mates. I knew it as surely as I knew my own name. Despite my skepticism, I couldn't ignore the voice that claimed each of them as my own. I couldn't ignore the possessive butterflies fluttering deep in my stomach as I glared at the back of Bash's head deep in conversation with a beautiful incubus girl.

Fuck.

Fuck.

Fuck.

Devlin gently grabbed my arm, pulling me in the direction of Dair and Killian, but I broke free of him as if his touch were toxic.

Not today, Satan. Not today.

I glanced helplessly at Diego, a couple of feet behind me, and he immediately came to my rescue.

"Out of the way, bitches. Zara needs some Z time."

Lupe growled, actually growled, when Diego wrapped his arm around my shoulders and pulled me towards an alcove. Devlin's glare turned from Diego's arm to Lupe's murderous expression, brows creasing in confusion.

Oh good lord. He didn't know. None of them knew.

Except for Ryland...

"What's the matter, sweet tits?" Diego asked in concern. I positioned myself so that I was facing the ballroom. Fortunately, none of the assassins seemed to be paying us any mind. Stupidly, if I did say so myself. Their attention fluttered between the beautiful, if not scantily-clad, women and the abundance of wine and food on the table. There weren't nearly as many competitors left as there was that first day. I counted only a dozen or so. "Is this about Mali?" he continued, pulling my attention away from the feast and onto him. "Are you sure it's safe for her?"

"Huh?" I asked.

Diego nodded his head towards the opposite end of the ballroom, and I followed his gaze immediately. Two figures were huddled in the corner, and I recognized the shock of dark hair immediately as Mali. Beside her, expression aloof, was Zack.

The assassin.

The man with the dead eyes.

They were whispering to one another, and Mali's eyes were wide. Not in fear, I realized blankly, but shock.

What the hell?

"I never told her to talk to that man. It's too dangerous."

I watched their interaction for a second longer, just in time to see Mali glide away from him. He stared after her for a moment before moving to sit at an empty seat near the end of the table. His body was held tautly, like a puppet on strings. Two girls leaned over the table, attempting to garner his attention, but he barely paid them any mind. His watchful eyes flickered from the food being served to the assassins watching one another warily.

Fear spiked down my spine as I took him in.

He almost seemed to be sheathed in a malevolent cloak. It didn't take a genius to know that this man, Zack, was bad news. Evil. That was the only word I could think to describe him. It seeped out of him like a dark, sticky tar.

Had he threatened Mali? Because of her relationship with Z? Why else would he talk to her? The mere thought of him hurting her made my blood run cold.

I could only hope that he didn't try anything at this dinner.

Thoughts of mates disappeared from my mind as I focused on Diego. I wished desperately that I could see his face behind the white mask. He'd always been so easy to read, and I yearned to know if he was as frightened as I was.

"Don't eat or drink anything," I warned him. "You never know if it's poisoned or not. Don't make eye contact with anyone. Don't engage in conversation—"

"Z, love..." Diego said, cutting me off mid rant. His hand settling on my shoulder, and he gave it an encouraging squeeze. "This is just dinner. I doubt anything is going to happen."

While I wanted to believe him, I couldn't ignore the nagging voice inside of my gut. Why did I have the feeling that this dinner was going to turn into an epic bloodbath?

Why did I feel like I was going to be helpless to stop

it? For the first time in my life, I was on the sidelines instead of leading the charge. It was terrifying.

"Be safe, Diego. Please." My voice broke on the final plea, and I hated myself for that brief moment of weakness. I had to remain strong.

Giving Diego one more cautionary look, I began to head in the direction of the princes' table. The last thing I wanted to do was sit next to them, next to these men I was beginning to believe were my mates, but that seat would provide me with a good view of the rest of the ballroom. I nodded at an empty seat directly in my line of vision, and Diego immediately slipped into the chair I indicated. There were two Matching girls on either side of him, and Bash was directly across the table.

Nobody would try anything with the Crowned Prince of Mages only inches away, right?

Right?

I hated this helpless feeling. I should've been the one dressed as Z, not him. I tried to remind myself that this was only a dinner and that the chances of anything happening to him were slim to none, but my intuition contradicted me at every turn.

Death. Death. Death.

The chant was impossibly loud, echoing on repeat in my head. I felt nauseous.

If there was a choice between Diego or me, the mission or Diego, I would choose Diego each and every time. He was my best friend, and I would be damned if my second identity cost him his life.

My resolve settling, I walked purposely towards the princes' table. A couple girls were attempting to engage the guys in conversation. One of them leaned forward eagerly, her breasts practically spilling out of her low-cut dress, and I resisted the urge to stab her in the face. Damn her. Damn them. Damn my own jealousy.

Mates.

I scoffed at the word. Hopefully, they didn't expect me to love them. Sex I could do, but love? Never again. I couldn't possibly invest myself in another person, knowing what heartache awaited me. Love was funny in that respect. You never really knew if the love was reciprocated until your heart was broken and you found yourself once again alone. There were walls around my heart for a reason, and mates or not, they would not be falling anytime soon.

Killian smiled brilliantly when he caught sight of me. He seemed utterly oblivious to the beautiful girl fawning over him only inches away. His eyes were on me, as if I were the only girl in the world. He would come to realize, as I did, that I wasn't the hero he so desperately wanted. I was the monster.

"You look beautiful," he said softly, his stutter more pronounced than previously. I wondered if it had something to do with the blonde bimbo taking up his personal space.

"It's amazing to finally see the girl behind the mask," Dair added. He, too, was staring at me with something akin to awe.

Goddammit.

Stop looking at me.

Look at me.

I leveled a glare at the girls fawning over them.

Mine.

Not mine.

Their faces paled instantly, and they scampered towards another table.

I tried to tell myself that it would be better if these men found love and happiness with girls like them—girls who weren't me. I couldn't be the mate they wanted and needed. Hell, I didn't even want to be their mate.

And yet...

The thought of them with anyone else nearly sent me over the edge. It was torture to imagine.

My emotions were everywhere. I couldn't quite grasp one without it immediately shifting into something else.

I'd spent my life hating these men, these strangers, only to discover that I was fucking meant for them. How could this have happened? Even with Lupe and Dair, two men that I'd only had one conversation with, I felt my body heating at the intensity in their gazes. It wasn't just lust, though there was plenty of that too, but the need to be with them and laugh with them and talk to them and—

Fuck!

I scrubbed a hand down my face, reluctantly throwing myself into an empty chair between Dair and Killian. I couldn't focus on them anymore, not when I had to protect Diego from Z's enemies, and Mali from herself.

"I've been wanting to introduce you to my brothers," Devlin was saying to me, a sly smile curving up his lips. Hatred briefly roared inside of me.

Had he known? That I was his mate?

Had he known?

One glance into his violet eyes, gazing at me as if I was the fucking light of his world instead of the darkness I knew myself to be, confirmed that yes, he was aware. He knew, and he'd still left me. He knew, and he hadn't bothered to tell me.

Fuck.

I was feeling too much, too deeply, too quickly. My breathing was turning shallow.

How could I have been so stupid? And how was I supposed to handle this now?

I wondered if I even should. If I ignored it, maybe the problem would go away. Maybe I would be able to push it into the far crevices of my mind, under lock and key with no hope of escape. It was what I did with my parents and S, after all.

Their deaths were now a small clenching at the top of my heart, a pressure. It was not overwhelming or loud, it simply sat there, mildly noticeable like a mosquito bite that didn't itch quite enough to scratch. The tears still welled in my eyes at times, sliding into the corners and blurring my vision, but they didn't fall. They didn't make tracks down my face like they used to.

I remembered the happiness before, and the immense hurting after. The guilt. The anger. I remembered when the hurt wasn't soft, but instead, it was unmanageable. These overwhelming emotions kept me from standing back up after such an intense fall.

Now that was gone. I could hold the hurt with both hands, and I knew I was strong enough to survive. I'd found the strength to carry on, a little emptier than before but still a glass that was half full.

I told myself that it would be easy to do the same thing with these nightmares. Cut them off quickly and forcefully, before any feelings were developed.

They would forget about me, and I would continue hunting their kind. Easy.

Not easy.

They were my mates, and I, theirs.

Maybe, just maybe, I could avoid the eruption that such a revelation would cause.

"This is my mate, Zara," Devlin introduced softly. Proudly. So fucking obliviously.

Cue the volcanic eruption.

Lupe jumped to his feet, eyes flashing gold. I'd seen a shifter like this once before, mere seconds before S was attacked, and it caused pinpricks of terror to shoot down my spine.

"Don't fucking joke about that."

"Excuse me?" Devlin slowly moved to his own feet, rolling up his sleeves in the process.

Don't look at them. Don't look at them. If you don't look, it's not real.

I kept my eyes on Diego. He was absently cutting at his chicken, but I was relieved to see that he hadn't taken a bite, nor did he address the girls trying desperately to get his attention. Bash was glaring at him, as if he hoped his eyes could physically penetrate Diego's mask.

As if he felt my eyes on him, Bash's gaze flickered towards me. He stared at me with absolute hatred before purposely turning his back on me to talk to the girl beside him.

My mate's an asshole, I thought before immediately cursing at myself.

Not mate.

Nope.

I couldn't even fault him for his behavior. I wanted to do the exact same thing. Ignore. Ignore. Ignore. If I didn't acknowledge it, it didn't exist.

"She's my fucking mate!" Lupe sneered.

"What the fuck, man?"

As the guys argued over me, I couldn't help but compare this situation to kids fighting over a toy. I wasn't a damn possession, and I had no intentions of being their mate. I would cut off my own hand if that would somehow remove this ridiculous bond I felt with each of them.

Lips pursed, I took a tentative sip of my water. I wasn't actually thirsty, but I was desperate to do something with my hands besides fiddle my thumbs like an imbecile.

"I knew she was my mate from the second I laid eyes on her," Killian whispered softly, and two furious eyes turned in his direction.

"She can't be all of our mates," Dair said reasonably, though there was a tightening to his voice I'd never heard before.

As if I fucking knew him.

I didn't know him. I didn't know any of them. It was the mate bond between us, a biological concoction designed to provide the most babies possible, not an actual connection. Feelings weren't involved. *Knowing* them wasn't involved. It was just a stupid bond. Nothing more.

Everything more.

Did they really have to talk about me as if I weren't there?

Diego was still sitting stiffly in front of me, listening to whatever Bash was saying. A girl draped herself over the mage's lap, and he tensed. I felt irrationally jealous at the two of them together.

Fuck.

Fuck.

Fuck.

"Enough!" I hissed, and the four men immediately turned to look at me, chests heaving. Under their combined stares, I felt my nipples harden and my pussy clench with need. I didn't know what I was going to say. Deny the bond? Scream at them? Admit my own confusion? Kiss the shit out of them? Instead, I merely picked up a chicken leg and bit into it.

Yup. I was going to eat chicken as a way to ignore my feelings. If it happened to be a full rotisserie chicken, more power to me.

"Are you going to say anything?" Devlin asked. What did he want me to say? Deny that I felt a bond with all of them instead of just him?

Instead of answering, I turned my attention back towards my chicken.

"Don't fucking ignore me, Zara," he said, slamming his hand on the table. "You're acting like a child!"

"Don't talk to her like that!" Killian's voice was as cold as I'd ever heard it.

Ignore. Ignore. Ignore.

"I just can't fucking deal with this right now," I hissed. "Not today."

Not ever.

"Figure out your own shit with each other, and then maybe we'll talk."

For a moment, I thought they were going to push the issue. It was Dair who relented first, expression sympathetic.

"You're right—this isn't fair, and you probably have a lot of questions."

I didn't want his damn pity. He was right though— this *wasn't* fair. Nothing about my life had ever been fair, but this just felt like a cosmic joke.

"Fine," Devlin said through gritted teeth. He jumped to his feet and angrily grabbed Lupe's shoulder to pull him up as well. "Let's talk, *brothers.*"

He said that word, a word that should've been said as a term of endearment, like it was the worst possible curse word he could think of. I flinched instinctively at the venom in his voice but did not tear my attention away from Diego.

Ignore. Ignore. Ignore.

Lupe wheeled Dair out of the room, and Devlin followed after him. He didn't even bother to look back at me, as if my mere presence disgusted him. As if I had a say in any of this.

Only Killian stayed behind. I could feel his eyes on my neck. He didn't say anything, I didn't look at him, but his companionship provided me with much needed comfort.

I hated it.

I didn't like relying on other people, and I hated people relying on me. I already had to look after Mali and Diego. Could I handle seven more?

No. I couldn't.

With a heavy sigh, Killian followed after his brothers. I briefly wondered if I'd hurt his feelings, but that thought was washed away by a tidal wave of anger. It didn't matter if I'd hurt his feelings. I had already accepted that the universe made a mistake when it assigned me as their mate.

Me. A mate.

A lover.

It was almost comical.

At some point during my mental breakdown, Bash had followed after them. He would hate me even more once he discovered the truth. They all would. Would they blame me? Would they think I was a whore, despite having no control over the bond? Why did it matter to me what they thought?

I felt his presence a moment before I saw his silhouette.

"You knew," I whispered, eyes still trained on Diego.

Ryland's answer was a breath against my neck.

"Yes."

"And you didn't tell anyone? Why?"

Why didn't you tell me? I wanted to say. In front of me, Diego shifted in his seat, moving to cross one leg over the other. I scanned the area around him, grateful when I spotted nothing unusual.

A large man a few tables over, however, was gagging, blood dripping from his mouth. His eyes rolled back into his head just as his body dropped like a bag of rocks. The girls around him screamed, and I noticed Zach smiling slyly into his own cup of wine.

Poison.

Another competitor down.

Besides the girls, nobody paid the dead man any mind. I barely processed it, though I wondered if it was because I was immune to death.

Mali stood in the doorway, eyes trained on the dead body in horror.

One down. Eleven to go.

"Reasons," Ryland whispered, answering the question I'd forgotten I had asked. Nothing made sense anymore. Not this competition, not this life that I was forced into, not even my relationship with the princes. I felt oddly numb as I sat at the now empty table that once sat four handsome men. Numb and alone.

They discovered the truth and ran.

They always ran.

Always left me.

Alone. So alone.

"You have to trust that things will work out," he continued. This time, I felt his nose against my neck. He was close. So close.

"What happened to your face?" I asked softly. I was still staring at Diego and the dead body noticeable over his shoulder. Death. So much death. I was surrounded by it.

I heard Ryland's sharp intake of breath, but I couldn't find it within me to care that I'd crossed some invisible line. I didn't care about anything anymore.

"I'm going to check on my brothers," he said, ignoring my question. "Make sure they don't kill each other."

And then he was gone, and I once again was alone.

My choice. I chose to be alone.

In a matter of minutes, I'd completely destroyed my relationships with each of the princes. If you could even call what I had with them relationships.

Relationships were like big ass orgies. Everyone was trying too hard, only a select few received pleasure, and the rest were left with nothing but crippling disappointment.

Instead of wallowing in my own self-pity, I focused on Diego. He absently stirred his food around on his plate. I wondered if he could feel my eyes burning a hole into his back. If he did, he didn't acknowledge it.

Good boy.

It was only because my attention was fixated on Diego that I noticed the figure walking towards him. Glinting in the artificial lighting, was a knife.

In that moment, I wasn't Zara or Z or Susan. I wasn't an assassin nor was I an assistant. I was just a girl attempting to save one of her last remaining family members.

I jumped from my seat, reaching beneath my skirt to grab my own dagger. The man was tall with a light splatter of blond hair on his chin and a predatory glint to his dark eyes. He moved with a grace that identified him as an incubus. The sexual power emitting off of him in waves was another indication. The incubus raised his dagger, intending to slash Diego's neck, when I charged.

I deflected the blade with a knife of my own, twisting my body so I could jam my elbow into his stomach. He staggered, the grip he had on the copper handle momentarily loosening. I jammed my head into his nose, listening to the satisfying crunch of bones being snapped. Both he and his weapon fell to the floor.

I was thrumming with an incandescent fury. This man thought he could hurt my friend? My family? He was going to pay for what he'd tried to do.

Mentally, I shuffled through the information I'd gathered concerning the remaining competitors. I knew this man to be James, and I knew him to be a powerful incubus. I also knew he'd raped countless women, including a nine-year-old girl.

Leveling a punch at his face, I hit him until his features were nearly unrecognizable. His eyes were bloated shut, and blood welled at the corner of his lips. I was dimly aware of girls screaming, Diego saying my name, and a cold laugh that could've only belonged to a psychopath.

Still, I didn't stop. All of my pent-up aggression exploded out of me with each punch to his once perfect face. I wanted him to feel the pain he'd inflicted on those women, the way he'd destroyed their lives. I wanted him to remember my face, my fist, before he died.

"Z!" Diego shouted. His hands were on my shoulders. I knew I should stop. I knew I had to.

Panting, I leaned over his unrecognizable face. He was hideous, the monster inside of him finally being reflected.

"You're disgusting," I whispered. My voice broke through the cries in the room like the crack of a whip. "I hope you burn in hell."

Without breaking eye contact, I brought the keen blade to his neck and sliced. His hands scrambled to his neck desperately in a futile attempt to keep the blood inside of him. Poor little James. Poor little incubus.

Poor little rapist.

His unseeing eyes stared at something above my shoulder. People told me that you needed to shut the eyes of the dead. It was a way to respect them. This monster didn't deserve my respect. I wanted him to stare up at me, the girl who'd killed him. I wanted the world to know he was dead and not merely sleeping.

I wanted him to suffer.

"He's dead. He's dead." Diego wrapped his arms around me and buried his face into my back. I turned in his embrace, inhaling the smoky scent that was uniquely Diego. He was no longer wearing the mask and cloak. There was no point to that anymore.

Everybody had seen me kill the incubus while Diego had cowered. They may not know exactly who I was, but they would soon find out.

Diego's eyes were warm as they scanned me, searching my body for any noticeable injuries. There was no judgement or fear in his gaze, only love. Blood stained my beautiful, purple dress. I could feel it in my hair and on my skin.

"He would've killed you," I whispered. I found that I needed to justify my actions. I wasn't a monster.

I *wasn't*.

Or was I?

I didn't dare survey the expressions of those around me. The shock and fear. The leers from the Damning competitors. I knew I'd just revealed my identity, the one thing that had made me safe, but I couldn't find it within me to care.

All I could focus on was Diego, alive and safe.

"Mali!" I scrambled to my feet, desperately scanning the sea of faces without sticking on any one in particular. "Is she okay?"

"I'm fine, but we need to go."

Mali appeared in front of me. Her hair was disheveled, and her eyes were wild. Still, she was okay. She was breathing.

Grasping her hand, I pulled her to me.

"We need to leave," I said. "We need to get out of here."

And I didn't just mean the ballroom. We had to leave the capital, this competition, this life. Now that my identity was revealed, it wasn't safe for any of us.

"Okay. Okay." Mali smoothed down my hair. "Just come on. You need to trust me."

Focusing on Mali, only Mali, I nodded.

I allowed her to pull me up and out of the ballroom. Diego followed closely behind, his hand pressing against the small of my back. The heavy doors swung shut behind me, and I winced at the sound.

And then the screaming began.

It was muffled through the closed door, but the noise was undeniable. Screams of pain. Cries of agony.

I broke free of Mali's grip and ran back towards the door. All of those people...

I knew for a fact that there were innocent people in that room. What was happening to them?

"I'm so sorry. I made a deal." Mali's voice was a mere whisper, barely audible over the screams.

"What the hell are you talking about?" Diego snapped.

Mali's face was pale, and guilt flashed in her eyes. Guilt. It was an emotion I was all too familiar with.

From somewhere behind her, a cold laugh reverberated through the room. The hairs on the back of my neck stood on end at the icy sound.

Zack materialized from the shadows, and his arm went to wrap around Mali's waist.

"Mali?" I whispered, stunned. She refused to meet my gaze.

"Hello, Z. Diego. It's a pleasure to meet you." His voice was as cold as his face. The apathetic sound sent goosebumps down my arms. "I believe you already know my mate, Mali. Now it's time for us to talk."

TWENTY-SIX

LUPE

Never in a million years did I believe that I would meet my mate. It was an elusive fantasy, something that was just out of reach. It was like trying to grasp air—impossible.

But then she barreled her way into my life. She'd been warm and real and vibrant, slowly melting the ice around my heart. For the first time, I wanted to do more than read books and scour libraries. I wanted to *be* more.

For her.

I should've known that I wouldn't get my happily ever after. Shifters rarely did, though I often wondered if our sin, wrath, had something to do with that. Getting angry over the smallest of things was a sure way to screw up every good relationship in your life.

I'd always known that there was a possibility I'd have to share my mate. The waning population of females made this a necessity. But to share a mate with my brothers?

All six of them?

I wasn't an idiot. Even with Jax being wherever the hell he was, I knew that Zara was his mate as well. It would explain his eccentric behavior and his talk of the "golden-haired warrior goddess." I didn't know how to deal with this information. She wasn't mine, despite me being hers, and she might never be. I knew she feared shifters. I could see the flicker of unease in her eyes and the way her body shied away from mine, as if I would ever hurt her. How could she ever learn to love me, or at the very least, care for me, when I had to compete against six other amazing men? Would she even want all of us as her mates? Or would she only want one of us? Or none of us?

"What the hell are we going to do?" Devlin asked in trepidation. His ponytail had come loose at some point, and his hair was now an unruly mess. It was strange to see our fearless leader so unkempt. His eyes flashed from face to face, unable to fully focus on anyone in particular.

In that moment, I hated him. I hated my best friend. He'd had her first, had her love, and he'd thrown it all away. I knew his reasoning. Hell, I even understood it, but I didn't know how to look at him anymore with anything but disgust. My bear growled restlessly in the confines of my mind. He wanted to roam free and find her. Claim her. He knew she was ours, and he would be damned if he let her out of his sight again.

"She's our mate. What even is there to do?" Dair asked reasonably. He was the only one who didn't seem perturbed by the aspect of sharing. I knew mermaids often had polyamorous relationships. His dad himself had five wives, something nearly unheard of in the super-natural community.

"I don't...I don't know if I can..." Devlin ran a hand through his hair. I watched my brother's jerky movements with narrowed eyes.

"So what? You're going to demand that she chooses only one of us? Demand that she chooses you?" My words were nearly inarticulate. I was losing control, fast, and my growl was just another indication.

"I don't fucking know! There's seven of us and only one of her!"

"Six," Bash said. He was sitting on the counter in the kitchen, watching our interaction with impassive eyes. He tried to give the impression that he gave zero shits about her, but I wasn't an idiot. "Don't group me into this equation. I want nothing to do with her."

I snorted.

He could deny it all he wanted, but even he wasn't immune to Zara's magnetic pull. It was more than just the bond between us. It was *her*. Her radiant smile, her musical laugh, the way the skin between her brows creased when she was deep in thought. I wanted to learn everything there was to know about her. I wanted to pull her apart, piece by piece, until her essence was bared before me. There was still so much I had yet to learn about her, and I had the distinct feeling that years of intensive studying would still fail to reveal who Zara was as a person.

It was only a matter of time until Bash realized that as well. He was hers, whether he wanted to be or not.

"So what do you suppose we do?" Devlin asked

tersely. "Share her? Pass her around like she's a damn possession?"

"We talk to her about it. Ask her what she wants to do. She's my mate, and I'm not giving her up." For the first time in forever, Killian spoke without a single stutter. His eyes were pure steel as he surveyed the room.

"I love her," Devlin whispered softly.

"So it's settled then." Dair glanced from face to face. "We talk to her. And we don't treat her like a possession. Everything is, and always will be, her choice. Is that clear?"

I couldn't help but snort.

"Oh, please. If she doesn't want to do something, she could easily kill us. I think it's safe to say that we know who wears the pants in this relationship."

The men smiled softly. Even Bash's lips curved upwards, though he quickly tried to hide it.

"She's gone! She disappeared, and I'll never find her again!" Atta entered the kitchen with an elaborate flourish. She dramatically draped herself onto a bar stool.

"What's your problem?" Bash snapped. He could never handle my sister's theatrics, not that I blamed him. There was only so much I myself could handle before I wanted to strangle her.

"My mate, of course," said Atta, as if the answer was obvious.

Bash rolled his eyes and muttered, "Of fucking course," under his breath.

"Please don't tell me your mate is Zara." Devlin pinched the bridge of his nose in exasperation. "I don't know if I'll be able to handle another person thrown into this equation." Atta raised her eyebrow in confusion.

"Nooo...that's Lupe's mate. Mine is her beautiful, sexy friend, Mali." She spoke the name wistfully, as if it were something sacred. I wondered if I said Zara's name with the same reverence.

"She looked as if she wanted to stab you in the eyes," I pointed out. Atta swiveled her head to glare at me.

"You're one to talk."

An earsplitting scream interrupted my retort.

From the ballroom.

Where Zara was.

Before I realized what was happening, my feet were propelling me back towards the room. I was dimly aware of the others following behind me, but I could barely concentrate on them. My entire focus was on Zara.

She had to be okay. She had to. The alternative was too horrible to even think about.

Fear, real, unrelenting fear, settled heavily in my chest, a leaden feeling. I couldn't recall the last time I'd felt such a strong emotion before. Fear—and your consequential responses towards it—was a funny thing. Each person had a fight-or-flight response that was only amplified when one experienced a strong emotion. For so long, I'd run away from my problems. Always running. Always fleeing.

This was the first time I'd ever been willing to fight. Maybe Zara was already rubbing off on me. My little fighter.

There was only one door that led to the ballroom, and it was unexpectedly locked. Not even my impressive shifter strength could open the door. After one more ineffectual shove of my shoulder against the wooden frame, I turned towards my brothers helplessly.

"It's spelled," Bash whispered, eyes narrowing.

"Can you break it?" Ryland asked from the shadows. He sounded as tense as we all felt. The carefree guy had been transformed into a prowling tiger out for the kill.

"Give me a minute."

"But can you break it?" Devlin asked. His eyes were glowing as if someone had lit a candle beneath the surface. His dark hair swayed in the breeze created by his own power. He needed to calm down before the entire building collapsed in on itself. We all needed to calm down. My own bear was pacing, clawing, gnawing in a desperate attempt to break free. I could feel my carefully constructed cage begin to break with each second that passed.

"Give me a damn minute!" Bash screamed. He squeezed his eyelids shut as he concentrated on the intricate spellwork.

"Can you feel her?" I asked Devlin. I knew that his bond with her was stronger than the others. If anyone would be able to feel her presence, it would be him.

"I don't know. I can't concentrate. I can't..." Once again, he pulled at his hair.

"Well fucking try," Killian snapped. Before Devlin could respond, the door to the ballroom burst open. I shoved Bash out of my way in my haste to get inside.

I needed to see with my own eyes that she was okay. For my own sanity, she had to be all right.

The sight before me...

It was something I would never be able to unsee. Bodies were sprawled across the ballroom floor. Though all of their faces were unrecognizable, I could distinctly make out dresses of various colors and fabrics. The Matching competitors. Innocent women. Mixed in with them were the bodies that could only be participants of the Damning.

And their faces...

Charred, black skin greeted me. Smoke filtered from their bodies, the pungent smell assaulting my senses. If I were to live a thousand more years, I would never see a sight as horrendous as this one.

"Another spell," Bash whispered. One of my brothers began to throw up behind me.

And yet, despite all of the death mere inches from me, I could only feel relief. Not one of these bodies had a purple dress on.

Zara wasn't there.

"She's not here." Devlin must've come to the same conclusion I had. Unlike me, he didn't sound at all comforted by the fact that she'd missed this brutal attack. Because if she wasn't there, then where the hell was she?

I knew, as surely as I knew my own name, that she was in trouble. I didn't know if it was my own intuition or the bond between us.

In a span of seconds, my body shifted from my human form into my bear one. He clawed at the air angrily, seven hundred pounds of pure muscle.

Nobody would hurt my mate.

I would make sure of that.

TWENTY-SEVEN

DEVLIN

I didn't know how to even begin to describe my panic when I opened the ballroom door and saw row after row of dead bodies. Most people would be relieved—after all, not one had on the purple dress Z had been wearing earlier—but all I could feel was a smothering fear. The intensity of such an emotion threatened to consume me, threatened to plunge me beneath wave after wave of icy water with no hope of escape. It slithered down my spine, this absolute terror, until I had trouble distinguishing one emotion from the next.

Fear.

Terror.

Heartache.

She wasn't there.

And if there was one thing I knew about Z, it was that she wouldn't have left all of these people to their gruesome fate if she'd had a choice. She fought for what she believed in, fought for the innocents. It was just the type of person she was. Though she had her own personal darkness, she also had a brilliant light that was too pure for this world. Too pure for me.

"Fuck!" I screamed. My hands once again pulled at my brown hair. Z had always joked that this was a horrible habit I had to break and that I'd go bald before I reached thirty. I would retort that I'd stop ripping my hair out the second she stopped chewing on her nails. Moments spent fighting with her were some of my happiest memories.

Taking a stuttering breath, I focused on the bond. I could feel it extending from my chest, reaching for the essence that was innately Z. I would describe it as a flame, a flicker of light in a darkened cave. Just as quickly, my connection to her vanished.

"Fuck!" I cursed again.

"Focus," Killian said from beside me. "You need to focus and find her."

I ignored him. I ignored Lupe's growl as his bear completely consumed him. I ignored everything besides the intermittent flicking of Z's vibrant light at the end of the bond.

I would find her. I had to.

TWENTY-EIGHT

DAIR

I'd never allowed myself to see my paralyzed condition as a handicap. It was merely something that was a part of me, like the fact I turned into a mermaid twelve hours every day. It was one of the many facets that made me...me. I'd long since accepted that I would never be able to walk again, never be able to dance again, never be able to run again. I was confined to my chair, and for the most part, I was okay with that.

Except for now.

As my brothers all ran towards the ballroom, they failed to remember me and my damn chair. This particular section of the capital had never been the most accessible for people like me, mainly because it was immensely rare to see a nightmare with any type of disability. We were designed to be the epitome of perfection. Predators. The top of the food chain.

Cursing softly, I watched my wheel get stuck on a section of carpeting. Movements erratic, I attempted to maneuver myself over the obstacle. At that moment, I hated myself and my weakness. How would I be able to protect Z when I could barely look after myself? The answer was simple—I wouldn't be able to.

"Shit," I murmured after I'd finally freed my chair.

"What has gotten you in such a foul mood?" a familiar voice asked slyly in my ear. Flinching, I glanced over my shoulder to see my brother's smirking face. It seemed to be perpetually etched across his features, that damn smile. Before I could respond to his taunts, he began to wheel me in the opposite direction of the ballroom.

"Where the hell are you taking me?" I hissed, my thin patience splintering. I normally considered myself a mild-mannered individual, but right now, I felt like a lion out for the kill. I needed to get to Z, my mate. I had to see for myself that she was okay.

I never expected the mating bond to be like this. I'd heard stories, of course, but they all paled in comparison to the actual thing. There was an ache in my chest to be with her, to see her smile, and to make her happy. I didn't think it was possible for me to be happy if she wasn't. Being away from her, knowing she was in danger, was torture. I'd barely met the girl, and already, she was consuming every single thought I had.

"Father would like to speak with you," my brother Tavvy said conversationally. At those words, my blood went cold.

God, no.

Not now.

"I have somewhere I have to be. Maybe later would be a better time," I said, attempting to dampen my growing panic. If there was one thing I knew about my older brother, it was that he had an acute sense for fear. The man relished in it, the sensation, as if it was his own personal fetish. I wondered if it actually was. I kept my features impassive and my tone nonchalant as I spoke.

"Quiet!" A blistering slap hit my cheek, and I squeezed my eyelids shut.

Don't react. Don't react.

"I apologize." My jaw ticked, but I continued on doggedly. "I shouldn't have spoken out of turn."

Pleased with my response, Tavvy wheeled me into the throne room.

The first person I saw was my father, a haughty tilt to his head and a fur robe adorning his body. I knew that the fur belonged to a deceased shifter. It was a power play, that robe. A game. The only problem was that there was no rulebook to the twisted politics that plagued the nation.

His five wives sat in semicircle around him. I recognized his fated mate, Elise, and her cold, unwavering stare. Beside her was my own mother, Juliet. She offered me a timid wave when she saw me, and my own lips instinctively curved upwards into a half-hearted smile.

My mother wasn't my father's mate. She had a mate, the father of my sister, but she'd been forced to leave him when Father became aware of her ethereal beauty. He was jealous, envious, that such a beautiful creature existed and wasn't tied to him. He stole her away that very night and made her his bride.

Peeling my attention away from my mother, I raised my eyes towards the domineering man that seemed to innately command respect and attention from everyone in the room. It wasn't just because he was a large and impressive man, though there was no denying that he was, but more so the amount of power that he emanated. Anyone with a brain would know that he was someone to be both feared and worshiped.

"Dair! My son! Welcome!" He extended his arms in greeting as if we were old friends instead of enemies. He may have been my father, but I hated him. I hated what he stood for, and I hated what he'd done to me and the people I loved.

"What do you want, Father?"

I prepared myself for the inevitable pain, my body tensing, my eyes twitching, and my mind closing down. All of these meetings ended the same way. The sooner I was tortured, the sooner it would be over, and the sooner I could find Z. It was the thought of her that gave me the strength and courage to meet my father's eyes. Eyes that were the exact same shade of azure as my own.

"I'm going to get straight to the point." He paused, his strident voice echoing in the spacious room. It was merely an attempt at dramatics, that pause. A pathetic one. "What do you know of the competitor Z?"

His words were like a bucket of ice water being thrown over my head. Whatever I'd expected him to say, it hadn't been that. My body tensed under his scrutiny, but I tried to keep my face apathetic. He couldn't have known about Z being my mate.

No. There must be another explanation.

"I know that he's a competitor for the Damning," I

said, keeping my voice indifferent. Shrugging, I added, "Besides that, nothing. Why are you interested in him?"

The smile he offered me felt like snakes slithering down my spine. Evil.

I always knew that my father was evil personified, but it had never felt more true than at that moment. Tavvy, behind me, began to chuckle darkly.

"No reason."

That same smile remained plastered on his face. The urge to punch it off of him was overwhelming. As I watched, the smile contorted itself into something I would almost describe as sly. It was one I was intimately familiar with, one that demanded pain.

"Come, my dear son. Let's have a private meeting in my study, shall we?"

TWENTY-NINE

Z

I stared up at the man I barely knew yet already hated with an intensity that was staggering. Zack's glacial stare begged me to submit, to fall onto my hands and knees in front of him, but I would die before I bowed down to that bastard.

"Come." With an imperious set to his chin, he turned and walked down the hallway, Mali beside him. There was no fear in his stroll, a stroll I would almost describe as carefree. He truly didn't believe I was capable of harming him.

And he was right—with his hand on Mali's waist, I knew I wouldn't risk my friend's life, no matter how betrayed I felt by her actions. I'd walk into the mouth of hell willingly.

"Stay here," I whispered harshly to Diego. He stared at me incredulously.

"No way in hell."

"Go grab the princes." When he still didn't move, I shoved at his shoulder. "Go!"

A new determination to my step, I hurried after Zack and Mali. I could only pray that Diego, for once, would listen to me.

The room Zack led me to was large and similar in appearance to my own suite. Mali moved around the room with a familiarity that made my throat close. How long had she been keeping this from me? *Why* had she kept this from me?

The door opened and closed behind me. Diego, expression fierce, gave me a nod of solidarity. Damn him. Didn't he realize I was trying to protect him? He moved to stand beside me, and I noticed Zack watching our exchange with curious eyes.

Ignoring Zack completely, I turned towards Mali.

"I thought Atta was your mate," I said. Simple and to the point. It was almost as if I were speaking to a stranger. I supposed, in a way, I was. I no longer knew the vampire in front of me. Tears welled in her eyes, but I didn't allow them to deter me. She'd betrayed me, betrayed us all. People were dead because of her and Zack.

"She is." Mali's words were choked, and she moved to wrap her thin arms around her waist. "They both are."

I watched her pathetic attempt at holding herself together. She would come to realize that the physical gesture would do little to soothe her mental anguish. It was impossible to hold together all of the fucked-up pieces of yourself. I would know.

Suddenly, I found that I couldn't look at Mali anymore. I couldn't bear to see the pain in her gaze, the agony, as if she wasn't a willing participant in this entire situation. She'd made her choice, and now she had to live with the consequences. I forged a steel barrier around my heart at that moment and turned to glare at Zack.

"Why am I here?"

"He promised that he wouldn't hurt you," Mali broke in desperately.

"I did, my dear." Despite his words being directed at Mali, he didn't tear his gaze away from me. There was so much darkness in his pitch-black eyes that it was like staring into an abyss. One could get lost in those eyes, and not in a good way. Down and down you'd fall, with no hope of ever escaping. There was no wisdom in that ancient gaze, only an evilness that would make even the devil look tame in comparison.

My heart hammered as I fully came to terms with how terrifying a man like Zack actually was. How dangerous.

"Unfortunately, I'm going to have to break this promise."

Mali's protest was cut off by a wave of his hand. One second, she was staring up at him, eyes hopeful, and the next, she was thrown against the wall. She let out a startled yelp, and I immediately ran towards her.

My feet stopped working after only one step in her direction, and I glared at Zack's display of power.

"You're going to kill me," I said. It wasn't a question.

Zack shrugged nonchalantly, ignoring the cries and pleas of his mate still pinned to the wall.

"I'm doing you a favor," he said. "The poison that was in your cup will take months to take effect. Months of absolute agony."

Poison?

I distantly recalled having a sip of water at dinner. I'd stupidly believed that it would be safe to drink. After all, nobody knew my true identity. Nobody, that was, except for Mali and Diego.

Mali was crying in earnest now, as if she'd just finally realized the consequences of her actions—my life.

"It's nothing personal," Zack continued. Despite his emotionless tone, there was a malicious gleam to his eyes that hinted that this was, in fact, very much personal to him. "Perhaps I would've even spared your life if Aaliyah hadn't insisted on your death."

"Aaliyah?"

It was the third time I'd heard her name.

"Why is she attacking the princes?" I continued. I didn't even know her, and I already hated that bitch.

At my question, Zack let out a whoop of laughter. The sound made unpleasant goosebumps erupt on my skin. It was the type of laugh you heard in your nightmares. There was no humor in it, just noise, as if he were a robot going through the motions. I supposed he was in a way. I didn't think a man like him was even capable of empathy, love, or joy.

"Stupid girl. The princes were never her target." His rancid breath hit my face as he leaned into me. "She was going after *you*."

I didn't have time to ponder this newfound information, as Zack had unsheathed a silver blade. I knew with absolute clarity that I was going to die. My body was immobile, held captive by Zack's power. There was nothing I could do to fight my imminent death, no pleas I could give that would spare me or convince him that my life was worth living. In a way, this death would be merciful, if what he'd said about the poison was true.

I was going to die. I'd found my mates, a near impossible feat, and I was going to be slain before I would get to know them. I would never able to kiss Killian's blushing cheeks, argue with Bash because he was an asshole, laugh at Ryland's antics. Would they find a new mate after I was gone? Would they even want to?

Did it make me selfish that I wanted them to hold onto our relationship as tightly as I was?

Three things happened in a span of seconds. First, Zack raised his hand that held the blade, and I braced myself for the inevitable pain. I knew it would be painful with a weapon as sharp as that. Second, Mali was able to break free of whatever restraints Zack had spelled on her. And finally, Diego threw himself in front of me.

I heard Zack let out a scream, but my attention was fixated on Diego.

Diego falling.

Diego with blood seeping through his shirt.

Diego with a sword, a sword that was meant for me, in his chest

With a cry of anguish, I dropped to my knees beside him. I didn't care that Zack was only inches away and could easily kill me. I didn't care that blood stained my beautiful purple dress and my hands like a second skin. I didn't care about any of that.

Diego's breathing was shallow as I shakily ran a hand through his brown hair.

"You're okay. You're going to be okay," I whispered. God, there was so much blood. It was *everywhere.*

I pressed my hands against the wound in an attempt to stop the bleeding.

"You're going to be okay. I promise. Okay?" I felt something salty hit my lips. Salty and wet. Tears? Was I crying?

Diego cracked a small smile, and I saw that blood stained his teeth.

"I love you, Z," he croaked out. More tears dropped down my face.

"Shut up. Save your strength. You're going to be fine." My hands were shaking so badly, but I still held them against his chest. The bleeding had to stop. It had to.

So much blood...

"Tell HH—" He coughed, blood dripping down his chapped lips.

"You can tell him yourself," I said, my resolve strengthening. "Because you're going to be fine."

"...that I love him."

And then his eyes closed, and his chest went still. I could feel my sanity splintering. My thoughts were an incoherent mesh of words and phrases.

No.

No.

No.

"Wake up!" I screamed, shaking Diego's shoulder. "You have to wake up! Wake! Up!" I punctuated each word with a slap to his cold face.

He was only sleeping. He had to be. He would wake

up, smile, and then make a perverted joke about my position on top of him.

But his eyes remained closed. His expression was serene, almost peaceful, and his black lashes were feathered against his cheekbones.

No. No. No.

"Wake up!" I was screaming. Crying. Hitting. "You can't leave me! You promised! You fucking promised! Get your ass back up right now!"

My screams turned into heart-wrenching sobs, and I threw myself over his body. Not Diego. Not him.

No. No. No.

He had taken him from me.

Something cracked inside of me just then. I wouldn't have been able to tell you what it was. My last hold on humanity?

I could barely think straight. A red sheen coated my vision with each step I took towards *him*. The monster. The murderer.

Mali stood over his prone body, body trembling as she stabbed yet another stake into his arm. I could tell she had no intent on killing him, just harming him and rendering him immobile.

He would not receive the same leniency from me.

Without a word, I grabbed a dagger from its sheath and unceremoniously stabbed it into his chest. There were no cat and mouse games. No playing. I wanted him to die, and I wanted my face to be the last thing he saw.

He laughed, the sound making my blood curdle, and whispered three final words before the life drained from his eyes.

"Long live Aaliyah."

And then he was gone.

Dead.

Just like Diego.

I felt a hand land on my shoulder, and I immediately went still.

"Z..." Mali sobbed. I jumped to my feet, the dagger I'd used to kill her mate inches from her throat. I barely registered the shock on her face.

"Don't," I whispered. "Don't talk to me ever again."

"I am so sorry," she cried, her words nearly inarticulate. I pressed the blade deeper into her neck, nicking skin in the process. She winced but didn't pull away. Her eyes were anguished when they met mine. "I didn't know. I didn't realize he was such a monster. Diego—"

"Don't say his name. It's your fault that he's dead. *Yours.* You betrayed us. You're lucky I don't kill you right now." My hand tightened over the copper handle. "I don't ever want to see your face again. You're dead to me."

"Z..." she sobbed.

"Go!"

"I'm so sorry!"

"Go! Get the fuck out of here! Go! Go!"

I could still hear her cries as she ran from the room. I hoped she remembered this moment—the moment when she realized she was all alone in the world. I hated her.

And I hated myself.

A sob rose up my throat as I took in Diego's body on the ground, blood a thick pool around him.

No. No. No.

I curled into a ball beside him and placed my head into the crook of his neck.

No. No. No.

Maybe if I denied it enough times, it would no longer be true.

THIRTY

RYLAND

I didn't think anything could possibly break me. My mind was an impenetrable fortress, and my heart was nearly as guarded. I'd never allowed my emotions to get in the way, never allowed myself to *feel*.

But walking into that room? Seeing Z sobbing into a dead mage's neck?

That nearly destroyed me.

For the first time in forever, I wished that I wasn't restricted to the shadows. She deserved the light, and I'd never be the type of person who could give that to her.

Devlin moved beside her, kneeling. He tentatively reached out to brush at the blood soaked hair sticking to her cheek.

"Baby..." he said helplessly. His eyes were wet with unshed tears as he watched her. I remembered when he'd been burning with jealousy over Z's relationship with Diego. Now, Devlin stared at the mage's body as if they were long lost brothers instead of strangers. I wondered if his bond with Z was advanced enough to the point where

he felt her pain. Even I could feel trickles of agony rever-
berating through the bond. I nearly gasped at the intensity of such an overwhelming emotion.

She'd loved him. Maybe not in the same way she'd
loved—and still loved—Devlin, but in a way that was
similar to what I felt for my brothers.

"He was alive." Her voice was so soft, I had to strain
to hear it. "He was alive, and then he threw himself in
front of me. Isn't that bullshit? His death is bullshit. He
should still be alive. He should still be..." She trailed off
as sobs shook her body. The transformation from a
huntress to a sniffling child was startling. I knew she
would hate herself later for displaying such vulnerability
in front of us. We were alike in that respect.

Devlin leaned down to pull her into his arms, and she
went willingly. Once her body was settled snugly against
his chest, he began to walk.

I could hear her sobs, muffled by his chest, and his
soothing voice attempting to comfort her. My chest ached
painfully. I yearned to hold her myself, to comfort her, to
kiss all of her tears away. But she didn't need me right
now, and she most definitely didn't need my darkness.

As I stared at her tear-stained face, I wondered if this
was something she would be able to survive. There were
only so many times you could break before it became
nearly impossible to pull yourself back together again.
She'd lost a member of her family, and I knew that was
something she wouldn't be able to forget.

There were only two options for her—survive or
succumb. I could only hope she would choose the former.

Bash moved to stand over Diego's body, expression

unreadable. He knelt down and tentatively reached for something in the mage's jacket pocket.

"What is it?" I asked.

Slowly, movements almost calculated, Bash held up a strange object. It appeared to be a bag twined tightly with hair. Inked onto the side was a familiar symbol—the same one we'd seen on the two dead men that had attacked Killian.

"It's a hex," he said, twisting the bag between his long fingers. "I've never seen such powerful magic before."

I ventured a step closer, struck by the awe and fear on Bash's face. It was such a strange combination that my hands turned clammy at my sides. If something was capable of scaring Bash, it must be bad.

"What does it do?"

I almost didn't want to hear his answer.

"It takes away your powers." Bash's inquisitive gaze flickered from the hex bag to Diego. "It makes you basically human."

A spell that dampened the powers of a nightmare? I shuddered.

It didn't even sound possible. If Bash hadn't told me himself, I would've laughed at the absurdity of it all. Our powers were a biological function, something that made us inherently different from one another. Inherently *us*. You couldn't just take away a mage's magic. It would be the equivalent of changing a human's eye color —impossible.

Only...it wasn't.

Bash shook his head, eyes still sadly trained on Diego's face.

"Do you think he knew, when he came here, that he would have no powers? Why would he do this?"

"Because he loved her," I answered easily. "And you would do anything for the people you love."

Something flickered in his eyes then. Something there and gone too quickly for me to decipher.

Hand clenching around the hex bag, Bash slowly ambled to his feet. His eyes were dazed as they surveyed the macabre scene before him. So much blood. It stained the walls. The floor. The two dead bodies.

"He loved her enough to walk into a slaughter." He couldn't seem to wrap his head around that concept. Taking a shuddering breath, he glanced once more at Diego. I knew he was seeing more than just a dead body, but a person who had risked it all for his family. A person who wasn't meant to die as early as he did. "Thank you."

My heart clenched.

"Yes," I whispered. "Thank you."

EPILOGUE

Z

ONE WEEK LATER
I stared at his sleeping face. He looked so peaceful like that. All of the stress and tension fell away in those brief moments when the sun had yet to emerge from behind the tree boughs. He didn't like falling asleep. I knew that. He feared I would leave him, leave *them*. He also feared I would lose the battle against my own mind.

He was right to be worried about me.

Turning away from Devlin, I faced my bedroom mirror once again. My face was paler than I remembered it being, and dark circles marred the skin under my eyes. When was the last time I'd slept? I couldn't remember. Hell, when was the last time I'd eaten? Devlin had been trying to get me to eat, and for the most part, I allowed him to believe it was working. He didn't have to know that I threw up the majority of my food only hours later.

He didn't have to know that I was slowly killing myself as a way to feel something, anything, that wasn't this depressing loneliness Diego's absence had brought into my life.

Grief had a way of strangling you until you craved the inevitable darkness. I grieved not only Diego, but also Mali. I'd lost everyone I had ever cared about that day. My body was a mere carcass of what it once was. A shell, almost.

I glanced down at the black tracksuit I had on, one that accentuated my breasts and hips. My ribs were more pronounced, I noticed, but I found that I couldn't muster the will to care.

Today was the day I would be declared the official assassin of the kingdom. Today, I would stand in front of the seven royal families and get a fucking gold star for my murderous tendencies. It occurred to me that this would be the first time meeting my mates' parents, men and women I'd already been preprogrammed to hate. I would have to look them in the eyes and act like I wasn't planning their gruesome deaths.

And they would die, of that I was almost certain. I could only hope that it would be my hand holding the knife when the life drained from their miserable bodies.

There was also Aaliyah I had to worry about. I'd contacted my sources back at the resistance, and I had yet to hear anything from them. That worried me tremendously. B was a timely man. Punctual to the extreme. The longest I'd gone without hearing from him was only a day. I told myself not to panic, that there were other things I needed to focus on.

Who was Aaliyah, and why was she targeting me?

Questions were running rampant through my head. There were just too many pieces I had to gather before I could even consider an answer.

A coughing fit nearly made me buckle over. I glanced towards Devlin, anxious that he had heard me, but he was mercifully still asleep. He must've been more tired than I realized.

Grabbing a tissue, I coughed until my throat was raw. Blood stained the white surface.

My blood.

Without a word, I tossed the tissue into the garbage can alongside dozens of others.

It was a problem I would deal with. Later.

Maybe.

For now, I had a commencement ceremony to attend.

Raising my chin, I stepped out into the hallway. I knew that my princes—*the* princes, not *my* princes— would be there already. Except for Devlin. He hadn't left my side since...

Well. I didn't want to think about that.

I didn't want to think about how everyone I'd ever loved had been pulled away from me. Love was dangerous, and I swore to myself I would never feel that emotion again. Even if seven princes were attempting to worm their way into my heart.

I may have been alone now, but I'd won. That had to count for something. B would be proud of me for completing my mission. Diego would've been too.

My throat closed, but I quickly swept those emotions away. Not today. Not ever. They had to stay so far buried that not even a necromancer could raise them from the grave.

I was Z.

Assassin.

Mate of seven men.

Competitor of the Damning.

Winner of the Damning.

Straightening my shoulders, I walked down the hallway to face my destiny.

ABOUT THE AUTHOR

Katie May is a reverse harem author, a KDP All-Star winner, and an USA Today Bestselling Author. She lives in West Michigan with her family and cat. When not writing, she could be found reading a good book, listening to broadway musicals, or playing games. Join Katie's Gang to stay updated on all her releases! And did you know she has a TikTok? Yeah, me either. Follow her here! But be warned...she's an awkward noodle.

ALSO BY KATIE MAY

Together We Fall (Apocalyptic Reverse Harem, COMPLETED)

1. The Darkness We Crave

2. The Light We Seek

3. The Storm We Face

4. The Monsters We Hunt

Beyond the Shadows (Horror Reverse Harem, COMPLETED)

1. Gangs and Ghosts

2. Guns and Graveyards

3. Gallows and Ghouls

The Damning (Fantasy Paranormal Reverse Harem)

1. Greed

2. Envy

3. Gluttony

4. Sloth

Prodigium Academy (Horror Comedy Academy Reverse Harem)

1. Monsters

2. Roaring

Tory's School for the Trouble (Bully Horror Academy Reverse Harem)

1. Between

2. Beyond (Coming Soon)

Supernaturalette (Interactive Reverse Harem)

1. Introductions

2. First Dates

3. Group Outing

4. Game Night

5. Exes

6. Truth or Dare

Kingdom of Wolves (Shifter Reverse Harem Duet)

1. Torn to Bits

2. Ripped to Shreds

CO-WRITES

Afterworld Academy with Loxley Savage (Academy Fantasy Reverse Harem, COMPLETED)

1. Dearly Departed

2. Darkness Deceives

3. Defying Destiny

Darkest Flames with Ann Denton (Paranormal Reverse Harem, COMPLETED)

1. Demon Kissed

STAND-ALONES

Made in the USA
Columbia, SC
14 January 2022

53508223R00186